into the normalcy of human oddity, in a night of partying turned twisted; activist and eroticist Cecilia Tan offers a similar glimpse of the haunting future of desire; the always shocking and real Ray Garton and John Everson set their tales along the line between violence and sexual gratification; the stories from D. Harlan Wilson and Erinn L. Kemper do a nice change of scenery, coming at the idea of "appetite" from a different angle; and finally I feel very pleased and honored to bring to you a brand new novella from Scott Edelman, which is one of the best meditations on the subject of death and desire that I've ever read. You will not forgot it.

On the nonfiction side, we have a wonderful article by Lawrence C. Connolly on Robert Aickman and Aickman's role in this current theme. John Palisano gives us an entertaining recap of *SHRIEKFEST 2014*. There are new interviews with Cecilia Tan as well as Del Howison and Joseph Nassise about their new Clive Barker-inspired anthology *Midian Unmade*. We return with our feature "Horror in a Hundred Stories," three short pieces of horror fiction chosen out of a hundred submissions and selected from our Hellnotes community. Also we have our next installment of the comic series by Joe McKinney and Patrick Freivald. And finally, there are columns exploring Sinister Appetites from our usual columnists including Donald Tyson who has joined the team; Tyson's new column Murmurs in the Dark explores occult fiction with Aleister Crowley as his focal point this issue.

So on with the show! Grab your popcorn, soda, and leather whip, then sit back and get ready to peer into the depths…

—Aaron J. French
Editor-in-Chief

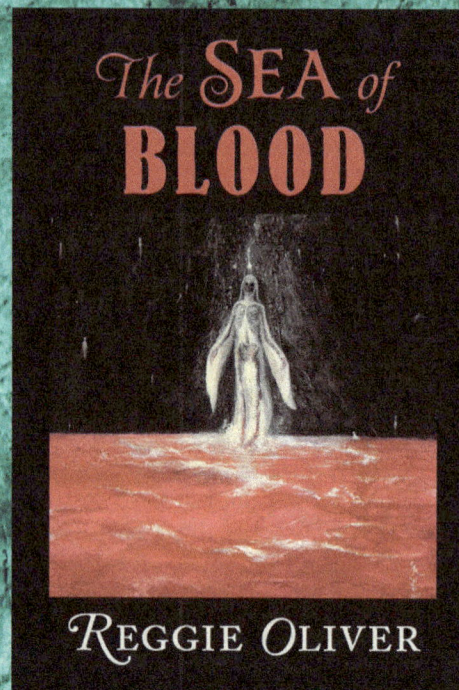

DARK DISCOVERIES

Publisher
JournalStone Publishing, LLC

Editor-in-Chief and Art Director
Aaron J. French

Contributing Editor
K. H. Vaughan

Assistant Editors
Nancy Kalanta (Reviews Editor)
Russ Thompson (Senior Submissions Editor)
Stuart Conover (Assistant Reviews Editor)

Layout, and Design
Paul Fry

Contributors

Storm Constantine	Jeff Connor
Scott Edelman	Rick Hipson
Ray Garton	Joe Nazare
John Everson	Catherine Bader
Erinn L. Kemper	Yvonne Navarro
Cecilia Tan	Richard Dansky
Del Howison	Michael R. Collings
Joseph Nassise	Aaron J. French
Lawrence C. Connolly	Leah Jung
John Palisano	D. Harlan Wilson
K. H. Vaughan	Donald Tyson
Gary A. Braunbeck	Joe McKinney
Robert Morrish	and Patrick Freivald

Founding Publisher and Editor
James R. Beach

Special Thanks

Cecilia Tan	Mickayla Pence
Lawrence C. Connolly	(Makeup Artist)
Del Howison	Leah Jung
Joseph Nassise	Scott Edelman
Nofar Avigdor (Cover Model)	Jeff Connor

Contributing Artists/Photographers
Bradley Thornber (Cover Photographer)
Steve Santiago (pg 5 & 38)
Greg Chapman (pg 44, 55 & 112)
Luke Spooner (pg 25 & 94)
John Palisano

DARK DISCOVERIES
(ISSN 1548-6842) is published (Qtrly) by
JournalStone Publications
439 Gateway Dr., #83, Pacifica, CA 94044

Copyright ©2012 and beyond by JournalStone
Publications, and where specified elsewhere in the
issue. All rights revert to the authors/artists upon
publication, with exception of the Logo and images
specifically created for the magazine. Nothing shown
can be reproduced without obtaining written permission
from the creators. All book/magazine cover images
and author photos remain the copyrighted property
of their respective owners. Direct all inquiries, address
changes, subscription orders, to:

Christopher C. Payne
JournalStone Publications
439 Gateway Dr., #83, Pacifica, CA 94044, U.S.A.
christophercpayne@journalstone.com.

Please make check or money order payable to:
JournalStone Publishing and send to the address above.
Credit/Debit cards via Paypal at:
christophercpayne@journalstone.com. Advertising
rates available. Discounts for bulk and standing retail
orders.

FICTION

Becoming Invisible, Becoming Seen by Scott Edelman	05
At the Sign of the Leering Angel by Storm Constantine	25
The Wanting by Cecilia Tan	38
I Believe I Shall Not Die by D. Harlan Wilson	44
Emily's Last Session by Ray Garton	55
Symbiosis by Erinn L. Kemper	94
Field of Flesh by John Everson	112

FEATURES

Nightbreed Rising: An Interview with Del Howison and Joseph Nassise, eds. of *Midian Unmade* by K. H. Vaughan	18
Fear, Desire, and the stories of Robert Aickman by Lawrence C. Connolly	21
Chasing Desires: An interview with Cecilia Tan by K. H. Vaughan	33
Driving into the Sun SHRIEKFEST 2014 by John Palisano	47
Exemplifying the Sinister: An Interview with Nofar Avigdor by Leah Jung	52
Horror in a Hundred Stories	54
Comic Series "Jade Sky" by Joe McKinney and Patrick Freivald	64
Inner Demons: Desire and Conflict in Horror by K. H. Vaughan	90

COLUMNS

Double X Chromosome: Perfection by Yvonne Navarro	29
...Can't Get It Out of My Head... by Gary A. Braunbeck	42
Why Sinister Appetites are *Sinister*... and Why They Aren't by Michael R. Collings	61
What the Hell Ever Happened to... Jeff Connor and Scream/Press by Robert Morrish	102
Murmurs in the Dark: Aleister Crowley's Magical Child by Donald Tyson	108
Erotic Horror in Videogames by Richard Dansky	125

REVIEWS

Hellnotes/Horror World Reviews	128

Editorial

Updates from the Fantastique...

Greetings and welcome to the newest issue of *Dark Discoveries*. This time around, our theme is Sinister Appetites, and if that sounds slightly ambiguous, that's because it is—intentionally so. We did not want the content for this issue to center on erotic horror only, although that certainly is included. Instead, we broadened the theme's description to include the host of dark passions, everything our "dark side" longs for us to carry out continuously, but which may not be socially acceptable to pursue. This includes certain sexual desires, but also other, dare we say, animalistic urges, or at least murky, unexplainable, instinctual ones? Wanting to hurt another person, for instance, during a sexual encounter? Or worse, wanting to kill another person to satisfy sexual urges?

Freud called this a Will to Pleasure, and he was convinced these uncontrollable drives dominated human actions. Consequently, in the field of mental health now anyone who exhibits such "appetites" is clinically diagnosed a psychopath. "Not me," says your average Joe Shmoe on the street, "I would never entertain such fantasies." But in my experience—and I have a lot of it—in dealing with my own inner darkness, as well as helping others shine the light through theirs—I have become convinced that *everyone* to some degree experiences Sinister Appetites, whether or not they admit it. In fact, most often they are ashamed and driven into guilt; hence the denial and secrecy. But what's really going on here? What lies behind these taboo wants and sometimes dangerous desires?

We mentioned the "laboratory" explanation: mental illness. Then there is the religious claim, that of demons and Satan and so forth. Saint Paul said, "...what I would, that do I not; but what I hate, that do I," indicating the warring spiritual forces within (Wo)Man. But there's more to it than that. Human beings are extremely curious and exploratory, hence our modern science, which is always poking and prodding into nature to see what we can find, attempting to tame and dominate Her. The same is true of the inner part of the human, what Freud brilliantly classified as the unconscious (coined by Schelling, incidentally, and only adopted into psychology by Freud). The world religions might call this the soul. I would like to think of it also as the interior depths. Just as human beings love to penetrate (pun intended) to sub-nature and fiddle around with protons and neutrons, so the same applies to the sub-nature of our being. This is a perfectly healthy activity, in my opinion. And yet... with the scientists' penetration into sub-nature, they return with the atomic bomb.

The authors and writers in this issue of *Dark Discoveries* have set out to plumb the depths of the human psyche and dredge up their own human atom bombs. And they've come up with an amazing collection of work, which really highlights what it means to be a human, drawn to "that which I want to do, but should not want to do," to paraphrase Pauly. The stories that follow sink down into your core and settle there, leaving you with your own incorrigible passions to ponder.

The enormously talented British fantasist Storm Constantine gives us a glimpse

Becoming Invisible, Becoming Seen

BY SCOTT EDELMAN

As Martin stood over Adrianna, her cold body entirely hidden from him by nothing more than a thin sheet which he imagined had previously covered other bodies equally as cold, he pushed away the image of those countless dead strangers and thought—

For years, I've lied to my family. I've lied to my friends. I've lied to Adrianna. And most of all, worst of all, I've lied to myself.

It's time I stopped lying.

Slowly, with trembling hands, he folded back the sheet to reveal her face, and only her face. He had stared at her longingly more times than he could count, but not one of those instances had been accompanied by such a sense of freedom. Because for once, he had no fear she would open those beautiful eyes to see him, really see *him*.

He had become invisible.

Hating that it needed to be this way, but surrendered to the fact that this was the way it needed to be, he lowered his face to hers and kissed those blue cheeks, which felt cool, comfortably cool, against his lips.

At last, he thought. *At last I get to find out who I really am.*

***

Martin was surprised at how little it bothered him when the rear door of the police car slammed. Even though he'd ended up locked in there by choice, he'd expected his first time in such a vehicle would be anxiety-producing. Instead, it was only the touch of that hand to his scalp, pushing him gently down to ensure he didn't bang his head, that raised his blood pressure. Martin didn't much like being touched unexpectedly, not even when that touch came from an old friend.

"Sorry," said Joe, pulling his hand back after Martin winced under his cupped fingers. "Habit."

Joe walked around the rear of the car and slid behind the wheel. Then, with a nod to Martin and a smile at Randy, his partner, he drove away from the station.

"Wish I could have let you ride up front," said Joe.

"No problem," said Martin.

The partition sealing him in the back seat didn't disturb him at all. In fact, he believed it would make the night much easier. He could set aside his usual struggle to keep up a front. The unceasing tension between his inner life and the mask he allowed others to see was exhausting. It was much better for Martin's plan if his friend could only catch glimpses of him in the rearview mirror. At that remove, perhaps Martin could continue passing for normal.

He'd known Joe since they were kids growing up on the same block, but had lost touch. It was Martin's fault, of course. He'd made a conscious decision to keep his distance, to not let others get too close. It was the only survival skill that made sense, once he realized his desires were so different from those of others.

So when Joe's name popped up online as a suggested friend, Martin was prepared to ignore him as he'd ignored all the others. Just as he was about to mouse-click Joe into invisibility, though, he noted that his old friend had become a police officer, something he'd never have predicted. Martin suddenly saw a way free from the prison he'd constructed around himself. He realized that if he tread carefully, Joe could end up being useful.

The serendipity led to some messaging, a couple of meet-ups for beer—filled with the kind of small talk at which Martin had always been miserable—and now this outing, which he'd been able to make Joe think was his idea, a ride-along so he could see what daily life was like for a cop.

"Thanks for doing this," said Martin, feeling something had to be said as they drove through the night.

"No problem," said Joe. "It's nice to have some company."

"Hey, what am I?" said his partner.

"Tell me a story I haven't heard a thousand times before, Randy, and then we'll talk." After a few silent moments, Joe tilted his head back toward Martin. "Hope you get what you want out of this. Things have been quiet lately."

Martin shrugged. What other options did he have to capture his goal? He tried to remain hopeful, even as Joe's predicted quiet continued. The two men had to stop to take a report from sobbing parents about their runaway. They shuttled a homeless man to a shelter. (Martin squeezed to the opposite end of the squad car for that, hoping the man wouldn't be insulted, wouldn't think it had anything to do with his homelessness. He'd have done that to avoid contact with any stranger, but didn't know of any way to say that without revealing too much.) They checked on a couple of burglar alarms which had gone off, but there ended up being no signs of break-ins.

The shift was almost over when a call came in that turned out to be the one Martin was hoping for, yet dreading at the same time.

When Joe parked the car at the mouth of an alley, Martin could see on the ground, not so very far inside, a woman. He instinctively reached for the door handle that wasn't there.

"This one you're going to have to stay in the car for," said Joe.

Martin stared as the two men walked deeper down the alley, wishing he could follow. He needed to see more, desperately wanted to be beside them as they stood above what he refused to call the corpse, because that would change everything.

The body.

As they circled her, Martin could glimpse through their legs that when she'd lived, she had been young, perhaps in her early twenties, though at that distance he could not be entirely sure. She was fully clothed, her blouse only slightly torn, her tight jeans undisturbed, which meant he could make out none of her skin other than the one hand flung in his direction and, because her head was twisted toward the depths of the alley, that soft spot on the back of her neck.

From what little he knew of how crimes like these turned out—knowledge gained from TV, sure, but for some reason he trusted TV when it came to such things—this appeared to be a case of violence, not sex. He knew those two often overlapped, but they didn't seem to have done so now. This relieved Martin because he didn't want to think of others having had her in that way. And thankfully, there was no blood. Martin didn't need blood, never imagined blood when he allowed his fantasies free rein.

He felt strangely cheated that the woman's unknown assailant (who would likely remain forever unknown based on what Joe had let on about the statistics of police work) hadn't allowed his victim to fall facing the street. He wanted to look in her eyes, to see the nothingness there. He wanted to rub the back of a hand across one still and cooling cheek. He wanted to place an ear against her lips and hear… silence. He was surprised by how many things he wanted now that he was at last in the presence of death.

His breath, coming more quickly than usual, had frosted the glass of the window, and he had to swipe at it with a sleeve so he could keep her in his sights. It was her fault he had to do that.

No. No, it wasn't her. He knew that. It was him. He had always known that. It was never about them.

As he devoured whatever it was of her he could see, he found himself squirming. Raw reality was having as much of an effect on him as his unsupported imagination previously had. He needed to adjust a sudden erection to make himself more comfortable, surprised he needed to, yet not surprised at all.

What he'd feared about himself, what he'd recognized in himself, was true. He may have had doubts, but his body had none. Bodies did not lie.

Joe returned to the squad car and popped open the rear door.

It wasn't until the cool air hit Martin that he realized how overheated he'd become. There was now nothing between Martin and the object of his desire save space and time.

"Looks like whatever happened here is long over," said Joe. "So it's probably safe for you to get a little closer if you want your first look at a dead body. Just be careful where you step."

"No," said Martin, a little too quickly perhaps, since his supposed curiosity was the reason he'd given for the ride-along. He'd love to gaze closely upon a dead woman for the first time. But to do so while others watched? That would be far too personal an act. Besides, at that moment, it would also be embarrassing to stand. What would be revealed about Martin's nature would surely revolt Joe. How could he possibly explain it? Martin's reaction just wasn't normal.

But since when had Martin ever been normal? He'd let Adrianna see that part of himself, slowly, and over time, but Joe? Never.

"I'm OK where I am," Martin added. "I don't think I'm ready to see someone like that after all. But thanks, Joe, really."

"No problem."

Joe slammed the door, locking Martin away once more with his lies and his desires and his unbearable sense of urgency.

Maybe I should be locked away, he thought, unable to take his eyes from the dead woman, unable to stop thinking of what he wished he could do to her. *But maybe… maybe there's another way.*

***

Martin slid his lips across Adrianna's cheek to press them against hers, which did not press back, did not push away whatever part of himself called to her in this state. He turned his head to listen for the exhalation which, if heard, would tell him… what? That she might speak, tell him to stop, remind him that his desires were disgusting? He was never entirely sure of the nature of what he feared. His needs were beyond reason. He only knew that there was a meaning to be found in silence, and in Adrianna's absence was the only place he could find his own presence.

He pulled the sheet further down her body, revealing her pale form, naked, unmoving. He'd seen her unclothed before, slept beside her naked body, had tried, had failed, to do more than sleep. He'd done that for her, for them both, more than once, but there was something about her, about any woman alive, from which he inevitably recoiled. He couldn't control it. (He didn't know at this stage in his life if he'd choose to control it even if he could.) But seeing her this way, seeing her now… this was different.

When he touched her cold hip, there was no reaction from her. She didn't smile, didn't open her eyes to pin him with her gaze, to possibly judge him. Oh, he knew that consciously judging him was a thing she would never do, she'd told him that endlessly, but inside Martin, beyond and beneath choice, there was always that fear. That fear of being seen. That fear of being recognized. But no one would see what they were doing here together, him moving, her unmoving, in this room. No one could stop what he was driven to do next.

Adrianna was… perfect. And, if he was being honest with himself (which he had moments before promised to be, sworn to be), she always had been. Until today, though, that perfection had been hidden behind a veil (or so he told himself), suspected but never fully seen.

But now…

He didn't take the time to undress, even though when he imagined this, when the scenario he thought would never occur played out in his mind, he'd always seen them both as naked. But here in the actuality, his erection was too insistent, painful even, for him to pause to strip down. He no longer felt quite himself, or maybe he was now finally fully himself, and so he hurriedly unzipped and climbed atop the table. He reached for the lubricant he'd left nearby, because he'd expected Adrianna would be beyond providing any of her own (he'd once read that nails grew after death, but surely *that* response did not continue), and then, almost faster than thought, he was inside her at last.

"Oh, Adrianna," he sighed as he thrust, and thrust again, feeling complete, finally complete, after all his lonely years. All those years of unfulfilled longing. All those years of disappointing himself and others. All those years of feeling broken somehow. They were exorcised from his reality, gone as if they'd never existed. For how could anything that felt so right, so real, so true, ever be wrong?

With Adrianna unmoving in his arms, Martin suddenly became certain that the missteps in his life before then were not the false paths he'd thought they were, that each had a purpose which had steered him straight to this. The things he'd thought were failures which had caused him to change schools, change jobs, change cities, change friends, his frustrating inability with all the other potential partners, all of it had led here, and his perceived mistakes had not been mistakes, but course corrections on the road to his eventual union with Adrianna.

The fullness of emotion brought on by this perception overwhelmed him, and as he continued his rhythmic movements, he did not know how long he could last. And after a lifetime of waiting, he wanted the moment to last forever. He deserved that.

But then—

Adrianna twitched, and the pretense ended.

Martin tried fruitlessly to ignore her signs of life, but could not, and his desire instantly fled. Instead of swimming toward her, he found himself flailing to get away. He deflated, both physically and metaphorically, and rolled off her, suddenly no longer in the morgue they inhabited together in his mind, but back in his bedroom, the scene of so many previous catastrophes. He began crying, and when she touched him, he shrugged her hand from his shoulder.

"I should have known," he said between sobs, sliding to the floor beside the bed. "I was a fool to think this would ever work."

"You're no fool," said Adrianna, sitting up and pulling the sheet around her shoulders, still frigid from the ice bath which had cooled her down for the attempted masquerade. "You know me better than that. Would I be with a fool? There's so much more to us than this. Next time we try, we'll get this right. I can do this for you. Let me do this for you."

"No," he said, swiping a sleeve across his face. "It's impossible. No one is that good an actor. Not even you."

"You've been that good an actor," she said. "You've been that good an actor your whole life. But you don't have to act with me. You know that, right?"

He gazed up at Adrianna and smiled weakly. "You're a good friend," he said.

"I'm much more than that," she said. "Do you know how difficult it is not to react when you touch me? Maybe it would be easier for someone who didn't feel about you the way I do, but… I didn't play along with this just out of friendship."

"I know," he said. "And I… I love you, too. Since that first day I heard you humming to yourself over the cubicle wall, and joined in, I sensed you were different from the others. When we stood and looked at each other, I knew, I guess, that there could be something more. And then there *was* something more. But…"

"But?" she said, sliding off the bed to settle down beside him.

"But I don't think your love, my love, any love can be enough. If love could have fixed me, I'd have been fixed a long time ago."

"But we can keep trying, can't we? I felt you inside me. That wasn't a lie. We can figure this out. We *can*."

She took his hand, gripping his fingers tight, and because he'd come to care for her as he'd cared for no other, he fought the impulse to pull away. He'd never wanted to hurt her. He never wanted to hurt anyone. So he held her and tried to think of what to say next. But when nothing came, he gently placed her hand into her lap.

"I don't know," he said. "I just don't know."

"You're scared," she said. "I get that. But I'm not going anywhere."

Which was, he realized, exactly what scared him most.

***

"I could lose my job for this," said Joe as he unlocked the door to the morgue. He looked up and down the empty hallway, then waved Martin in. "If the video cameras weren't busted, I wouldn't even think of it."

"I know," said Martin, trying his best to sound sympathetic, but not really caring, even though he knew he should. What would be learned that night inside the brightly lit room with its metal tables and niche-lined walls was more important than any job, any friendship. This was the night he'd discover whether he could be made whole, and nothing else mattered. "I appreciate it. I do."

"You really sure you'll be able to sleep in here?" said Joe as he looked around and shook his head. "There's no way I could. The dead don't bother me out there, but in here… I don't know, there's something that feels wrong about it."

"I can only try," said Martin, cradling a duffle bag that contained a blanket and… other things. "We'll know one way or the other by morning."

Yes, thought Martin. *We'll know.*

What he would know, and what Joe thought would be known, were two different things. He'd shared with his friend a traumatic incident from childhood, an incident which had never really happened, but which he'd made sure was rich with the ring of truth.

How he'd been trapped in an elevator with one of his aunts, how that had caused her to have a heart attack, and how he'd been stuck in there with her body for hours.

How he'd had nightmares ever since, and great difficulty in getting a good night's sleep. How that had affected his entire life, and how therapy had availed him nothing. How the serendipity of his finding Joe again after all those years and learning his occupation made it occur to him that if only he could overcome that fear, the whole of his life might change.

Lies. All lies.

But Joe was his friend, or believed he was, at least, and so had accepted them. Or even if he hadn't fully accepted them, had been willing to go along with Martin's suggestion, which he'd done his best to make seem spontaneous.

"You sure you want to go ahead with this?" said Joe. "You sure your shrink's OK with the whole idea?"

"She's fine with it," said Martin. "Don't worry."

Martin wasn't seeing a psychiatrist, hadn't since he was a kid and his parents insisted he visit one because he'd seemed so withdrawn. What point would there be? He already knew what was wrong with him.

He leaned on the door, desperate to close it, the nearness of his goal making casual conversation even more difficult. He didn't want to come across as too excited, but was appearing reserved even possible? Hopefully, Joe would think his change in demeanor was only a case of nerves.

"See you tomorrow," he said.

"That's what I'm hoping," said Joe. "I don't want there to be a reason for me to get any phone calls before then, understand?"

"Got it."

And then Martin was alone.

Well, not entirely alone. For behind each of the rectangular metal doors, stacked three high and the length of the room wide, were bodies which had once held souls. They'd lived lives which had sculpted their personalities onto their flesh, etching each moment of their existence onto malleable, ephemeral skin. They were gone, and yet, they were also not, because the evidence remained. Now all Martin had to do was use the signs of what had been left behind to make the right choice. Behind one of those doors was the woman which would either cure him, or prove him irrevocably broken.

He studied the doors with their labels listing names, ages, heights, weights, and causes of death. But that information was too little to delineate a life, and certainly not enough for him to decide. He had to see for himself. He had to judge. The one meant for him, for this moment, couldn't be just anybody. Or, he thought, any body. (This time he allowed himself a smile.) But there was no denying that it would have to be someone… special.

Stacy. He'd start with Stacy.

He wrapped trembling fingers around a door handle, wondering if he was truly ready. But even as he hesitated, he knew that whether he was up for this or not didn't matter. There was no other direction in which he could go. It was either this… or end it all. And end up on a slab himself. And that he was really not ready for.

He grimaced, swung open the door, and slid out Stacy's slab.

She was a young woman, or had been a young woman anyway. Her dark hair pooled around her shoulders, and she was covered by a sheet pulled up to meet that hair. She'd be naked underneath, they'd all be naked, he knew, but he wasn't going to take advantage of the situation and peek. It didn't seem proper for him to see anything more than what this woman would have chosen to have him see during their first meeting in real life, had they ever met. His interest, however much it might have seemed that way when he'd tried in the past to explain it to others, was not prurient.

What he sought, the missing piece of his puzzle, would only be found above the neck. Only then, once the connection had been made, would he go further.

He studied Stacy's face, which even in repose, told him that she had not been happy. He could read that easily. Had she known that when she'd lived? Seeing her history sculpted there made him pause and wonder—what was his life imprinting on his own face even at that moment? What were others deciphering about his inner life when they looked in his direction?

He shrugged that thought away. This was definitely not the time for self-analysis. All that was important now was that he end up with someone who'd led a mostly happy life. He slid Stacy back where she would remain until her family, or some person who loved her, he hoped, claimed her, and slammed the heavy door shut. It echoed more loudly than he wished.

Next came Brianna, with red hair and a crooked grin which had survived even though she had not. She had died in her early 50s. Though she seemed serene, the writing on the card in her door tagged her as an apparent suicide. Yet there was nothing about her that indicated she had been distraught. Perhaps, thought Martin, that was because she had fully chosen her destiny, as he was attempting to choose his. He should have felt a connection with her, he knew, because he, too, had occasionally contemplated taking that way out. Instead, and to his surprise, he found himself judging her. Hypocritical of him, he knew. But he couldn't deny the emotion, and he wouldn't pretend otherwise. His time for pretense was over.

He looked at four more women, Alyssa, Christiana, Rafaella, Vanessa, rejecting each, surprised he could afford to be so choosy when finally afforded this opportunity, worrying that perhaps the one he needed was still out there, not yet ready to be brought to this place—before he found the one that seemed… perfect.

Was that a smile, a warm genuine smile, he saw on her lips, or was he just imagining it? He had enough self-awareness that he knew it could be either, but in the end, did it really matter? Her eyebrows were full, and even completely relaxed as she was, for no one is so relaxed as in death, one was slightly higher than the other, as if she was considering him with an almost quizzical expression. Her eyes were closed, and he let them remain that way. He preferred those windows shut. Her earlobes, which he could tell had once held numerous piercings, now were as naked as the rest of her, and that those had been stripped from her made him sad, sadder, strangely, than the far more permanent fact of her death.

He pressed one palm against a cold cheek, and smiled. It fit perfectly, as if they had been designed for each other. She was his and he was hers. There was no point in him searching or delaying any longer. She was the one.

He struggled to squeeze down beside her on the narrow slab, but it wasn't quite wide enough for them both. He had to turn her onto one side so that she faced him, and then slide her over, so that they could both fit together there. She was so heavy, far heavier than she appeared, dead weight for the first time literal rather than merely metaphorical, but then, he'd never touched a dead person before, so he had nothing to compare it to other than the living he'd touched in life melded with his dreams and fantasies.

The rolling slab creaked beneath the two of them, and he worried for a moment that it wouldn't be able to hold them both, but it would have to, wouldn't it? After all, she was a small woman, and he was only slightly larger. Certainly many of the dead who passed through that room were not, and some surely even outweighed them combined. He decided he had to risk it, even as he knew he was long past deciding anything. What was to happen next was beyond choice.

He reached under the sheet to grasp her wrist and used it to fling her arm around his chest. She did not hug him once he placed it there, could not hug him, but though that arm did not move from where he set it, it did not make her embrace less real. It comforted him like a snug blanket. He held her tight, sheet still mostly between them, pressed his cheek against hers, listened to the beating of his own heart. That he could hear no beating within her sped his thrub-dubbing faster than he had ever known.

He whispered her name, learned just moments before from the index card on the door to her compartment, in her ear, filling the syllables with the love of a lifetime. He knew he was saying it for himself, that she could not hear him, but he imagined that she could. And it was far more exciting to imagine that she could than if she actually could.

He pulled the sheet entirely away, let it drop to the floor.

He bent one of her knees, forcing it over his hip. It wasn't that easy, as she had stiffened, but then… so had he.

He didn't need to wait any longer. There was no need to postpone the inevitability with foreplay. He unzipped, and slid on a condom, so no evidence would be left behind. As crazed with passion as he was, he still had sense enough for that. The act of doing so, though, almost got him off all by itself, so intense was his excitement.

He forced his way in, apologizing as he did so, and even though he was hard, it hurt. But he didn't mind the pain, which only reinforced to him that this was really happening. He was happy it didn't hurt her, though, glad she was beyond knowing such things.

Once he entered her, it didn't take long. It couldn't. All it took was one thrust, then two, and he exploded. He bit into his forearm to muffle a scream. He tasted blood, his own blood, telling him that he was alive, and then, almost immediately, began to cry. Not, as he'd always thought he might when contemplating his reaction as this finally occurred, out of self-hatred, but out of happiness.

For the first time Martin could remember, he was truly happy.

***

Martin was thinking of Stacy again, the woman who'd completed him in a way he'd never dared dream could happen, not really, when Adrianna startled him by snapping her fingers under his nose, bringing him back to the familiar coffee shop where they were in the middle of one of their lunch breaks. He had to take stock of where he was for a moment, almost as if he'd been woken groggily from a nap, needed to remind himself, *Oh, here I am.*

He'd been drifting away from Adrianna frequently, and not just her, but most everyone he knew, since the events of the weekend, submerging often into a kind of fugue state, drawn there by that impossibly deep connection he'd felt with another human being for the first time. He could tell she believed he was pulling away—not understanding that rather, he was being pulled—and so their time together this week had been strained, as she fought to prevent him from vanishing into himself.

"Sorry," he said. But he wasn't, not really. He'd much rather be lost in those memories at the moment than focused on having lunch with Adrianna. Not something he would tell her, though. Just because he'd finally found what he'd been looking for didn't make it necessary to hurt her. She'd been good to him in a way no one ever had been before, seen something in him he did not see in himself.

"What's going on?" she asked. She leaned across the table and spoke in a whisper. "Are you still thinking about… the other night? About us? We can try again, you know. We *should* try again. I've been practicing. You know. Holding my breath. Remaining still. Not moving a muscle. *Any* muscle. We can get this right. I know we can."

She appeared so vulnerable in her hope that he was touched, and he tried his best not to react. Not yet. There could be no right between them, he was sure of it, not now that his night in the morgue proved beyond a doubt that whatever Adrianna could deliver to him would be just a pallid imitation. He'd have to lie to her, now and forever, and though he had spent a lifetime lying, knowing the right lie was not an easy thing.

His recent lies were taking him into unfamiliar territory. Like the lies he'd had to tell Joe about what had happened, both in the morgue and after, how he'd felt he was approaching a breakthrough, lies both small and large that were necessary so that his friend would let him return for a repeat performance. (Because he'd have to return. He'd have to.) They were lies he couldn't even begin to share with Adrienne, because on learning them, she'd see how false they were. She knew him for what he was, which meant that upon any mention of a morgue, she'd know exactly what he was doing in that room. His prior openness would make it hard to hide now. He had a momentary regret that he'd opened his soul to her, even though that decision had given him great comfort at the time.

"Well?" she asked.

"No," he said, in a single syllable that trailed off, promising more to come. But he had no idea what that should be, and so sat there looking at her as she looked at him expecting an explanation.

"No what?" she said. "We can't stop now. We can figure it out. No one should have to continue living the way you do. You deserve for us to work it out. I know what it's like to need something you can never have. It's not good."

He wanted to tell her that she'd misinterpreted what he'd just said, that his no didn't mean they should stop trying, but rather that they should just… stop. He had found someone else. Some*thing* else. But he didn't want to hurt her by telling her that, especially not considering the unique nature of the person he'd found and the type he would find fulfillment with in the future. He'd dated before, had broken up with women before, but it was never due to a reason like this, and usually, he was broken up *with*, because they'd tire of what he could never fully give them. So he just let his "no" hang there for a while, took another sip of his coffee, and tried to think of a way to say what needed to be said.

But before he could, she reached across the table to touch his hand. He looked into her eyes, and what he saw there made him stop looking for the words. He thought, *I can't hurt this woman.* And so he instead decided to say things he did not believe.

"Sure, we'll try again," he said, and her smile brought him a surprising amount of happiness. "Of course. Just… not immediately. I need to get my head straight first. Let's wait a bit. Let's wait."

But even as he spoke, he was also wondering how

quickly Joe would let him return to the morgue to do again what he'd done before.

***

Stacy, the woman he'd made love to the previous week in the morgue—and yes, he thought of it as making love, even though he knew how ludicrous that would sound to anyone else—was gone. But then, of course she'd be gone. As he stood in the center of the room once more, scanning the wall of doors and the new names which had taken the place of the ones with which he was already familiar, he knew it was foolish that he'd thought, even briefly, she might have remained, knew that bodies cycled through the morgue quickly on the way to their final destinations—but still, that twinge of disappointment was there. There would never be a second encounter, a chance for rediscovery, a deeper exploration. She was gone, and he would never see her again.

But there would be another. Many others, in fact, or else… what? He didn't know the alternative for sure. He only knew that having achieved what he'd desired, losing it would be worse than never having had it at all.

Martin had convinced Joe to let him spend a second night at the morgue with yet another fabulation, this time explaining how his first night visit had helped him, the way his nightmares had lessened in both frequency and intensity, the encouragement he'd received from his (non-existent) shrink, who (or so Martin claimed) had been happy with his progress and suggested he continue with the extremely unorthodox treatment. Martin had draped enough believable detail on his story that Joe had been convinced. Joe was a good friend. At least one of them was.

Thinking of Joe, of their one-sided friendship, Martin flashed on Adrianna, and it occurred to him that though he had been a lousy friend to them both, he'd been especially deficient with her. But then, he always had been. He knew that.

Was this thing of his which had finally become a reality instead of a dream the impediment that had all along prevented any true closeness? Was that why Adrianna and all the women who had come before her were such better friends to him than he could ever find it in himself to be to them?

Maybe. Probably. But in the end, it didn't matter. It just *was*. And this was not the place to spend thinking about such things. He didn't have time to waste.

He was aware he'd been lucky the previous week, knew how much of a risk he'd taken, yet here he was taking another one. The locked door behind him wouldn't have stopped anyone who needed to deliver a new body. He understood that. And he got that if he was caught in the act—an act which he wasn't really sure how to name, because necrophilia sounded so cold, so clinical, so stripped of the love that he felt motivated him—being arrested would be the least of his worries.

But he couldn't retreat from his plan now. It would be like willingly returning to a life in a cage. And he'd already had too many years of that life.

He slowly opened the first drawer, inside of which the card promised he'd find a woman named Trinity, and was filled with a combination of hope and dread, one strengthened by the success of his first experience. What if he found no one special this night? What if there was no one meant just for him waiting to be revealed? He needed more than a random compliant form. Whoever he chose had to be exactly that. Chosen. She had to have that certain slant of chin, earlobes with just the right amount of fleshiness, those lashes resilient under his thumbs.

Which poor Trinity definitely didn't have. She appeared starved and beaten, and seemingly went out of this world with a struggle. She made him realize how lucky he'd been the first night that he'd been able find someone not showing signs of a violent end. That wasn't usually how people ended up here. No, it couldn't be this one.

He pushed the first drawer shut, then quickly caught it before it clanged too loudly. His desire was clearly making him careless. He hurriedly move to the next niche.

No, not Alyssa either, with the large bruise on her left cheek. (*Who could do that to a woman*? he thought, knowing all the while that some might ask the same question about him.) Nor Jasmine with a gunshot wound just under one breast. Not even Tiffany, for whom the cause of death wasn't quite so evident, but whose teeth forced her lips into a frown.

He considered and rejected each one with less deliberation than he had the last time. Because, he guessed, having experienced Stacy, he knew there was someone out there waiting for him.

And then… there she was. Mia.

He only had to look at her for an instant to know that. How had she died? He did not care. It did not matter. Seeing her stretched out before him brought back memories of that song his father had sung to his mother about seeing a stranger across a crowded room… though if Martin had seen this stranger across a crowded room when she'd been alive, there would have been none of the magic he felt at this moment.

Tears rolled down his face from the richness of his emotions, and one dropped from his cheek and onto hers. He kissed the spot where it had fallen, then climbed on top of her and gazed down into that calm face, staring lovingly at the lids of those closed eyes which would never open, never cry again. Another tear fell, giving her the appearance of being as happy as he was. He flattened himself upon her, stroking her close-cropped hair, tucking his chin into one side of her neck, whispering something into her unhearing ear which surprised him even as it came.

He didn't remember having said "I love you" before and having meant it. Had he said it to Adrianna? He wasn't sure. He thought he had, but the love he shared with Adrianna was a love which could never be fulfilled, never be carried through to completion, not like what he had with Mia. He just wasn't made that way.

He slipped his left hand under her back and used it to balance himself as he moved his right down her side to one hip. His fingers tingled as they slid along her smooth and slightly clammy skin. He couldn't help but laugh as giddiness overtook him. He moved his free hand to his waist, and was about to shift his weight so he could unzip, when he felt something against his stomach…

What?

There rose a strange kind of (at first) nearly imperceptible vibration, one he'd never known a body to make, which grew into a trembling in her gut, then exploded into a rumbling. How was a body even capable of that? He jerked slightly back at first, but when the movement subsided, he decided to attribute it to nothing more than trapped gasses moving through her recently deceased body, gasses set free by his act of laying upon her.

He'd heard of such things, so when the sounds and movements began again, he assumed this was an inevitable byproduct of the path on which he was now walking. He smiled lovingly and waited for her movements to pass. But this time, they did not.

Then she turned her head toward his cheek so swiftly and urgently that his own head was shoved aside, and he screamed, pulling back from where he'd been nuzzling her. He fell off her and off the slab onto the hard floor and looked up in horror as the woman, seemingly dazed, sat up, her movements jerky. For a moment, Martin, puzzled, uncomprehending, imagined this was one of those cases he'd heard about in which a coroner misdiagnosed as dead a person who was not, and fear spiked in him that she would report what he had been doing. But then Mia's eyes snapped open, and she looked at him steadily, unblinkingly, and he knew… not knowing how he knew… that she was hungry.

Her jaw began to chatter, clacking open and shut so fast and with such force that a tooth flew from her mouth to bounce on the linoleum. Her arms then rose and reached out for him, causing her to fall from the slab, collapsing forward in a jumble of clumsy limbs. As Martin skittered backwards across the floor, he could tell to his horror— she wanted him. And not at all in the way in which he'd wanted her.

He got up to his feet far more quickly than her stiffened body allowed. She had trouble rising, and once upright, she staggered back against the slab, which gave him time for a frantic scan of the room. He needed a weapon, but saw none. (Where were all the knives? Where were all the bone saws?) He backed away, bumping into a desk, and swept his hand behind him without taking his eyes off the woman. He grabbed something and threw without thinking… but it was only a stapler, which bounced off her chest. She kept moving forward, mouth impossibly wide, growling loud enough that the sound of it hurt his ears.

Hating to take his eyes from her, but knowing it was his only hope, he turned and ran for the door, which he barely had time to unlock before she caught up with him. Her fingers ripped through his loose shirt and she dragged him across the room. As she climbed his back, he curled away from her, hoping that by bending he'd put his neck out of the reach of those teeth, but there was only so far he could go. She was much too strong for him.

As Martin rocked with all his strength, trying to shake her from his shoulders, he heard the door being flung open, followed by Joe's startled voice.

"Jesus, Martin. What the hell is going on in here? What are you doing?"

"Help me, Joe!" Martin shouted, hearing her teeth snapping the air behind his ears. "Get her off me!"

"Is she alive?" asked Joe.

"Yes," said Martin. "No. I don't know. Do something!"

Martin could feel Joe peel the woman from his back. He turned to see him push her across the room. Joe then grabbed one of Martin's wrists and yanked him to his feet. Martin watched with horror as Mia slowly climbed to her feet, her eyes still filled with hunger.

"Shoot her!" he screamed.

"Who do you think I am?" said Joe, backing slowly away from the woman. "I don't go around shooting everything I don't understand. Maybe she's just sick."

"It's more than that," said Martin, his voice cracking. "She was dead. And now she isn't."

Mia spring toward them, and Joe pulled Martin out of her path. If not for that, she'd have landed where Martin had been a moment before.

"Let's get out of here," Joe said, as she began to rise once more.

Joe pushed him out of the room and quickly followed, locking the door just as the woman slammed against it. She hammered at the barrier with a strength that seemed impossible for her size, but though the door bounced on its hinges, she still wasn't strong enough to break through.

"I came running as soon as I heard the noise," said Joe. "You're lucky I was still in the building."

Joe put a hand on Martin's shoulder, turning his focus away from the threat.

For a moment—but only for a moment—Martin felt such relief he thought he'd tell Joe everything that had occurred from when his friend had left him in the room, and not just that, but *everything*, back to when it all truly began— or at least when he realized it had—but he immediately realized his behavior would be more horrifying to Joe than anything the woman had done or become. Better to be silent. It had always been better to be silent.

"I have no idea what happened," he said, knowing that he was lying, yet feeling as if he was being truthful at the same time.

But then Martin could hear other sounds, the movement of more of the dead, awakening (or whatever it was) and trying to break free from their cubicles… and he suddenly did have an idea. A very depressing idea. For if the dead were no longer staying dead, what that would mean for him would be…

No. Better not to think about it. Better not to think at all.

***

Martin had begged. He'd pleaded. He'd told Joe how close his help had brought him to a breakthrough. But none of Martin's attempts to convince Joe to allow a return to the morgue had been successful. With the dead suddenly and inexplicably coming back to life, and with the lengths of time before each return varying and unpredictable, Joe insisted there was no way he would let Martin try again what he'd tried twice, but only succeeded at once.

And with all eyes—and the newly repaired cameras— in the station now on the morgue, there was no way they could even think of sneaking him in and out. This was no longer a world in which rules could be bent.

And besides, said Joe, as bad as the nightmares were,

was a cure really worth risking your life for?

It was. At least a cure for what *really* ailed Martin.

In what had to be the crummiest case of bad timing ever, the world chose to change right after *he* had changed. It was almost as if the universe was laughing at him. In the days after Joe had saved his life, Martin had called in sick from work and did nothing but watch television. He was too morose for much of anything else. And watching the news, which too often interrupted the regular programming that might have distracted him, made him even more morose. All the talking heads agreed—the dead were coming back to life, which made him feel dead himself. Because where did that leave him? After what he'd finally been privileged to feel, he refused to accept what the world seemed to be telling him—that he would be allowed to feel it no longer. Surely there was a space between death and rebirth into which the future would allow him to insert himself.

"I don't know what to tell you," Joe had said during their most recent conversation, when his friend had to disappoint him yet again. "We're all going to have nightmares about the dead now. You're no longer alone there."

But what Martin couldn't tell Joe was that he *was* still alone, because what he was having weren't the nightmares he'd lied about, but fantasies. Fantasies suddenly, miraculously realized. Fantasies that he needed to continue realizing.

And so, the following week (the waiting had been unbearable, but that's how long it took Martin to do what needed to be done) he found himself sitting in his car, listening to a stolen police radio, hoping his salvation hadn't been snatched from him just when he'd finally learned it was even possible. That was the only way he could think of to learn for sure. Eavesdropping in darkness on deserted streets, waiting to hear reports of a murder (and doing more than just waiting, but hoping for it, praying for it), he felt more guilty about his theft of the radio than he did about any of the things he'd done or was about to do.

As he listened anxiously to the disembodied voices, it seemed an unusually quiet night, with much less chatter than the time he'd ridden in the back of Joe's police car. It was disappointing, but it did make sense. Fear was keeping many people home, and he figured he might have to wait a while before those adventurous enough to wander out ran into not quite the adventure they were looking for.

So he was relieved when a call came in near dawn about a stabbing at a bar, and a woman's body the owner wanted the hell out of there. Martin raced to the scene before the police could… or likely even wanted to from what Joe had let on. No one except Martin was in any hurry to rush to the side of the dead these days.

When he arrived at the bar, the only one there was the nervous owner, who smoked a cigarette as he paced the street out front. All of the man's (living) customers had fled, and with no one knowing how long it would be before this particular corpse came back, even he wanted to get away as soon as possible. Which was lucky for Martin—it meant the man didn't particularly care that the person who arrived to pick up the body showed no signs of being a police officer. He never even questioned it. And

so Martin was easily able to persuade the man to leave him alone there, as long as he promised to lock up as soon as he was done.

"She's right by the television," the man said, handing Martin the keys. "I didn't touch her."

Martin entered, locking the door behind him. It took a moment for his eyes to adjust, but then, there she was, right where the man had said. Apparently, the woman had stood on tiptoe to change the channel on the television, someone hadn't liked it, and it ended with her dead on the floor. He still had trouble understanding why people did such things. But the why of it didn't bother him so much at that moment. He may not have understood. But he was grateful.

He knelt beside the woman, lifting her chin so he could get a better look. Her eyes had remained open, and her gaze, no longer under her control, was focused through and beyond him.

She was pretty, with high cheekbones and a smile that had survived her death. Not quite his type, though, but she would have to do. He could no longer afford to be picky. (Could he ever truly have afforded to be picky?) He tried to scoop her up in his arms, the first time he'd ever done anything like that, and failed, falling to the floor beside her, narrowly missing the pool of blood that had spilled from her wound. Seeing no other option, he tucked his hands into her armpits and dragged her, feeling as he pulled her along that she deserved better. Her shoes peeled off as they staggered awkwardly together to his car, but he left them where they'd separated. She wouldn't need them ever again, and neither would he. Shoes had never played a part in his fantasy.

The streets were still deserted, and no one saw him place her—clumsily but gently, ever so gently—in his trunk. He wished he could have set her beside him in the passenger seat, but thought… no. It wasn't that the blood, which still occasionally dripped, bothered him. Rather, he didn't want to chance her sudden reawakening while his eyes were busy on the road.

At his apartment, after first checking he wouldn't be seen (the streets there were deserted as well, so in that moment at least, his curse was also his blessing), he took her upstairs and laid her out on his bed, the same bed where he and Adrianna had so recently pretended. But this would be no act. He unbuttoned her shirt, dark with blood, and beneath the damp cloth saw for the first time where she had been stabbed. As he washed her wound, he marveled at how so small a cut had such a large effect. People were like balloons, he guessed. Prick them and they explode.

Once her skin was clean, he draped a sheet across her side so he would not have to see the evidence of what had ended her life. He didn't like thinking of her violent end, of anyone's violent end. He preferred to think of her as simply having fallen asleep and not having woken up.

He closed those staring eyes, wiped away her makeup, and sitting beside her, wondered how much time he had. He could have hours. He could have days. He could have no time at all. He knew he was playing Russian Roulette with a dead woman as the bullet, but he didn't care. He only hoped whatever time remained would be enough.

He felt safe behind the locked door of his own apartment, or as safe as anyone could sanely feel beside a dead body that would soon come back to life, so he was comfortable undressing, unlike at the morgue, where he had to be alert for interruptions. He folded his clothes neatly and laid them on the end table beside the hammer and butcher knife he'd previously placed there. He hoped neither would be necessary, that he could get done what he needed to do before the inevitable, but it was best to prepare for all eventualities.

As he lay atop her, he felt himself grow hard immediately, as he expected he would. He wanted to enter her quickly, but he also wanted to make this time last. So even though his body urged *stay, stay, stay*, he rose from the bed and found her bloody clothes. She didn't carry a wallet—her pants had been much too tight for her to do so—but in one pocket he found a credit card and driver's license.

Maxine. Her name had been Maxine. It was a good name. And she deserved a good name, especially now.

Martin returned to the bed and called her by that name, imagining as he did so that she was able to hear it. That its syllables, spoken slowly and repeatedly, comforted her. He massaged her temples, kissed the space between her breasts, stroked her thighs, whispered that name over and over until it lost all meaning, became all meaning.

Then he could bear to wait no longer, and it was time.

Maxine hadn't been dead as long as his first discovered lover, but dead was dead, and a lubricant was still needed, which he retrieved from a drawer. He shuddered as he entered her, but having entered her, moved no further. He paused, as devoid of movement as his partner, and took several deep breaths to regain his composure. As soon as he was sure of himself, sure he'd hold back until the moment was right, he began to move again. And then, slowly and steadily, he loved her.

What was he looking for here? Why this not that? He'd questioned himself for years, starting as a teenager, as others did of themselves, but he never came up with an answer. As he moved rhythmically above Maxine, Martin knew in reality what he'd always hypothesized—that the question was its own answer. There are some things that exist in a place beyond reason, and as he dotted Maxine's forehead with little kisses, rubbed his cheek against hers, lifted one of her feet so an ankle dug into his back, he knew that he was what he was, and always would be. And he felt no shame in that. He had finally found himself.

Thank you, Maxine. Thank you, Maxine. Thank you. Thank you. Thank you.

He was about to finish, could feel his skin tingling as the moment began to overtake him, when to his horror, her vaginal muscles snapped tight around him, both halting his orgasm and trapping him against her. He was doubly horrified, because not only would that reaction, or any reaction coming from any sexual partner, have repulsed him, but also the movement meant she was alive again.

Martin flailed against her, trying to roll off her as yet only partially reanimated body, but could not. He was painfully engorged, and stuck. He lunged toward the end table, but couldn't get quite close enough, so instead of grabbing either of his prearranged weapons, he ended up

sweeping them to the floor.

He was naked, defenseless, and pinned inside a dead woman. Which meant, he knew, that he would soon be dead himself.

Her eyes snapped open, and this time, he saw to his horror that she was no longer looking flatly through him, but directly at him. Her lips peeled back, revealing teeth which soon would be aiming for his throat, and he shrieked. He snatched the pillow from under her head and pushed it over her hungry face. Laying an elbow across the pillow, he struggled to keep those teeth from his flesh, at the same time rocking himself to one side and fumbling at the floor with his other hand. He managed to graze the hilt of the knife with his fingertips, but in doing so only ended up pushing it further away. Maxine, or what had once been Maxine, reached her hands around his back and pulled him closer. As she did so, he could feel through the pillow the dull gnawing of her teeth against his cheek. It was clear that slim protection wouldn't keep him safe for long. She would surely chew through soon and that would be the end of him.

He screamed, and hurled himself to the side, unbalancing their conjoined bodies so that he fell off the bed and pulled her over on top of him. Near hysteria, he quickly rolled once more so that she was under him again—but now she was on top of the weapons, and they were still out of his reach. She kicked wildly, her legs hammering against the floor as she tried to launch herself up at him. The pillow was still wedged between them, was managing to keep her head pinned against the floor, but he knew his strength wouldn't last forever. And meanwhile, his erection, trapped in the vise of her corpse, refused to diminish and release him.

Then came a banging at the door, and the shouting of his name.

Adrianna.

"I don't know what's happening," she said, her voice muffled. "But I'm coming in."

She still had a key, though she hadn't used it in weeks, and he hadn't had the heart to ask for it back. Thank God for that. He heard the thunder of her footsteps behind him, even over the banging of Maxine's limbs, and then—

"Move your head," Adrianna said. "Move it! Now!"

As he craned his neck to the right, Adrianna yanked the pillow away, and before Maxine's teeth could rip into Martin's neck, she brought the base of a lamp down against the dead woman's skull.

Once, and Maxine shuddered and wailed.

Twice, and she quivered and hissed.

Then a third time, and she stopped moving, this time permanently. Her body relaxed once more into death. And Martin was free.

Adrienne helped him rise from the corpse, but they didn't stand long, for together they tumbled to the floor, their backs against the bed, the dead woman at their feet. Adrienne reached behind her to pull the sheet from the bed and drape it around his shoulders.

"Tell me the truth," she asked quietly, and then paused so long he wondered if she'd changed her mind and decided she really didn't want to know. Only after she looked away from him did she say with great precision,

"Did you kill her?"

"No," he said loudly, offended she would think he was capable of such a thing, even as they sat before the evidence of exactly what he was capable. "I would never do something like that. I could never. You know that."

"But you'd do something like *that*," she said, tilting her head behind them toward the bed where Maxine's reanimating had interrupted their lovemaking.

"But… that's different," he said. "That doesn't hurt anyone. I would never hurt anyone. Don't you understand? I thought you understood."

"Oh, I understand," she said. "But you *are* hurting someone. You're hurting yourself. And you're hurting… you're hurting me."

Adrianna leaned her head on his shoulder. He tensed, but she did not lift it, though she had often previously responded to those types of signs. She sighed, then spoke as if to a child. A child that was loved. But still, a child.

"What are we going to do with you, Martin?" she said.

"There's nothing to be done with me." He shifted uneasily, wishing she'd move her head, but knowing no way to tell her to do so, not after she'd saved his life. That she was still there after what she'd seen was remarkable. He didn't know that he'd have had it in him to remain by her side had the situation been reversed. "This is who I am. This is who I'll always be."

"But don't you get that this is not going to work? You can't go on like this. Especially not with what's started happening in the world. What you want, it can't be made real. Not anymore. You and me, that's real. I've been watching your apartment, waiting for you to realize that. If I hadn't, who knows what would have happened."

"I know what would have happened."

"Well, it didn't. And you know what that means. It's a sign. It's the universe telling us something. We've got to keep trying."

He shook his head, pulled the sheet more tightly around his shoulders, wishing he could enclose himself in a cocoon.

"No," he said, trying his best not to sound mean, just totally honest, which is what she deserved. But he knew his best wasn't good enough. It never had been. "We both know it will never work. You do, don't you? If you know me, really know me, then you also know that. There's no way we can fix this."

"There *is* a way," she said. "There's got to be a way."

He felt dead inside. Thinking that, and of those who actually were dead inside, almost made him smile. Almost. But the events of the night showed him he'd have no reason to smile again. He'd been bent one way all his life, and now that he'd finally figured things out, the world was suddenly bent another way, and despair was the only sane reaction. Dead inside felt just about right.

"I love you, Martin," said Adrianna.

"And I love you," he said. "I've told you that. But I also told you that love is not enough. Love was never enough. If it had been, we wouldn't be…"

He gestured at the twice-killed body before them.

"…here."

He leaned away from her, letting her head slide from his shoulder. He closed his eyes, hunching forward. There

was no future for them, could be no future for them. He saw that. Why couldn't she?

In a few moments, he could hear Adrianna, without a word, without a touch, getting up. Then he heard the closing of his apartment door.

And then he was alone.

With Maxine. But alone.

And alone, more alone than he had ever been, was, horribly, the way it was going to have to be from then on.

***

It took Martin longer to dispose of Maxine's body than he'd originally thought it would when he first picked her up what seemed like a lifetime ago. Not because of the difficulty of the mere physical act of loading her back into his car, transporting her, and then abandoning her, but due to the time it took for him to fully commit to the decision that, yes, she had to go.

After Adrianna had left, he seemed to fall into a fugue state that prevented any action, even as he told himself repeatedly to get on with it. When that finally passed, the first thing he was able to rouse himself to do was replace the pillow over Maxine's face so he wouldn't have to see the mangled results of his rescue. The second thing he did was remove the sheet from around his shoulders, the sheet which Adrianna had lovingly wrapped there, fold it neatly, and then place it over Maxine's stomach, hiding that wound, too. The third thing he did was less something he did by choice, and more a thing that occurred beyond his doing of it. It just happened uncontrollably.

He looked down at Maxine, all signs of the violence which had been done to her, first by a stranger, and then by his friend, obscured, and felt his attraction returning. For an infinitesimal sliver of time, he was actually thinking of continuing with his original plan and seeing it all to completion.

Then, before he could turn that impulse into action, the thought disgusted even him, and all the shame and embarrassment over what were his essential drives, a shame and embarrassment which he'd thought had been erased through his recent actions, came flooding back. That he'd considered acting out on his fantasy in that instant, however briefly, sickened him, and he thought, now he knew how the world would regard even the least of what he'd done. He swore to himself he'd never give in to such a thing, as doing so would turn an act that was supposed to be beautiful into something sordid.

And yet.

And yet…

He found he could not, no matter how much he thought he should, immediately part from Maxine. And so he sat beside her all that day, and into the next as well. After his most recent moments of temptation and his rejection of it, she no longer called to him in that way, and when he looked at her, she was not a sexual object, but rather a symbol of his horribly lonely future. That empty future floated before him, filling his mind. She was more than just a dead body. She was physical proof of the void to come, the period at the end of his sentence. And his sentence was life.

It wasn't until she began to decay and her smell grew overpowering that he was finally able to let her go. He clumsily dressed her back in the clothes in which he'd found her, clothes now stiffened by her dried blood, and used a hat and scarf which Adrianna had left behind to hide the head wound. He then hustled her down the stairs and into his car once more. This time he allowed her to sit up front, her head tilting against the glass so that anyone who spotted them would assume she was napping.

He still wasn't entirely clear about what he wanted to do next, and so at first drove aimlessly, wondering where he should take her. Where he should *leave* her. He knew one easy answer was to just return her to the bar where he'd picked her up, even though before everything had gone wrong he'd initially rejected that idea. But it occurred to Martin that, after all, the bar owner probably deserved to end up with the disposal of the body being his problem simply because he hadn't helped that night, hadn't intervened to prevent Maxine's murder. And he certainly should never have let a stranger like Martin walk in and whisk away her body, even with the way the world had changed. Not everyone would have had the same pure intentions. (Remarkable. Even with the state of Maxine's body, he still believed his intentions were pure.) Martin pushed away those thoughts of making some sort of cosmic point, though. He knew in his heart that she deserved better.

We all deserved better.

He eventually found himself at a nearby hospital, not quite sure how he'd gotten there. He gently carried her to a bench which was partially in shadow due to a bulb that had gone out. He forcibly folded her into a seated position, and then placed her hands together in her lap, weaving her fingers together. He sat beside her on the very edge of the bench. But only briefly.

"I'm sorry things had to turn out this way," he said. "You were probably a very nice person."

As Martin drove off, he glanced from the road ahead to her form in the rearview mirror until she shrunk too small to be seen. He made his way back to his apartment, wiping away tears with bloody fingers.

At his building, he took the elevator to his floor and walked slowly down the hall, exhaustion finally having overtaken him. When he got to his door, he pulled out his key, but discovered—the door was already unlocked. He would have sworn he had locked it, it was an ingrained habit with him… and there was only one person he'd ever trusted with a key.

Adrianna.

Even after what he'd done to her with his actions, his words, and his silences, even after all of his crimes of the heart and crimes of the body, she still hadn't left it behind when she walked off that last horrible night. He pushed the door open, but remained outside, uncertain he had the strength to confront the accusations—loving accusations, but accusations nonetheless—he was sure he'd find written on her face.

"Adrianna?" he called from the hallway.

There was no answer. With no other alternative, he entered his apartment, continuing to say her name, continuing to hear nothing in return. Once he reached his darkened bedroom, he noticed a sliver of light streaming from under the closed bathroom door. As sure as he was that his front door had been locked, he was even more certain he'd turned off that light.

He crossed the bedroom quickly, but having done so, pushed the door open slowly, whispering her name once more. Inside, he found his answer as to why there'd been no answer.

Adrianna was submerged in the bathtub. Naked. Unmoving. No bubbles breaking the surface of the water. On the bathmat, next to an empty pill bottle, a sheet of paper.

He leapt past them both and yanked her from the water, soaking his clothes, but not giving a damn about it. He kept calling her name as he carried her to the bed. She did not answer. (He knew she would not answer. But that did not stop him from calling her again and again.) He touched two fingers to her throat, pressed an ear to her ribcage, held one of her wrists tenderly, but… nothing.

Adrianna was gone.

He staggered back to the bathroom, where he knelt beside the note, its writing smeared from his failed attempt at rescuing her the way she had rescued him. He could barely read it through his tears.

She loved him, she said. She understood him, she said. And she wanted to be with him forever, she said. But she knew… this was the only way.

Do quickly what you feel called upon to do, what we both want you to do, she wrote. Before what inevitably will happen inevitably happens.

Stunned by what she had done, uncertain at first how he felt, he returned to the bedroom, the writing on the damp page growing blurrier in his hands. He gazed at her, imagined her watching his apartment, waiting for her moment to, with her death, bring their future to life, and considered this impossibility, this inevitability.

She understood, he thought. *I never truly believed anyone could.*

She was so beautiful lying there, so serene. But for how long? How long would she lie there like that before changing and taking back the gift she had given him?

The amount of time that remained was meaningless. She had given herself to him in a way no one else could. He could not scorn something that precious.

He slowly removed his clothes, savoring the fullness of what was to come. He refused to rush this. He folded each item neatly, stacked them on the table beside the bed, and placed her note, by now no longer legible, atop them. He retrieved a towel from the bathroom, sat beside her on the bed, and tenderly patted her skin dry.

She looked peaceful there, as if she knew where she was and what he had begun to do, and welcomed it. He smiled, and wondered—if she could see him now, would he appear peaceful, too? He thought he would, and he wished she *could* see it, could see what she had done for him, though at the same time realizing that if she could, then she'd paradoxically have nothing to see.

He stretched out beside her, and studied her profile. He'd never been able to see her quite like that before, had never managed to catch her unawares. Oh, they'd playacted at it, but neither of them could fake it well enough to pull it off, not convincingly. She knew that.

So she had made it real.

He kissed her cheek, gently. She did not stir, did not turn her head to kiss him back, which was as it should be. Which was as it had to be. He lifted one of her hands, fanned out her fingers, and spread them across his chest.

That was all the touch he needed from her to be ready.

He rolled onto her, rolled into her, crying out as he did so, feeling for the first time complete. He'd thought what he'd had with the others had already completed him, but he'd been wrong. The others had been strangers, and whatever communion they'd had was but an imitation of this solemn, this euphoric, this liberating act chosen freely by both parties. He gazed at her, the woman who loved him so greatly that she was willing to lead him to this place, and he never wanted their dance to be over. And yet, it had to be over. Because that had been the point of her gift.

Martin balanced above her, alternating between moving slowly and not at all, pacing himself, waiting for that movement in death which he would never have welcomed in life. And when it came, when she fluttered, when he felt the subtle vibrations that signaled her return… rather than retreat, he thrust forward, dove deep, dove for her soul.

She opened her eyes. She looked at him. She saw him, he thought. There was a hunger there, yes. But there was also love. Wasn't there?

"I love you, Adrianna," he said. He knew it, really knew it, at last. It had been Adrianna. It had been Adrianna all along.

And then her lips peeled back into a smile. At least, Martin allowed it to be a smile. And he smiled back. She hugged him tight, and under the pressure of her embrace, he could feel the cracking of first one, then another rib. The pain was exquisite, but he no longer cared. She lifted her head, and he bent his, allowing her to bite into his neck, and as she chewed until his blood flowed, he came, letting go of the burdens of a lifetime, releasing all his misery, releasing all his loneliness, releasing all his love.

He knew, as consciousness faded, that he would be back. And he was sure that when he returned, Adrianna would be there.

No. He *knew* she would be there.

She would be there.

She would be there.

She would.

"Obsessively dark and razorous, these graphic takes on life, faith, illusion and self-delusion open paths where you need to watch your step."
— Tanith Lee, recipient of 2013 World Fantasy Life Achievement Award

"Aaron J. French leads his readers on dark and dangerous journeys, where the destination is never sure."
— Storm Constantine, author of the *Wraeththu* books

Aaron J. French

ABERRATIONS of REALITY

Available now in Hardcover, Paperback, and Digital formats

amazon.com   BARNES &NOBLE   www.crowdedquarantine.co.uk

Nightbreed Rising: An Interview with Del Howison and Joseph Nassise, eds. of *Midian Unmade*

By K. H. Vaughan

No issue with a theme of "Sinister Appetites" would be complete without some reference to the work of Clive Barker. This summer, TOR will release an anthology of original stories set after the destruction of Midian in the novella *Cabal*. Introduced by Barker and edited by Joseph Nassise and Del Howison, *Midian Unmade* features 23 stories of the Nightbreed. Joe and Del agreed to tell us a little more about this landmark contribution to a core horror mythology.

KVH: How did the *Midian Unmade* anthology come about?

JN: As I note in the introduction to *Midian Unmade*, *Cabal* was the book that introduced me to Clive's writing. The tale of the Nightbreed stuck with me for years and eventually I developed a writing career of my own. I had always dreamed of writing stories about the Nightbreed in the years following the destruction of Midian, answering some of the questions *Cabal* had left me with regarding the Nightbreed: Where had they gone? What had they done to survive? Who or what were they devoting themselves to now?

As chance would have it, I had the opportunity to reconnect with Clive years later when I was serving as president of the Horror Writer Association and several times after that through my friendship with Del Howison, owner of the Dark Delicacies bookstore. Del had edited several well-praised anthologies of horror by the time I started thinking about approaching Clive with my idea to do the *Midian Unmade* anthology and Del seemed the perfect person to partner with on the project. We got in touch with Clive, hashed things out, and then took it to market. Tor stepped up and what had only been a dream was suddenly a reality.

DH: Joe contacted me to see if I would be interested in working with him on the project. I immediately said "Yes." I'd known Joe for several years but this was the first time we had ever worked together.

KVH: Midian has been an important part of the horror landscape for decades now. Why is it so enduring? What is it about the Nightbreed and the Midian mythology that you respond to most?

JN: The big draw for me was this sense of unbelonging that I think is inherent to the lives of the Nightbreed. They are the eternal cast-offs of society, neither wanted nor noticed, and I felt that there was both power and sorrow to be found in a situation like that. I wanted to tell those stories, to connect with that sense all of us have had at one time or another of being different from everyone else.

DH: As a person who grew up in the late sixties and seventies I like the conundrum that being an outsider tends to make you cluster with other outsiders thus making you an outsider no longer. Very few of us are a true lone wolf.

PHOTO COURTESY OF JOSEPH NASSISE

KVH: It must have been a challenge to select stories that would be fresh and fit with the original. How did you approach this? Were you looking to evolve or advance the mythology or more toward a paean or throwback to the original?

DH: First off let me say that Joe and I read over 1000 stories. One of our main thoughts was to diversify. Clive said that in his novel and film he was only able to deal with a few of the denizens of Midian but that it was a democracy of monsters. So we were allowed to spread our wings as far as possible. Of course we wanted stories that covered the characters everybody was familiar with, but we also wanted to touch on other residents of Midian. So there are many new creations for the readers to discover. We also wanted the tales to touch on different themes and personalities and not be repetitious in nature. We didn't want 6 stories featuring Babette, for example.

JN: This was the hardest aspect of the project for me. We wanted to be certain we had a good balance of stories, stories featuring the characters from the original book, those from the film *Nightbreed*, and new characters that the writers created just for the project. I think we did that. We wanted a diversity of themes and of subject matter—I think we did that, too. We wanted to talk about what the Nightbreed were doing in today's world, how they were adapting to the growing challenges of modern society. I think we did that, as well.

Del mentioned that we read over 1000 stories. Some were definite no's and some were definite yes's, but we had quite a few that were solid tales that were worth considering. At that point the discussions over the pros and cons began. If we take this story, we can't take that one. This one features a new Breed but that one does a fabulous job with a known character. Oh, look, another Babette story, and so on. One of the best parts of working with Del on this project was that he understood the point of it all and was as determined as I was to deliver excellent stories that truly honored the world we'd been allowed to play in.

KHV: It's a different cultural landscape today than the late 80s when Barker wrote *Cabal*. Is that reflected in the stories you selected?

JN: I'm not so sure that I'd agree with you there. The details change but the themes of our lives stay the same. Love and loss, the longing to belong and the longing to be left alone, the mix of emotions that both comfort and plague us all the days of our lives. Clive wrote about those themes in *Cabal* and we like to think we brought them back into the light again with *Midian Unmade*.

DH: Human nature, love, hate—it's all the same. But the overall sense I got from putting this collection together with Joe was of longing. Longing to belong. Longing to reconnect. Longing to love. Longing to hate and kill. In some cases, longing to be left alone.

KVH: Why are horror and desire so entwined?

JN: This a tough one for me and I'm not sure that I have a decent answer for it. I suppose it's because they are diametric opposites and, as in life, opposites attract.

DH: They are one razor sharp edge of a two-sided sword. They are emotions that are honed to come together as one.

KVH: What is the role of desire in your own work?

JN: In my work, a character's desire is usually his largest motivating influence and therefore it lies at the core of all my characters do.

DH: I believe that it is what drives everything we do, whether it is sexual, monetary, power-driven, or the need for pleasure.

KVH: The anthology *Hellbound Hearts* was inspired by the Hellraiser universe. Do you think there are other settings that would be good candidates?

JN: Oh yes. I think there is more to mine in just those two settings, never mind all the other wonderful worlds that Clive has created in his fiction to date. I would love to do an annual Nightbreed anthology or have the chance to play in some of his other settings, such as the setting for the books of the Art.

DH: I believe the world of Clive Barker has only been scraped and not really cut into. Shall I say, there is a lot of meat on that bone?

PHOTO COURTESY OF DEL HOWISON

KVH: What other projects do you have on the horizon?

JN: Harper Voyager just released the second book in my Great Undead War alternate history series (World War One with steampunk and zombies!) and I'll have two books in the Rogue Angel action adventure series out this year in March and September, respectively. In between will be the release of the sixth book in my Templar Chronicles urban fantasy series, Fall of Night.

In other words, it's going to be another busy year and I'm thankful for it.

DH: Personally I am just finishing up a Western novel that I'll be shopping around and I've had a few short stories released in other editor's anthologies such as Eric Miller's *Hell Comes to Hollywood 2*, and Jonathan Maberry's *Out of Tune* which was published by JournalStone.

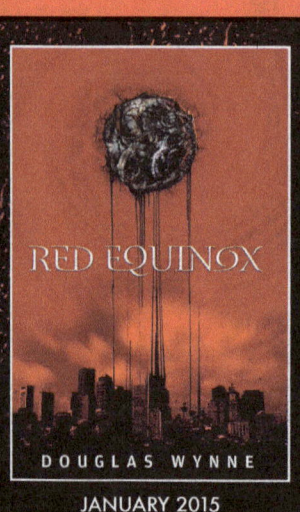
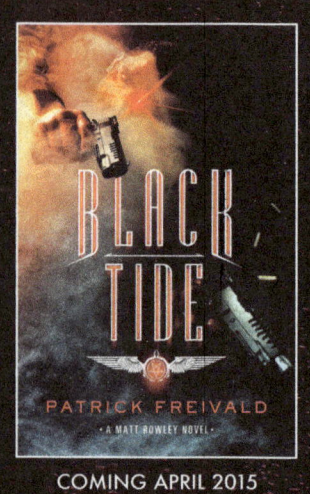

Lawrence C. Connolly with Sword, at World Fantasy Convention, Brighton UK, November 2013

Fear, Desire, and the stories of Robert Aickman

BY LAWRENCE C. CONNOLLY

"Know thyself," the oracle tells us, speaking through a chiseled inscription on the Temple of Apollo at Delphi. It's good advice, but perhaps easier to chisel than put into action. The problem is that we, like so many things in our world, are a collection of conflicted forces, sinister desires, suppressed fears.

Consider the male mantis, compelled to mate with a female who will likely devour him in the process. He arrives prepared, bringing an offering, a dead insect that he places before her. Then he retreats, scurries around, mounts her from behind. If he's lucky, the gift will keep her occupied, feeding her appetite while he satisfies his own. Sometimes it works. Other times, she reaches around with her sling-blade arms and helps herself to his head and prothorax, leaving his lower body to finish the act.

I remember seeing this courtship play out as a child, at a time when I was still too young to grasp its complexities, but old enough to wonder at the insect's name. *Praying* mantis, a creature that *prays* and *preys*, at once devout and devious, pious and terrible. The revelation provided an early glimpse into the duality of existence and the ambivalent forces that govern our lives. But nature was not my only teacher. Like other children, I had nightmares.

Writing in his autobiography *Erinnerungen, Träume, Gedanken* (translated as *Memories, Dreams, Reflections*), Swiss psychologist Carl Jung recalls one of his earliest childhood dreams, a nightmare of sexual premonition.

The dream begins in a meadow, the ground broken by an open grave. Standing on the brink, a child discovers a stone stairway leading deep underground. Though the image frightens him, he descends the stairs and arrives at a portal covered with green curtains. Too curious to turn away, he pushes the curtains aside to reveal a stage standing in the center of a large chamber.

What he sees on the stage is startling enough on its own. But keep in mind, Jung claims to have dreamed it as a child of four.

> On this platform stood [...] a magnificent throne, a real king's throne in a fairy tale. Something was standing on it which I thought at first was a tree trunk twelve to fifteen feet high and about one and a half to two feet thick. It was a huge thing, reaching almost to the ceiling. But it was of a curious composition: it was made of skin and naked flesh, and on top there was something like a rounded head with no face and no hair. On the very top of the head was a single eye, gazing motionlessly upward.

Unable to comprehend what he is seeing, the child stands transfixed before the giant phallus until he hears his mother calling from beyond the chamber. "Yes, just look at him," the mother says. "That is the man-eater!" Rather than clarifying the image, the words compound the terror, and the child wakes, overwhelmed by the harbingers of sexuality that will consume him in years to come.

So what caused the dream?

According to Jung, such images are the manifestations of collective unconsciousness, archetypes of humanity's deepest desires, darkest fears. They call to us in our dreams, and we follow them, drawing ever closer until the weight of their mystery drives us away, sends us fleeing back to the waking world to ponder their significance and perhaps—eventually—understand them.

In this way, they are much like the stories of Robert Aickman.

By way of an example, let us consider "The Swords," a story currently available in a Farber and Farber reissue of the classic collection *Cold-Hand in Mine*.

The story opens on the eve of a young man's first sexual experience, at a time when he is "raw as a spring onion," inexperienced in matters of love. We find him wandering through a dying town, restless and alone. Music plays in the distance, drawing him toward a dingy carnival pressed between factory walls. Here he finds the familiar attractions—games, vendors, carousel—childhood diversions. But there is something else, a tent with a curtained doorway and a hand-painted sign reading: "The Swords."

Pushing the curtains aside, the protagonist steps through to find himself standing before a stage. A performance is in progress, one involving a carnival barker, a seated woman, and a collection of swords. Unable to make sense of the entire scene, he focuses on the woman.

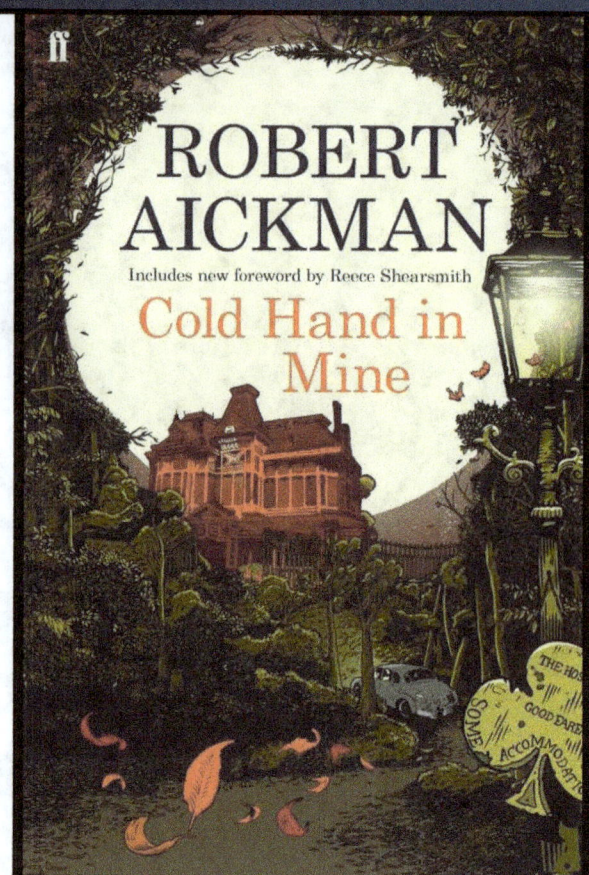

Cold Hand in Mine, Farber & Farber, 2014. Cover art by Tim McDonagh

> She was dressed up like a French chorus, in a tight and shiny black thing, cut low, and black fishnet stockings, and those shiny black shoes with super high heels that many men go for in such a big way. But the total effect was not particularly sexy.

Compounding the image, the woman appears to be covered with a green powder that makes her look "more sick than spicy." In all, the effect is what Sigmund Freud calls *das Unheimliche*, a term usually translated as "the uncanny," the impression that something is at once familiar and strange, attractive and repulsive.

Such impressions lie at the heart of Aickman's stories, for he is a master at crafting familiar images that come off as slightly wrong. Thus, though aspects of the woman's costume seem alluring, the combined effect is something else. Rather than being drawn toward her, the protagonist feels repelled, a sensation further enhanced by the nearby collection of swords.

> There was nothing gleaming about them, and nothing decorative. The blades were a dull grey, and the hilts were made of some black stuff, possibly even plastic. They looked thoroughly mass-produced and industrial, and I could not think where they might have been got. They were not fencing foils but something much solider, and the demand for real swords nowadays must be mainly ceremonial, and less and less even of that. Possibly these swords came from suppliers for the stage, though I doubt that too.

Note the play against expectations, the layering of familiar details running counter to the norm. The swords seem unsuited for ceremony, performance, or combat. So what are they for? Like the child in Jung's dream, the protagonist is too naïve to understand. Yet he remains transfixed before the stage, watching as the barker challenges one of the attending men to draw closer, select a sword, and run the woman through. "Go on," the barker shouts. "Stick it in."

The volunteer complies, but as he does he turns in such a way as to block the protagonist's view, masking the act of penetration. The protagonist only hears the blade

going in, cutting the woman's skin, thrusting deep. Then, as the volunteer withdraws the sword and steps aside, the protagonist sees the woman sitting with "hands […] pressed together against her left side, where, presumably, the sword had gone in. But there was […] no sign of blood."

And the protagonist notices something else too.

> [T]he strangest thing was that she now looked not only happy, with her eyes very wide open and a little smile on her lips, but, in spite of that green powder, beautiful too, which I was far from having thought in the first place.

At this moment, the balance between revulsion and attraction tips. The protagonist finds himself desiring her, though not enough to take the stage. He remains in his seat, watching as more volunteers perform the act of woundless

Jamie Foreman and Amanda Ryan in "The Swords." Directed by Tony Scott for The Hunger. Scott Free Productions, 1997

penetration. Then, realizing his turn is approaching, he flees into the night, back to his lonely bed in a shabby boarding house. It is a classically Freudian reaction, the young man rejecting the uncanny by seeking refuge in the mundane. Yet the image of the girl lingers, and the next day he arranges a private encounter, one involving a more conventional form of penetration.

Unfortunately for the protagonist, the act leaves him with a sense of disappointment, an emptiness "for which there is no exact word." He pulls away from the woman, then grabs her hand to lift her into a final embrace. But the attempt fails. The woman's hand separates from her arm, coming off in his grip while the rest of her remains on the bed, no closer than before.

The story offers no explanations. Like a nightmare, it seems built on archetypes whose interpretations may only become clear in retrospect, much in the way that dreams acquire meaning through psychoanalysis. The similarity may have been intended, for as Aickman tells us in *The First Fontana book of Ghost Stories*:

> Dr. Freud established that only a small part, perhaps one-tenth, of the human mental and emotional organization is conscious. Our main response to this discovery has been to reject the nine-tenths unconscious more completely and more systematically than ever before. [... But] the ghost story, like Dr. Freud, makes contact with the submerged nine-tenths.

Like many readers, I initially found "The Swords" confounding. And yet, as with a haunting dream, it has revealed itself over time. Reflecting on it now, I sense that it speaks to the tragedy of men doomed to desire that which they can pierce but never grasp.

And there's more.

In the story's dénouement, as the protagonist ponders the details from a later point in life, he recalls a promise that the carnival barker delivered when collecting payment for the private encounter. "We'll meet again," the barker says.

Yet in the story's final line, the protagonist assures us that "so far, despite what he said, our paths have not recrossed."

They will, of course, for a sword may as readily represent death as sexuality. The protagonist may have come to terms with one of life's primal imperatives, but another awaits. It will come to him, but the story ends with him denying that it ever will.

Denial is considered more prominently in another Aickman story, one that originally appeared in the collection *Sub Rosa: Strange Tales*, and is currently available in a Farber and Farber reissue of *The Wine Dark Sea*. Titled "The Inner Room," the story, like "The Swords," opens with an innocent protagonist (this time a young girl named Lena) searching for something.

It is Lena's birthday. Her parents have promised to take her to the sea, but car trouble leaves them stranded in a dusty town where they come upon a shop selling toys and groceries. Her father tells her to select a gift, and she wanders amid the clutter, searching until she comes to a curtained window that stands between the storeroom and what appear to be the proprietor's living quarters. There, through the lace partition, she glimpses "the façade of an enormous dolls' house." She senses it is not a toy. On the contrary, it is "the most grown-up thing in the shop." She tells her father she must have it, and soon it is installed in a spare room in her family's home.

Although Aickman never gives Lena's age, he drops sufficient hints (the girl's insistence that she is too old for dolls and that the house is "not meant for children") to indicate that she is entering adolescence. The significance of her age becomes clearer as she realizes that the house cannot be opened. She can peer through its doors and windows, spy on the strange dolls that inhabit its furnished rooms, but nowhere can she detect the presence of clasps and hinges that might give her access to the interior. And there is more. By measuring the outside walls, her brother determines that the house contains an inner room, one completely hidden from view, detectable but inaccessible.

Once aware of this hidden place, Lena begins dreaming about the dolls coming for her at night, but the nightmares end when her father sells the dollhouse and the story leaps forward some thirty years. We learn of Lena's abbreviated career as a dancer, her childless marriage cut short by war, and what seem to be more than a few bouts with depression. Finally, we come to a point where a middle-aged Lena loses her way on a back road and finds herself in the presence of a full-size version of her dollhouse. Is she dreaming? Lena considers the possibility, denies it, then admits that it must be so. In any event, she enters the house to find it inhabited by women who resemble the dolls from her childhood. They seem irritated at her, accusing her of being a neglectful caretaker. Then one of them offers to take her to the inner room.

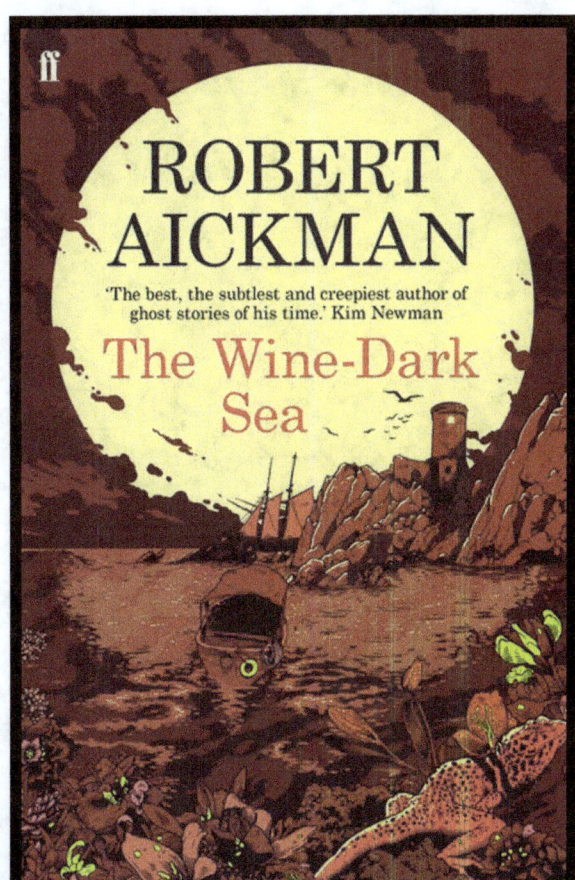

The Wine Dark Sea, Farber & Farber, 2014. Cover art by Tim McDonagh

"It is the room where we eat," the woman tells her. "I may almost say where we feast."

But Lena refuses to go. Instead, she flees into the night and continues along her previous path.

Again, the story offers no explanations, but one interpretation may be found in parallels between the inner room and Lena's barren womb. Indeed, at a panel on Aickman's stories at the 2014 World Fantasy Convention, scholar Rebekah Brown acknowledged that the dolls in the house may represent the children Lena never had. Beyond that, the references to the eating and feasting within the inner room may point to the sexual appetite Lena has kept locked away for too long.

In any event, simple answers and one-to-one correlations are not Aickman's stock and trade, and perhaps all we can say for certain is that he, like Freud and Jung, writes of the presence of an inner region of the self. For Freud it is the Id, a vault of suppressed instincts and drives. For Jung, it is the curtained storehouse of the universal unconscious. For Aickman, it is both carnival tent and inaccessible room. For all three, it is a place we can enter only in dreams or stories, a region of the self that holds the desires that drive our lives, and the fears that tug at us from beneath the surface of the real.

Author Bio:

Lawrence C. Connolly writes about fears, desires, and suppressed memories in his latest novel *Vortex: Book Three of the Veins Cycle* (2014). His other books include the novels *Veins* (2008) and *Vipers* (2010) and the collections *Visions* (2009), *This Way to Egress* (2010), and *Voices* (2011). *Voices* was nominated for the Bram Stoker Award, Superior Achievement in a Fiction Collection. He serves twice a year as one of the residency writers at Seton Hill University's graduate program in Writing Popular Fiction and blogs about fiction, performance, and rock-n-roll at http://LawrenceCConnolly.com.

THE ART OF STEVE SANTIAGO

WWW.ILLUSTRATOR-STEVE.COM

At the
Sign
of the
Leering
Angel

By Storm Constantine

'*These* aren't my shoes!' A thick-set man, wobbling on women's spiky heels, filled the entrance to the building. Arietty could see—and sense—the crowds behind him. The tall old house was a smoky hive; humming, throbbing. Heat and dim light pulsed out of it, yet its top third story was in darkness. People seated on the front steps in the late summer night were laughing uncontrollably at the shoe man's antics. He struck a dramatic, supposedly feminine pose, laughing so much himself he must surely fall over soon.

'Idiot,' said Zinsa beneath her breath. She linked her arm through Arietty's elbow, dragged her up the steps. Sprawling limbs moved sluggishly from their path.

'*These* aren't my shoes!' the man told them.

Zinsa bared her alarmingly white teeth at him.

The shoe man grinned, spat, 'Oooh, get her!', guffawed, and turned back to his friends.

Arietty really wanted to go home. She wasn't so much tired as people-drained, exhausted by all the faces, the yapping mouths, the heat and stinks of others, in bars whose names she could not remember, where baleful music thundered like the howl of demons, and there were too many glittering eyes.

Zinsa had turned up at Arietty's flat earlier that day—they'd been friends since school. 'Your trouble,' Zinsa had said, pointing a perfectly-groomed talon at Arietty, 'is that you're just rooted in your room, growing pale and yellow like a mushroom. You don't do anything, except sit in front of that computer.'

Arietty had never been as dark as Zinsa. She was naturally paler, owing to a white grand-mother. She didn't bother to argue about her genetic inheritances, however; merely braced herself against the onslaught.

'You should go out more,' Zinsa said, then smiled to soften the lecture. 'Anyway, that's not a suggestion. Get ready. We're going out *now*.'

Zinsa meant well but she didn't understand Arietty's world—that of the virtual realms of the internet. She didn't know about Arietty's artwork, all the online friends she had made, the virtual galleries in which her creations were displayed. To Zinsa, as the pictures weren't created in reality they undoubtedly wouldn't count as real. 'Do some proper painting,' she'd probably say—if she knew about them.

And so Arietty had been dragged into the circles of the city to suffer its torments in the name of fun.

After the bars had been exhausted, Zinsa had been told about a private club—the Leering Angel—which apparently was one of *the* places to go. *Whatever that means,* Arietty thought sourly.

'Great name,' Zinsa said.

The tall skinny man who had offered the information flicked his fingers and a card appeared, as if in a magician's trick. A pass. A key. The magic artifact that would provide entrance into a mysterious realm. Arietty had already decided to make the best of it all by imagining her excursion as some kind of fantasy quest. The man with the card was a trickster, probably not to be trusted.

So here she and Zinsa were, in a narrow road of towering old terraced houses, only one of which spewed light and noise and had a sign above its door: the Leering Angel. This was painted—quite expertly Arietty decided—upon a board, which had been fixed above the door. The picture was of a tall, skinny man, dressed in black leather, sprouting black wings from his shoulders, and winking at the viewer. Leering, Arietty supposed.

Passing the revelers on the steps and proceeding into the hall, Arietty guessed this must be a student house, because it didn't look like a club, rather somewhere people lived, albeit somewhat squalidly. A bicycle was shoved against the wall below the maw of the stairs. The old black and white tiles underfoot were grimy. One of the stained glass panels beside the open door was broken and patched with cardboard and tape. This was a house that had once been grand, but was now infested with vermin and rot. Sad. Arietty could see an illustration of it in her mind already; its walls leaning rather more than they did in reality, its dark windows like mournful eyes.

A long corridor led Arietty and Zinsa past three rooms, apparently full of people; in one of them dancing. They emerged into a large kitchen, brightly lit, where a table was covered in beer cans and vodka bottles, plus an array of lurid 'alcopops'. People were still yapping here, like in the bars. Their faces looked bloated. They were fizzed up with booze and recreational drugs.

I have nothing in common with any of them, Arietty thought, and glanced at Zinsa who was already chatting with some Asian girl covered in red tattoos. *Not even with Zinny anymore? Have I moved so far away? How is any of this fun?*

A voice spoke close to her ear. 'You want the next floor.'

'What?' She looked back, but whoever had spoken had already turned away, or perhaps they hadn't even been speaking to her in the first place. Her imagination wanted to believe it had been a disembodied voice and that this was the beginning of a strange adventure, but of course that was unlikely. The people here, although trying hard to be the opposite, were desperately unstrange. The crowd had moved in behind her, closing the path she and Zinsa had taken to this room. She was trapped. And where was Zinsa? The room was crammed with bodies. Arietty's friend had been swallowed by them. She decided to worm her way back outside, call a cab. She could make her excuses to Zinsa tomorrow.

***

A girl was vomiting at the threshold to the house, braced by one hand against the door frame. Again, Arietty could see an illustration forming in her mind: the shadowy forms, the dark, merging colours. All that was clearly visible of the girl was her stiff, supporting arm and the gleam of light on the viscous pool at her feet. Dimmer, losing focus, her bare legs were splashed with vomit. Her long pale hair, knotty with extensions was blurry and wet, hanging over her face. She wore no shoes. Perhaps the man outside was wearing them. Arietty noticed others observing the girl, one or two reaching forward to assist, others drawing back with pinched expressions. They were frozen as if in a photograph. The girl was a prophet, half feared, half revered. Her visions made her sick. This was a painting of the time she predicted the end of the world. Beyond her, far above the skyline of the city, the night was gartered with a band of deep red.

But not in reality. This was merely a pissed up student, who if she had any shred of self-respect would wake up tomorrow cringing at herself. She would call a friend: 'Did I do anything embarrassing last night?' *Yes. Yes you did.*

Arietty glanced behind at the stairs, reluctant to edge past the retching girl. *Perhaps we have to make our adventures,* she decided. *There are pictures and strangenesses everywhere, but they're in the eyes, the heart, the mind. They're in dreams. We can follow them.* She put a hand upon the sticky stair rail. Again a picture came to her: a fragile girl, shadowy as the sepia dark above her, staring up into the unknown.

Arietty needed the bathroom, and this was as good an excuse as any to find herself on an upper floor, looking for a queue of people, or an open door with light spilling out. She found neither. There were wall lamps with old-fashioned fabric shades, from which little pom-poms dangled, but most of the bulbs had expired. The carpeting underfoot was merely the memory of a floor covering and would have to be removed with a metal scraper, should anyone ever bother to renovate the house. Sad ghosts might walk this corridor, sickened by what humanity had become, wishing they didn't have to keep walking and witness it.

This upper floor was quiet, but not watchful, as Arietty hoped, simply empty, worn out. She walked along the corridor, trying doors. Two were locked, but one opened onto a room full of crates, with a window blind so torn that the street light glow came in as if through filigree. Arietty held up her hand towards the pane and it seemed that light came out of her fingers. She backed out of the room and closed the door.

Next she came to another flight of stairs, which was narrow and potentially frightening. There were more rooms to investigate on the floor she was on but she opted to go higher instead. She could *decide* she was led. There would have to be something to find.

The stairs came to another corridor, where attic rooms must have been converted into rented bedsits. Here, Arietty could hear faint music, not modern but classical. To her right, some yards ahead, red light fanned from a doorway. As Arietty drew nearer she saw legs sticking out of the room, a woman's legs. She paused a moment, staring.

This must be it, what she'd been led to.

The legs were still, lifeless, but perhaps their owner was simply unconscious. The feet wore no shoes. Arietty approached cautiously. She was intrigued, curious, but also aware there might be others around of whom she should be wary. If these were dead legs, why did she feel so detached? She didn't feel there was a picture in what she saw, which was odd. The scene was weirdly prosaic. She wouldn't know why until she saw everything there was to see. She reached the door, peered in, and her stomach clenched.

The legs had no body. For a few horrified moments she imagined they were amputated, but then the coolest, most sensible part of her mind pointed out there was no blood— no flesh, in fact—and that the thighs of the legs ended in devices clearly designed to attach them to a human body:

a legless human body. Arietty put one hand against her stomach. Where was the owner of these legs? Why would someone who used them leave them here like this, sticking out of a doorway?

The room was empty of living presences, although possessed the watchfulness Arietty hadn't felt on the lower floor. There was a bed, rumpled, with a duvet cocooned in scarlet imitation satin. Beside the bed was a small cupboard covered with a fringed shawl, supporting a lamp with a red shade and bulb. There was no other evidence to suggest someone had been there recently, but there was another door to the left of the bed. Perhaps this led to a bathroom.

The music Arietty had heard had grown faintly louder. She knew that when she opened the door she wouldn't find a bathroom. She would find what the clues had drawn her to, nothing more.

The glow within was also red, but extremely dim. Arietty saw the lights first, small brass lamps that perhaps held night lights or candles. The room contained a mattress on the floor, strewn with rugs and shawls. The walls were similarly adorned. On the bed…

Was this a picture?

The woman had shoulder length, black hair cut severely straight on the brow into a fringe. Her skin was leper white, her eyes panda'd with black and diamante. Her lips were astonishingly red and wet, somehow bigger than should belong in her face. She wasn't pretty, because her chin was weak, nor even particularly striking, despite the metal spiked corset she wore—and the legs. These were black, chitinous, multiply-jointed, like those of an insect, ending in claws. This female creature regarded Arietty from where she fawned against a seminude, emaciated male, this one rigged up in a patent leather harness, with a mask over his face. His nipples were pierced by rings, from which screaming faces in silver depended. He wore a shiny black false phallus that reared decoratively from his crotch, but one very human testicle peeped half squashed from the edge of this device.

Arietty's mind wasn't taking pictures. She simply stared, numb, at what she saw.

The woman leered. 'Cat got ya tongue, honey?' She held a glass with a lurid cocktail in it.

The man laughed, muffled.

How could a cat take my tongue? Arietty thought. *Those words are meaningless. Why do people still say them?* 'I'm looking for the bathroom,' she said.

'You can piss on me,' drawled the woman, encouraging another grunt from the male, who behind his mask might possibly be gagged in some way.

'Where is it?' Arietty asked. 'The bathroom?'

The woman straightened up a little, moved her insect legs. 'Two doors down, love.'

'Thank you.'

Arietty stared at the scene before her for a few more moments. She didn't want to forget. 'I'm sorry,' she said.

The woman reached for a cigarette from the packet lying on the bed, lit one. 'What for?'

Arietty shook her head. They wouldn't even understand.

'We too weird for you, love?'

'No.' Arietty paused, but didn't speak her thoughts.

That's the trouble. You're not weird at all. You're... ordinary. She went back to the corridor, down to the cramped bathroom, where two aged toothbrushes embraced in a broken glass on the shabby sink, alongside the body of a crushed toothpaste tube that lay contorted on its back. Arietty peed gratefully, glancing round herself. Old blue slippers behind the door, a toweling bathrobe in faded pink leopard skin hanging from a hook. There were holes in the vinyl flooring. A tap dripped into the bath.

They were bikers, Arietty told herself. *She lost her legs in a crash.*

But maybe that wasn't true. Maybe she'd been born like that. So sad.

***

Downstairs, the sick girl was now sitting on the steps with other revelers, drinking from a bottle of spring water. The oracle soothed, her prophecies spent. Arietty paused before her. 'Say something to me,' she said.

The girl grimaced, bleary eyed and confused, then smiled a little. 'They weren't his shoes,' she said.

Arietty took out her purse and put a coin in the lap of the pale-haired girl. 'Thank you. You've inspired me.'

'Wow,' said the girl, uncertainly. Her fingers closed over the coin.

Double X Chromosome

BY
YVONNE NAVARRO

PERFECTION

© December 2014

This issue's theme is hunger. Being a (mostly) horror writer, the first things I think of are vampires, zombies, werewolves, and a host of other munch-on-your-face monsters. But there are worse hungers, ones that are *real*, like the need for too much food, alcoholism, drugs, sex, perversity, killing. These are all hungers of the mind and soul. Others, like OCD, are just as devious. On the surface they seem mild, but I'm here to tell you they aren't, because they can alter the course of your life.

You've guessed by now that I'm talking about wanting to be perfect. I'll be the first to admit I don't know poop about the pathology or treatment of OCD, and I'm sure there are millions of people who have it worse than I do. My little fraction of OCD probably seems ridiculous by comparison, but as I thought about it while I considered what to write for this article, I realized my form— my hunger for perfection—has had a huge and not advantageous effect on my life.

I'm a writer, and I'm also a painter. In the past I've been other things: a waitress, an accounting clerk, a legal secretary, plus a few other office-type things. In those,

Photo courtesy of Yvonne Navarro

great.

If you're a new writer and you're reading this, you're thinking I'm crazy. I am, but not in the way you expect. Yes, you need to make those manuscripts the best they can be, check for every typo, punctuation mistake, and nonsensical antecedent-to-pronoun. But there's a point at which you should stop re-reading and re-editing; you inhale and send that sucker into the world to see if it can run, or at least walk. Then move on to the next project, because if you're still holding your breath while you wait for a response, you going to make a great corpse in the opening scene for a someday re-launch of *Six Feet Under*.

That's bad enough, but I'm talking about those of us who take the pursuit of perfection too damned far.

I've had twenty-two novels and well over a hundred stories of varying lengths published, plus articles and introductions, yadda yadda yadda. Based on the principle

being a perfectionist was an asset. It helped me do a good job, get recognition, praise from my bosses, raises.

Demanding perfection in writing and painting? Not so

that experience brings skill, I like to think that the last thing I've written is always the best ever. This sounds great, but subconsciously I believe this attitude has backfired and resulted in a significant decrease in output. Why? Because I expect my writing to not just be good, but *perfect*, to meet some high-rise standard that my brain has set as the

"If I waited for perfection, I would never write a word."

Margaret Atwood

default for self-evaluation. The result is I've gotten more and more reluctant to write, to start anything even though I know a deadline is approaching. Let's be clear: this is *not* "writer's block"—I've plenty of ideas for stories, and if I know a particular project is coming up, I automatically start thinking about the opening line for it. They pop into my mind one after another, no problem. The issue is that I have this soul-deep fear that what comes out at the end is going to be… *mundane.* Ordinary in the realm of a world where everyone can be a writer thanks to the Internet and Amazon and Lulu.com and iUniverse, but the really good ones shine like a full moon on a cloudless Arizona night. Ordinary in the sense that I'm no longer *special.* This personal form of OCD has cracked my self-confidence, and that crack turned into a chasm when, as so often happens in the career of an author, the publishing industry's politics resulted in the cancellation after two books of a series I had worked on developing for years. The reviews were good, I did marketing and promotion, and readers wanted more. They *still* want more, but the publisher's contract had been with a book packager they weren't working with anymore. Something inside me whispers that if the books were good enough, the publisher would have continued

Perfection is the obstacle of creation and the enemy of achievement.

Neale Donald Walsch

the series anyway. Another publisher bowed out because of the challenge in getting the rights to the first two books. So now, unless I self-publish, this series is dead. D.E.A.D. And while I'm paddling around in that pity pool, my traitorous brain reminds me that very rarely does a review of an anthology in which I have a story specifically mention

my tale—I always seem to be in the "includes other fine authors" arena. Writers thrive on praise from fans and reviewers almost more than money (second only because money buys food). It's a good bet that I'm in the bleachers on this because I don't promote myself as much as some other people—I've always been kind of an introvert, the shy, quiet girl with big glasses and curly hair. That I've grown into my glasses and learned to use a blow dryer is beside the point.

And it all comes back to me thinking I'm just not perfect enough.

It drives my significant other, who's also a well-respected and popular author, batshit that I want everything in my office just *so* before I can write. My desk must be clear of anything that doesn't have to do with the project I'm working on right now. In a perfect world, I would have all projects completed so that the perpetual To-Do List in my head would list nothing else. In the real world, however, that list is numbered 1 through 752, and when I cross off something, three more things appear. What the hubby doesn't realize is that this isn't something that started in the 1980s when I got ticked because I couldn't find something in my eight-month-old pile of unfiled papers.

I might have thought so, but a bit of memory searching provides the truth:

> I'm a freshman in high school, and the science project I've been putting off for weeks is due tomorrow. I know my stuff and I know what and how I want to do it, even what to write. I'm three pages into the single-spaced text (back in the day of writing by hand in a notebook that is given to the teacher), and I misspell a word. I have to cross it out and keep going. But I don't. I rip out all three pages—yes, ALL THREE—and start over, because I suddenly don't like my own handwriting, even though it's always been clear and readable. It isn't right, it doesn't look good enough, it isn't PERFECT.

In truth, I don't think that was the beginning. I have vague memories of similar actions previous to that, going as far back to third grade.

This nasty self-hunger for perfection also affects my artwork. I was an artist (to the best I could be without training) long before I became a writer, and my first memory is of drawing. The desire for perfection is even

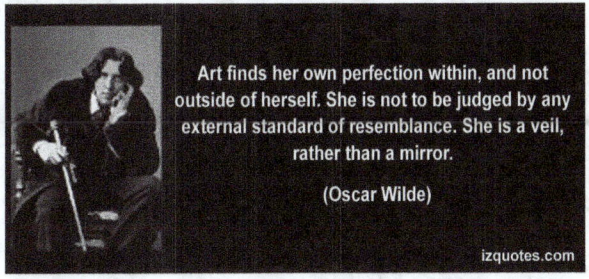

Art finds her own perfection within, and not outside of herself. She is not to be judged by any external standard of resemblance. She is a veil, rather than a mirror.

(Oscar Wilde)

izquotes.com

STRIVE FOR PROGRESS. NOT PERFECTION.

more damaging to the artist in me, because while the craving to create visual works screams for release, the evil perfectionist within knows, absolutely, that I'll never be able to satisfy myself. Drawings are never finished, sketches are never *started*, because they'll never be just right.

"Draw this map," commanded bulldog-faced Mrs. Holmes, my mean-spirited fourth grade teacher. So I labored over my map, reconstructing it beautifully. We're not finished in one period, so I write my name at the top like we're instructed and Mrs. Holmes collects them. We work on them for several days. On the last day, she passes out the in-progress maps and tells us this is the last day to work on it. Bu the map she hands me isn't mine. It's a scrawled mess, and even to 9-year-old me, it's obvious the original crayoned name has been sloppily erased and my name has been written over it. It isn't even close to my handwriting. I'm terrified of this woman—one time she slapped me across the face—but I finally get up the courage to take it to her toward the end of the period. I find my real one in the pile on her desk and anyone with a quarter of a brain can still see where my name faintly shows under Carmen Something-Or-The-Other's. I don't remember Mrs. Holmes's response, but it was along the lines of "Don't be ridiculous." I refused to work on that mess of a map, so I got a big fat F while "Carmen" got my A.

And again:

I'm in seventh grade, and it's my favorite time: art period. I even like my teacher at this school to which I've recently transferred. Our assignment is to use crayons and create a drawing made entirely of dots. My work is tiny and meticulous as I make my dot-drawing of a colorful totem pole set up at the front of the room. But being detail-oriented is painfully slow, and we've been told that anyone who fails to finish in the allotted number of art periods will fail. My urge to be perfect prevails and I can't finish.

> " $\mathcal{P}$ ictures of perfection make me sick and wicked."
>
> Jane Austen

Another F.

Maybe I'm stretching (maybe I *need* to), but I think these are where the hunger for perfection begins to turn in the wrong direction. The fourth-grade me couldn't believe Mrs. Holmes had never paid enough attention to my artwork to not *know* "Carmen" had stolen my map and substituted hers. The seventh-grade me couldn't believe my teacher wouldn't see my artwork merited an exception. And the grown-up me, even though I've learned the skill of accepting rejection, as every writer must, can't believe the publisher didn't love my work so much it would continue my series.

I don't really know where I'm going with this other than to serve as a warning to the newbies out there, and to the pros, too. When you're reworking that sentence, paragraph, page, story, or manuscript for the umpteenth time, or when you tell someone you've been working on your only novel "for five or six years now," don't be proud of yourself. Be brave. Escape the hunger for perfection. It's insidious, and if you don't curb it, it will grow into a monster. Finish the damned thing, revise it once, then read it aloud and fix the last of it. Give it to one or two readers who *aren't* your spouse or your mother. Consider their feedback honestly, fix it *one more time,* and then send it out and move along.

Because the search for perfection will never satisfy your hunger.

To get your hunger satisfied, pick up the first two volumes of *V-Wars*. The first volume has Yvonne's story, "Epiphany," and the second volume, *V-Wars, Blood and Fire,* continues that adventure with "The Hunger Within."

Comments? Questions? Suggestions? Yvonne Navarro can be reached via her website (yvonnenavarro.com), Facebook page (http://www.facebook.com/yvonne.navarro.001), or at her Dark Discoveries email: yvonne@journalstone.com.

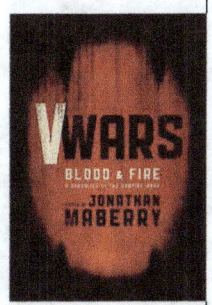

**Between the Devil and
the Deep Blue Sea**
by April Tucholke
apriltucholke.com

The End Games
by T. Michael Martin
tmichaelmartin.com

Sanctum
by Sarah Fine
sarahfinebooks.com

CHECK OUT THE HOTTEST TITLES IN YA HORROR!

CHASING DESIRES:
AN INTERVIEW WITH
CECILIA TAN

By K. H. VAUGHAN

Cecilia Tan, writer

Photo by Thomas S. Roche

First things first: Your novel *Slow Surrender* recently won the RT Reviewers Choice Award and the Maggie Award for Excellence, and Circlet Press was co-winner of the Bi Book Publisher of the Year at the 2014 Bisexual Book Awards. Congratulations!

CTAN: Thank you! It's rather interesting to suddenly feel like the world is catching up with me. That's the story of my life, though. Each subculture I've been a part of that was formerly "underground" has gone mainstream in my lifetime: goth, BDSM, even science fiction fandom! It's very odd to go from being a part of something that would be difficult to explain to Muggle relatives over a holiday dinner to something they've now heard of because it's a part of pop culture "everyone knows." And they still get it wrong, but it's like now they at least know it exists. "Oh honey do you go to that Comicon thing where everyone dresses up as super heroes?" Er, well, no Aunt Mabel, but thanks for making the effort to acknowledge the customs of My People.

DD: In a 2000 interview with *Strange Horizons* you said that erotic science fiction is not horror, but shares a kinship with it. Can you elaborate?

CTAN: OK, first off, to me the main distinction between science fiction and horror is in the basic DNA of the genres. I believe I first read this in an essay by Melissa Scott. Science fiction is about breaking the status quo. All other genres are about re-establishing it. In science fiction the world you have built ends up irrevocably changed by the end of the story. In horror, at the end the world has to be restored to the way it's supposed to be: evil is vanquished and everything goes "back to normal." Same with mystery: murderer caught, justice served, everything goes back to normal. So where's the place of sexuality in erotic science fiction versus erotic horror? In both cases it's the thing that shakes up the status quo, but the message is quite different.

When I founded Circlet Press to publish "erotic science fiction" (and fantasy) there were a couple of markets where you could publish erotic horror (the "Hot Blood" series, for example) but there was nowhere for erotic sf/f, as if all science fiction had to be acceptably "clean" or safe for any 14-year-old (or their concerned mother) to read. The big difference was that horror isn't supposed to be "clean" or "safe." It's obviously supposed to shock and horrify you. So eroticism or graphic sexuality had a foothold in horror but had been purged from sf/f. I didn't want to inject sexuality into my stories as a way to shock or horrify. I wanted to celebrate sexuality, especially marginalized sexuality. When you can build your own world, your own society, that's the perfect opportunity to create plotlines and situations where sexuality that is oppressed in the real world can instead be crucial or sacred—or at the very least openly represented!

Remember that back in 1992 finding an actual gay character or relationship (much less a sexual one) in a science fiction book had become rare. The experimentation of the 1970s, the free-loving bisexuals and gender-swapping aliens, had been

pretty well beaten out of the genre during the Reagan era. You could read a book like *Swordspoint* by Ellen Kushner which had to understate the relationship of the two male main characters so much that some people who read the sex scene between Richard and Alec didn't even realize sex was happening. (It's masterfully written!) I thought the only way to change this state of affairs was someone had to start publishing actual erotica so people couldn't blink and miss it. I wanted unmistakable, undeniable sexuality to be central in the stories I wrote and I founded Circlet Press to publish the same. So that people could no longer try to tell me science fiction was "for children" or that sexual writing couldn't be stimulating to the intellect or the political passions.

DD: Why are people so often ambivalent or even horrified by their appetites and desires?

CTAN: I think Americans are taught culturally not to want. Maybe it's our Puritan roots? We're taught guilt over any

gratification. I don't just mean sex, I also mean the sensual enjoyment of food, for example. How many times do you see a TV commercial for a deep dish pizza, and then see a Facebook update from a friend berating themselves for eating too much? These two things exist at the same time, the same way we have rampant commercialization of sex and desirability but also deeply repressive, judgmental attitudes about sex. I'm not only talking about what is labeled "alternative" sexuality, i.e. BDSM or gay or lesbian sex. I'm talking about "mainstream" heterosexual sex. People are so freaked out to think that what they want might be "weird" because they are so afraid to be judged by it. So they go around policing themselves and others when if instead they were just open about what they wanted, they might find out what they fear is "kinky and weird" is actually "normal"—i.e. desired by a majority of people.

What the massive explosion of popularity of *50 Shades of Grey* proved is that way, way, *way* more people were interested in BDSM than anyone in the mainstream thought—but which those of us in the BDSM underground knew was a groundswell waiting to be tapped. We need a new definition of "normal" desire that embraces diversity and a lot more flavors than vanilla, but people are afraid they'll be judged, afraid they'll be treated the way gay or gender variant folks are treated by the homophobic. There's a way in which this is a valid fear: queer and trans people are killed every day in this country for being perceived not to conform. But do I have to tell you my mantra is Conformity = Death? And science fiction is the genre which flips the status quo on its head. It is, and should be, the genre that encourages people to break the chains of conformity.

DD: Control or loss of control is often a factor in horror fiction: it is taken, lost, and may or may not be restored by the end. Is the dynamic in erotica or BDSM more about negotiating or ceding control? How does that compare to more mainstream bodice rippers?

CTAN: Okay, first of all, you need to hear that "bodice ripper" is considered a very derogatory term for romance. That's like if I characterized all science fiction as bug-eyed alien invasion pulp, with an extra layer of misogyny and sex-negativity added on top. Do you know the actual reason why so many bodices got ripped? When romance first exploded as a genre with the "Avon Ladies" (who sold in the hundreds of millions) and books like *The Flame and the Flower* (1972), which set the template for the historical romance genre, it was a plot necessity for heroines to be raped because there was no other way for a female character to lose her virginity and become sexually active while still retaining the sympathy of the reader. A female character could not "give it away" willingly. This is the legacy of the idiotic sex-negative attitudes of our culture that essentially forced women into these plot locutions because you simply COULD NOT WRITE a sexually empowered heroine: no one would publish it and if they did, you could expect the book to be banned, burned, etc. (Viz: the banning of Erica Jong's *Fear of Flying*, published in 1973.) Of course once the dreaded virginity is out of the way, the heroines were often then free to grab a kind of sexual agency that the readership perhaps couldn't.

Anyway, with that background knowledge in place, I can tell you in today's mainstream heterosexual romance the bodice no longer has to be ripped. Your typical romance heroine today is not even a virgin. She's usually 27 years old and already sexually active, but not yet emotionally fulfilled. When you add BDSM to the mix it can go one of two ways. In *50 Shades of Grey* it's like an old school throwback, what with the virginal heroine thrown into a situation with a powerful man, it's very evocative of the old "sold to a sheik" trope. But as anyone who knows anything about BDSM will tell you, the so-called "BDSM" in *50 Shades* is fantasy dreck, it's made-up stuff that isn't the way real-life BDSM happens and isn't the way the BDSM community sanctions it. The other way it can go in BDSM romance, and the way it is in the vast majority of the ones I've read, is more realistic, where instead of the "dom" being a stalkerish, pushy asshole who always gets his way, the kind of role playing and extreme sensation play that is the basis of BDSM also becomes the basis of emotional bonding and fulfillment for the characters. Which is how it tends to work in real life BDSM. Just sayin.

DD: Not all cultures deal with sexuality in the same way. Japanese kids animation doesn't have the same rigid barriers American kids programming does, for example. It's more integrated.

CTAN: They set their barriers in different places. I think they're just as rigid, but we may not be as aware when we're seeing a boundary since it's not a boundary for us. Our culture is hung up on sex for a number of reasons. One is we're a shame-based culture. Remember I said we fear being judged as different by others because we may be ostracized from the group or lose our social standing? The Japanese have that same fear, but theirs is a face-based culture rather than a shame-based one. My friend Midori, who is a writer and sex educator, gives a presentation on this subject and about sexual culture in Japan. She expresses that this is the crucial difference: shame-based versus face-based. In Japan you have love hotels equipped for the most perverted scenarios and no one is ashamed to use them. They'd be ashamed if someone FOUND OUT because then they would lose face, but not by the doing of the act itself the way an American might. An American does something pervy and feels guilty about it—shame wells up inside, it creates self-hate and negativity. The Japanese person need not feel any guilt because they have done everything correctly to preserve the social order and not make waves. It's still quite rigid, but the rules of behavior act on a different vector.

DD: An awful lot of people seem more offended by

sexuality than violence. Children's movies can feature a lot of violence and death, even genocidal violence, but as soon as a nipple makes an appearance it gets an adult rating.

CTAN: So true: we're a culture that glorifies violence and quashes sexuality. These two things are actually related though: they're BOTH expressions of a patriarchy that builds up a myth of violent masculinity as the "norm" and objectifies women as property to be protected. In cultures where women have agency, and where they participate traditionally in leadership and decision-making, rape is almost unheard of and violence is not condoned. In those where they don't, or where the male population outnumbers the female population, you see heavy swings toward conservatism and rampant rape. See India, which has been in the headlines so much these days. We need to imagine, and believe in, a different way of living, a different way of being. That's where science fiction and fantasy are important. The only way we can experience the dynamics of a female-centric culture, perhaps, is through the books of Diane Duane, or of gender-variant parenting through Samuel R. Delany, or of BDSM as sacred practice through Jacqueline Carey.

DD: I remember as a teenager in the age of cable you could always count on a slasher film to give you a few minutes of nudity, but I can't think of a lot of mainstream SF, fantasy, or horror in which sexuality is well-integrated in a mature, sex-positive way.

CTAN: Well, you have the problem also that TV and movies have such different rules from written literature. It used to be that you could depend on that few minutes of FEMALE nudity in any action film not just slasher films: it was part of the formula just like the car chase and the boss fight. It HAD to be in there. Watch any Steven Seagal film from the 1990s and you'll see they come up with SOME way to get the female lead topless. Sometimes it was as ridiculous as she was a stripper who pops out of a cake. I'm not kidding. The nude scene was that *de rigeur*. What's happened since then is now you don't get the TOTALLY GRATUITOUS nude scene. If there's going to be female nudity they try to write it into the actual plot. However if the sex scene is CONSENSUAL you'll get slapped with an X or NC-17 rating. If it's a RAPE scene however, oh, that's merely an R-rating. I am not kidding about this. In the film *Sucker Punch* there was supposed to be a consensual scene. They had to change it to a rape scene or they wouldn't have been able to get the film distributed. Too many places won't even show NC-17. That's how twisted the rules are governing visual media. So if we're going to talk about films in comparison to the written genres of sf/f/horror, we have to accept that's going to be a driving factor in what we see on screen.

DD: Then you have the use of sexual assault of a female to drive the male protagonist's narrative, let him be a white knight, or to show that he's the "good" guy.

CTAN: I think that's just another example of how a lot of

mainstream media is written by men for men: it's almost like female characters only exist in a lot of these films to give the hero someone to rescue or protect. Which brings us back to the idea that we live in a violent patriarchy that sees women as objects instead of as fully functional people. That's not just in slasher films, either: it's in pretty much all the genres aimed at male audiences.

DD: I see a lot of stuff possibly wrapped up in that. Slasher films that punish sexually active women and let the virginal final girl survive, voyeurism or rape in which the point doesn't seem to be that it is scary and intrusive, but to identify with the perpetrators POV... Could this be about displacing desires or fantasies into a horror context, or teaching ourselves that some kinds of behaviors are wrong, or is it more titillation and the expression of misogyny and sex-negative ideas?

CTAN: Unfortunately I see it as largely an expression of misogyny and sex-negativity. I wish I could tell you that having more sex scenes in horror films or action films was part of some kind of sex-positive revolution or loosening of the moirés, but it's just not. Not the way they're being presented by Hollywood. I still see science fiction as the place you're most likely to see the tropes subverted, but maybe that's just Joss Whedon breaking the curve with characters like Buffy. Then again, he tried to do other female-centric projects that didn't pan out (*Firefly*, *Dollhouse*), but give him a property like the Avengers (all guys with one ass-kicking chick) and he's on top of the world again. The Marvel movies overall have been interesting because they were absolutely not afraid to court the female audience. It's Thor himself who gets topless gratuitously in both Thor movies, not Natalie Portman, and I feel it was a very conscious choice to give her a female sidekick in the character of Darcy, who basically speaks the part of the fangirl chorus. Or look at a movie like *Pacific Rim*. Guillermo del Toro knew exactly what he was doing turning the hero-heroine dynamic inside out: it's the male character who is all puppy-eyed ("We're drift compatible!") and the female character who has the hero's journey to overcome her fear, draw her family's sword, and vanquish the monster. So it should surprise no one that female fans came out in droves to see a "dumb monster movie." And the thing is, I feel like science fiction and fantasy BOOKS do that sort of thing all the time. It just rarely makes it into the mainstream movies.

DD: I see a lot of Lovecraft pastiche that involves tentacle rape, which doesn't have a whole lot to do with Lovecraft.

CTAN: I think you may be missing the fact that Lovecraft is one convenient platform for tentacle rape stories and that this is only the tip of a very large and varied tentacle porn genre you haven't explored...? I find it highly likely that the genre of tentacle porn dwarfs the genre of Lovecraftian homage in terms of volume. Although I also wouldn't put it past many of those writing Lovecraftian homage these days to be quite adept at saying everything Lovecraft left unsaid. Saying "tentacle rape doesn't have a whole lot to do with Lovecraft" is a bit like saying "sex doesn't have a

whole lot to do with Dracula." Put mildly: oh yes it does.

DD: What makes for a good erotica-horror cross-over? How are fear and arousal related?

CTAN: Fear and arousal are not only related neurologically, there is the whole element of opening one's self up to emotional harm through intimacy. That's fertile ground for storytelling and I think there is a lot of room there for metaphoric journeying, too. The thing is for it to be horror, the trust has to be broken, the damage and harm has to occur, the thing that is feared has to become manifest in the story. For it to be erotica, the trust has to be maintained or restored, the roller coaster has to bring everyone back safely to the platform, with no missing limbs.

DD: It's been a long time since you founded Circlet. Is the market more open to mixing genres, or has kink become more mainstream?

CTAN: Yes and yes! There is much more mixing of the genres these days. Thank goodness. If I've been pounding one drum consistently for over 20 years it's that freedom of expression is important, it's that Conformity = Death. That's true both in life and in being true to one's sexuality and gender expression and in fiction, in art, in creating something new and fresh and emotionally urgent, as opposed to merely running in the tracks of dead clichés. Postmodernism and remix culture are well established now as a way to shake up the clichés. Using one genre to break the conventions of another is a tried and true method.

DD: I often hear about horror writers and fans getting a negative reaction about their interests. "You must be messed up to want to write or read that" responses and so forth. Is that a similar issue for people in the BDSM or erotic fiction community?

CTAN: Less and less. I used to hear it in the '90s a lot. What few cranks were still whispering it a few years ago were pretty much silenced when *50 Shades of Grey* became the bestselling book in the history of the English language. It's a pretty terrible book in a lot of ways but the sheer size of the phenomenon legitimized both BDSM and erotica in one fell swoop. We've seen a huge influx both into the BDSM community and into the erotica writing ranks.

DD: Do you have any favorite authors of dark fantasy or horror?

CTAN: When I was a kid (in the 1970s and '80s) it was the "classic" days of Stephen King, I read books like *Firestarter* and *The Dead Zone*. I didn't even think of them as "horror" so much as contemporary fantasy, which was what I wanted to be reading but it was like the genre didn't exist yet. Then came Anne Rice, who was sort of closer to what I wanted, but I didn't enjoy her prose style much. The Vertigo comic books of the 1980s were the only place I felt like I was finding the stories I wanted to read: Neil Gaiman's *Sandman*, and Alan Moore's *Swamp Thing*, which birthed John Constantine into *Hellblazer*. I fell headlong for Tim Powers, though: *Last Call* to me was what Gaiman was doing in *Sandman* but in a fantasy novel. *Last Call*, I thought, should have started a revolution in fantasy the way the success of William Gibson's *Neuromancer* kicked off a revolution in science fiction. And maybe it did, sort of. Laurell K. Hamilton's early Anita Blake books were taking off then, before they got erotic, back when the sensuality was all sublimated into horror and violence. Those were some books that took the mixing of genres to new heights! And Tanith Lee, I must mention Tanith Lee. I don't think it's a coincidence that she pioneered dark fantasy and also pioneered injecting alternative sexuality into her narratives. It's ripe territory.

DD: For readers who don't know your work, what's a good place to start? Speculative or erotic? Do you have stories that you think might cross over into horror or dark fantasy more than others?

CTAN: Okay, here's a secret: I'm working on a project for a major publisher right now that will be dark fantasy/urban fantasy AND have BDSM in it, which I feel will pull together everything I've ever done into one epic trilogy. But I can't tell you more about it because the contracts aren't signed yet. So shhhh it's a secret. Until then, let's see… I feel like I need an infographic of my work that would let people pick which parameters they want as a starting place: BDSM, gay, magic, bisexuality, etc.? How dark is dark?

This is the thing I should say explicitly: my fiction often goes very dark places, even into rape and situations of dubious consent, but it's built to be a roller coaster. It's built to be the Perils of Pauline and to send the reader into some very painful and dark situations—which is why I think readers of horror and dark fantasy often enjoy the ride—but I put the reader/the main character back on the platform safely at the end. For me that edge between consent and questioning consent and limits is where the interesting conflicts in the story are. I keep thinking one of these days I'm going to go too far and they're going to take my "Safe, Sane, Consensual" badge away (I'm a lifetime achievement

award winner from the National Leather Association), but I think because I always make it so central to my work—asking and answering: what is consent? where are the lines? when are they being crossed?—that even when non-consensuality appears in my stories, the story as a whole is still held up as an example of BDSM-positive. I guess that really is what I have in common with horror: my characters are ultimately always banishing the evil and restoring the power of good, only in my worlds consensuality itself is the power of good and non-consensuality is the power of evil. Somehow, in this day and age, introducing the idea that consent should be central to all relationships is still seen as groundbreaking.

Anyway: If you want urban fantasy mixed with sex magic and don't mind bisexuality, then Magic University is the place to start. (Think if Harry Potter went to college to study sex magic.) If you want high fantasy with BDSM and very dark magic but don't mind gay, *The Prince's Boy* is the place to start. *Black Feathers*, one of my short story collections, has a smattering of vampires and curses and 90s goth sensibility. If you want the BDSM antidote to *50 Shades of Grey*, that's *Slow Surrender*.

DD: What's on the horizon for you?

CTAN: I'm working on a BDSM romance trilogy for Hachette right now, mixing BDSM and rock stars as a follow-up to the success of *Slow Surrender*. The series will be called Secrets of a Rock Star and the first book is currently titled *Taking the Lead*. First book will be out in January 2016. And then the BDSM/urban fantasy/dark fantasy series I mentioned will come after that. I'm making notes and percolating ideas like crazy for that one. It's going to be gorgeous and terrifying and sensual and full of razors and leather and magical secrets. But you'll have to wait for it.

The Wanting

By Cecilia Tan

Her voice floats up to me like a wisp of smoke, insubstantial, almost imaginary. I am standing at the casement window of our fourth floor suite, looking into the dark valley, a precious few lights twinkling from the other side, assuring me that people are out there. Melissa is lying on the bed only a few feet from me, but her voice could be coming from much farther.

"Daniel, are you there?"

The sky is moonless; there is not enough light to show my silhouette there in the window. "I'm here."

"Make love to me," she says.

"Is that what you really want?" I fear she is offering herself to me for all the wrong reasons. She is as beautiful as the day we met, and my desire for her has never dimmed. If anything, the thought that the end might be near only sharpens my desire, and I imagine falling upon her like a ravening animal, driving into her and taking her with all the urgency I have bottled up inside.

No.

***

When people had first begun to disappear—from the world, I mean, not just our little piece of it—many explanations were floated. Aliens were abducting people from their cars as they drove, leaving empty wrecks but no bodies on lonely roadsides. A cult was brainwashing them into picking up and leaving their lives, walking out with two kids in the other room watching TV and the kettle whistling on the stove. But as the disappearances increased, there were more and more witnesses. No aliens. No cult. But no explanation either.

Earlier today, I watched it happen to my own brother, Kevin. Melissa was upstairs painting, but most of us were gathering in the dining room for dinner, as we do every day around sundown. Kev had been helping with the cooking. Ariana had picked the garden clean of its last greens for salad. Phil had roasted a turkey and I had joked with him that it was too early for Thanksgiving.

"Dan, I give thanks every day," he replied, too serious for the moment, and I knew something was wrong.

"Who?" I asked. Not what, but *who*, because when something is wrong that is the first thing that comes to any of our minds.

Before he could answer, Kevin came through the wide swinging doors from the kitchen and took a few steps toward us.

Suddenly we were looking at an empty space where he had been; his image winked out like the bulb had burned out on a slide projector. My heart jammed my throat as I stood up out of my chair.

Then he was there again, in mid-stride. He stopped, though, and stood still for a moment. There must have been four or five of us staring at him, and he looked down at his shirt. Then he smiled sadly and looked back at the rest of us. "I was hoping I'd spilled something." He shrugged and came over to me.

I went rigid like a drugstore indian. I wanted to rush over to him and hug him while he was still real, but I couldn't make my muscles move. Instead he put his arm around my shoulders. "You hungry?" he asked, almost a whisper.

"Not anymore." I could barely answer.

"Let's take a walk." No one else said anything as the two of us left the room, leaving us to what could be our last conversation.

Kevin had been there at the beginning, when I'd hatched the idea to take over the abandoned hotel, and gather people together. We walked out on the verandah, where the autumn chill was descending. The hotel looked much the same as it had that first day, the red brick exterior grand and old but not decadent, the rose bushes and azaleas lining the round drive poorly-pruned. There had been five of us, then. By the end of the year it was twenty, then twenty-five. People sang and painted and wrote. But like populations everywhere, our numbers dwindled, one by one. No matter how much I wanted them to stay, they usually moved on.

Kevin sat on the bench and I sat next to him. He lit a home-rolled smoke to ward off the chill and I accepted a puff from it. Of all the things that had changed in the world, it had become tough to get cigarettes, but not butane lighters. He flicked it on and off, watching the flame dance in the October breeze. "It's going to be okay, Danny," he told me.

"What do you mean, it's going to be okay? You're..." No one called it dying. *Going.* We called it *going*, but the result was the same. Disappearing. It was the same as dying.

"I mean, you'll be okay." We were sitting so our shoulders touched. "We always knew it could happen."

"God, how can you be so calm?"

He gave that infuriating shrug of his. "There's nothing I can do but accept it, is there? Once it happens, no one's ever come back. And it's not as if Penny will miss me."

"What?"

"She broke up with me this morning."

"What?" I repeated, this time unable to keep the accusation out of my tone.

Kev started walking along the porch. I followed, not finished saying what I had meant to say, and yet realizing he had more to tell me. The railing circled half the building and then I went down some stairs to the back and the trail to the south face of the hill, where our gardens were. We walked together, our breath fogging in the chill and dew brushing our boots.

In the twilight the pumpkins looked almost like they glowed. There were miles of zucchini vines. I heard a goat bleat from off to our right and I remembered there was a gate I needed to fix. We circled the pumpkin patch and he tossed the butt onto the wet ground. It burst in a few red sparks and then he ground it out.

Finally, I heard him exhale behind me, an *oh-come-on* kind of sound. "I'm sure it has nothing to do with Penny."

"Come on, Kev..."

"Penny and I have been essentially over for months already."

"But is it a coincidence that you made it formal today? There has to be a reason."

"Does there? Maybe it's just my time, that's all." He picked up a loose branch and swished the grass with it as we walked.

"That sounds like something they said to us in the hospital when mom died. 'It was just her time, son.' "

The words were bitter in my mouth. She'd died of the old horror, cancer, when I was in med school and Kev had been just starting college. The result was we had a familiar, and familial, way of talking about morbid things.

"I wanted there to be a reason then, too," I said.

"And was there one?"

"I don't know. Smoking? Asbestos? Cosmic rays?"

"All things beyond your control." He was staring at me now, frowning, like I was a puzzle that needed solving. "If Penny doesn't love me anymore, so what? Is there something you, or I, could do about it? Or is it me who doesn't love her anymore? There's no way to force it to last. When the time comes, the time comes."

I handed the stick back to him because I didn't want to drop it on the ground. Who knew if he had hours or days left with us? If he wanted to carry a stick, I wasn't going to deprive him. "You know, I always wished mom could have met her."

"Me, too." He looked up at the hotel, where there were lights on in some windows. Penny might be up there now, on the third floor, moving her things from the room they had shared into one of her own.

He took hold of my sleeve. "I guess I better talk to her, huh."

"What are you going to say?"

"I don't know. Someone's probably told her by now."

"You've probably got a few days left," I told him, trying to be optimistic. "We'll have a bonfire for you tomorrow night."

He nodded and didn't look at me as he went in the back door of the building.

This much we know. We couldn't determine for sure why Kevin or any other person would flicker and then disappear from existence forever, but folks could make some generalizations. People often disappeared after breaking up or having their hearts broken, a high percentage of others would go while trying to quit smoking or kicking alcoholism, some after a major disappointment in life—others after achieving major goals. The year we came to the mountains, both soccer teams from Argentina and Brazil had disappeared to the last man within six months of the World Cup. Now, there was no World Cup, nor were there enough people to fill the stadiums. But there were no guarantees as to who would disappear or why. It seemed to have to do with wanting something, but was it about wanting too much, or not enough?

I found Melissa in her studio on the top floor, the windows cracked open to vent the fumes, candles lit for the hour when the electricity would be shut off. It's amazing, in some ways, that the power is still on at all, but somehow a shell of a government, public utilities, even mail service perseveres, as if civil servants can't stop doing what they do for fear that they'll disappear, too.

She had stretched a canvas taller than she was, and was painting what looked like an archangel, given the outline of wings and robes I could see. The face had not yet been done. Actually, she was finished painting for the night, and was cleaning up, and she smiled at me like she was glad to see me. She went up on tiptoe and hugged me with

her forearms around my neck, her hands not touching me so as not to get paint on my clothes. As she settled back onto her heels though, she gave me a penetrating look. "Something's wrong."

I nodded and my voice came out gravelly. "Kevin."

"Oh no…" she said softly, almost as if she hadn't meant to say it out loud. Now the paint didn't matter and she gave me a real hug, pulling me down to her, and burying my face in her cloud of dark hair. I did what I only did with Melissa, which is cried.

Sometime later we went to our bedroom and talked, and then when the place had gone dark, went down to the kitchen to eat what was left of that night's meal.

We sat at the butcher block counter at a candle and she put a plate with a drumstick in front of me. She held a small bowl of cranberry sauce in her hands and picked at it with a fork.

"Well," she said, her thin shoulders slumping, "We knew the Red Death would come to the ball some time."

"It's not even like it's the first time," I said. "Remember Gerald?"

She snorted. "I don't think he went, in the literal sense. He just took off. Couldn't handle his share of the work."

"You really think so?"

"Yeah." Her lips were red with berry juice. "Lazy. Stupid. Good riddance!" She smiled. "And what was her name, Mary Ann, she's still living in Wilkes-Barre with that guy she met."

"Still?"

"Well, last I had heard anyway."

I bit into the meat but didn't really taste it as I chewed. "Soon there won't be anyone left."

She put the bowl down sharply. "Don't talk like that."

"What do you mean? It's true. People will either leave, or fade away, and I'll…"

"And you'll be alone? Is that what you believe? Oh Danny, take it from an artist, that's depression talking." She forked some of her cranberry sauce onto my plate and nudged me to keep eating.

"Shouldn't I be depressed? My brother's… dying. The family, the community I tried to build is dying. The world's dying."

She snapped her fingers at me. "Hey, hey, didn't you found this place so that art that celebrates existence could be created?"

"You're the only one who's getting anything done."

She pursed her lips, not sure whether to refute that or not. "That's beside the point. Without you, this place doesn't exist. I don't paint. Ariana doesn't write." She stopped as she realized she was treading close to a subject we had argued many times before—I was the only non-artist in the place.

"Listen," she said, "we need you."

But I couldn't shake the feeling that was settling over me, that I'd somehow failed, and I told her so.

"Depression," she said, nodding like the doctor I was supposed to have become, a lifetime ago.

I felt helpless. "What do you think, should I take some of your Prozac?"

She shrugged and said nothing, and I felt she was keeping something from me.

"Well? Should I?" There were two bites out of the turkey leg and I felt my throat was too tight to eat more. "'Lissa," I said, trying to sound calm, "do we have more?"

"A little," she said.

"How much is a little?"

"Maybe a week's worth…" Her eyes were downcast

with a little guilt, a little sorrow. "I was taking less of it for a while there, but then it was getting harder to get out of bed…"

I got off my stool and went around to hug her. "I'll get more."

She squeezed me tight around my middle. "I don't want you to leave. You were gone a week last time."

"I'll go down to Wilkes-Barre and see what I can find there."

"You know you're going to have to go farther than that."

"Maybe." My chest tightened but I held the sob in. I couldn't stand the thought. Kevin would be gone in hours or days. Who knows, maybe Penny would follow. And Melissa, too? Too many, too quickly. How could things fall apart so fast? It was my job to try to put it back together. If I didn't find what she needed in Wilkes-Barre, and she was probably right that I wouldn't, I could be gone for a month. How long would she last? "I'll leave tomorrow."

"No. You should be here with Kevin. I'll be okay, really."

"And if you aren't? I'll blame myself forever."

She looked up at me. "We'll talk about it in the morning?"

"All right."

So we came upstairs to bed. She had hung the suite with gossamer and gauze, surrounding the bed with long sheets of white like some giant lotus blossom. I wondered if, downstairs, Kevin and Penny had made love one last time or if they were each alone.

I stroked Melissa's hair, wanting to ask and not wanting to ask at the same time, wanting her, but not wanting to break the fragile equilibrium that our relationship had reached. She drifted off to sleep while I stroked her hair, and then I got out of bed.

I remember a conversation Kevin and I had a long time ago, when we were still in the city, when we were trying to decide what to do with ourselves. He had already left school and I was contemplating doing the same. We were sitting on a stone wall behind the student center, and the conversation quickly became existential. What was intelligence? Could animals create art? Why did humans behave irrationally if they had reason and intellect?

It was Kevin who said it first. "The reason people are disappearing is because there is no meaning to human existence. We simply exist, and there is no meaning. No meaning, no reason to stick around."

"That's ridiculous," I countered. "If that's what you think, why are you still around?"

"No idea. But think about that for a moment—no meaning, no reason to stay. Why are you in medical school?"

"I don't know."

"Suppose a long time ago you'd thought to help people. Develop a new treatment for heart disease, or Alzheimer's, or whatever. But what's the meaning in that, if people are merely going to flicker out like bad light bulbs?"

What I didn't say then, because the wound of mom's death was still recent, was that the only reason I was in med school at all was because it was her idea, and the only reason I had stayed was in her memory. But he had a point, if there was no meaning, why stay? It was shortly thereafter that we went to find our own meaning. Art seemed like a good bet, a good reason for humans to exist.

What's my reason to exist? I wonder. I see lightning flicker from the other side of Camelback; weather always hits the other side of the mountains first.

"Daniel?" Melissa is not asleep after all. Her voice is quiet, muffled by all the gossamer hung around the bed.

I turn toward the sound in the dark.

"Daniel, are you there?" I can hear the urgency in her voice, now, even though it seems far away.

And suddenly there is light, as she finds the lighter tucked behind the pillows. The flame looks like it dances on the end of her upturned thumb.

And as her mouth falls open and her eyes go round, I see now what she sees.

She is alone in the room.

And I am gone.

"... Can't Get It Out of My Head..."

By
Gary A. Braunbeck

Obsession.

How many mysteries, suspense novels, and horror stories use that single affliction as a jumping-off point? *Psycho, The Killer Inside Me, The Tenant,* brilliant movies like *Taxi Driver* and even such ham-fisted films like *Fatal Attraction* are, at their core, about a central character's inability to focus on anything besides his/her monomaniacal drive to achieve a single goal, be it the answer to why a young woman commits suicide by throwing herself out of an apartment window (*The Tenant*) or ridding the streets of a city of the ugliness and filth that robs existence of any meaning or decency (*Taxi Driver*). An argument could be made that stories and films focusing on obsession are reactionary (like Brain Garfield's *Death Wish*), statements about the current state of you-should-pardon-the-word society and the way it chips away at the power and worth of the individual—or, at the less cerebral end of the spectrum, are morality tales delivered with all the cleverness and subtlety of a sledgehammer against one's forehead (*Fatal Attraction, Basic Instinct*).

What's always puzzled me as a writer, a reader, and a film buff, is how quickly the subject of obsession—especially in recent years—is frequently (sometimes automatically) interpreted as *sexual obsession.* Not to come across like faux-Victorian prude, but I find the subject of obsession so much more fascinating when it concerns itself with more than the shrieking wide-eyed psycho-bitch murdering because she's not getting the man-meat or the sweaty, slobbering, unshaven pervert stalking the ingénue of the month because he thinks that her smiling at him on the street one afternoon means she's ready to do the Horizontal Mamba and wants him and only him as her dance partner, even if she doesn't know it yet.

Yawn.

By now you've figured out that this issue of *Dark Discoveries* concerns itself with erotic horror and obsession. I've no doubt that at least one of the stories here will fall into the category I described in the previous paragraph and it might even be a story that manages to transcend the obvious (as the great Ramsey Campbell did in his collection *Scared Stiff*), we shall see—but if you want an example of a story that magnificently transcends the standard sexual obsession formula, look no further than John Fowles' debut novel, *The Collector,* wherein we meet the outwardly mild-mannered clerk Frederick Clegg who kidnaps the object of his obsession, Miranda Grey, and holds her hostage in a "dungeon" that he has built specifically for her: it has clothing in her size and her tastes, her favorite books, he even prepares her favorite foods, etc. Half the novel is told from Clegg's warped point of view (that the reader soon begins to uncomfortably understand and even sympathize with), the other half of the book is presented through Miranda's journal entries. What makes this novel so powerful is the expert way in which Fowles illustrates how each character, slowly, inexorably, begins to comprehend the mind of the other; so much so that, by the two-thirds mark, the reader begins to wonder if Clegg's plan won't succeed after all, because maybe, *maybe* Miranda is developing genuine feelings for her captor.

Talk about your Stockholm Syndrome.

What makes *The Collector* arguably unique in the sexual obsession sub-genre (a sub-genre that probably didn't exist until this novel was published) is that, while the desire for physical intimacy is intensely present throughout the narrative, it is enriched by Clegg's desire for an intellectual, moral, and spiritual communion with Miranda, an organic connection that will make the much-hoped-for physical intercourse meaningful; Clegg sees himself as a true classical Romantic in the Byron/Shelley/Donne sense, while Miranda sees him as an object of disdain, pity, and the embodiment of nearly everything she's feared since she was a child.

The point that I'm probably hammering into the ground is that stories that deal with obsession should not restrict themselves solely to the area of the sexual, although in many of them the sexual element is a necessary part of the groundwork—take the John Hopkins play *This Story of Yours*, later made into a brilliant film entitled *The Offense* by Sidney Lumet. This 1973 film is one of the most nerve-wracking and emotionally devastating studies of how obsession leads to moral and psychological deterioration ever filmed. Sean Connery, in hands-down the most intense, multi-layered, and moving performance of his career, stars as Detective Sergeant Johnson, a bitter, angry, hard-drinking London Police Force detective whose tenuous grip on sanity is finally pushed past the breaking point during his interrogation of a suspected child-molester (the late Ian

Bannen, who matches Connery every step of the way in an equally powerful performance). Decades of dealing with rapes, murders, beatings, and other serious crimes he's had to investigate have made Johnson obsessed with the seedy side of existence, and left a terrible mark on his psyche. His rage and disgust have been suppressed for far too long, and during the course of the interrogation he reveals that the state of his own mind is just as bad, if not worse, than that of the suspected child-molester's (and it is heavily implied that Johnson himself harbors pedophilic tendencies).

The Offense does not unfold in a traditional linear fashion; there are flashbacks, flash-forwards, and scenes that appear as brief fragments reflecting the crumbling state of Johnson's mind. (I firmly believe that writer/director Christopher Nolan had to have found at least part of the inspiration for *Memento*'s structure from watching this film.) The sequence where Johnson breaks down in front of his wife and delivers a shattering, stream-of-consciousness monologue (wherein he begins mixing up the specifics of various cases until they all become one massive, bloody pile of bodies) was and remains Connery's finest moment on the screen. The entire cast is first-rate, Lumet's direction is tense and claustrophobic, and Hopkins' brittle, literate dialogue is some of the best you'll ever encounter. When anyone asks me to name the five most terrifying movies I've ever seen, *The Offense* is always one of them. It is also—like *The Collector*—a disturbing study in obsession that, though it has the element of sex as part of its core, is concerned more with the psychological effects of that affliction.

It is my hope that after you finish with this issue of *Dark Discoveries* you'll seek out films and novels about obsession that cast a wider net than the plethora of mouth-breather-baiting programming found on the Investigation Discovery channel. It is a subject that has yet, in my opinion, to be truly and thoroughly grappled with in modern dark fiction. Or maybe it's something that I just can't get out of my head. Luckily, at least I'm not a compulsive, as well.

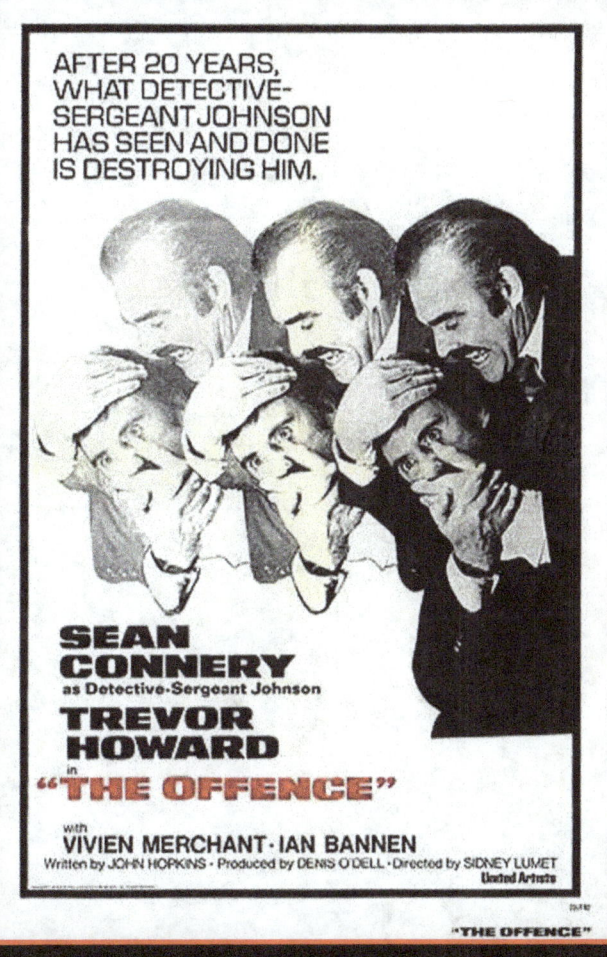

AFTER 20 YEARS, WHAT DETECTIVE-SERGEANT JOHNSON HAS SEEN AND DONE IS DESTROYING HIM.

SEAN CONNERY as Detective-Sergeant Johnson
TREVOR HOWARD in "THE OFFENCE"
with VIVIEN MERCHANT · IAN BANNEN
Written by JOHN HOPKINS · Produced by DENIS O'DELL · Directed by SIDNEY LUMET
United Artists

"THE OFFENCE"

I BELIEVE I SHALL not die

By D. Harlan Wilson

The Experience marked me beyond repair. The weight of its memory seemed to press down on my shoulders, imperiling me, threatening to wreck me once and for all. I barely made it to the bed, and I collapsed, and I took deep, stertorous breaths, rolling onto my back and blinking away the vertigo.

My ears rang like broken instruments. Decibels flooded my sensorium and multiplied with a viral intensity and hate.

I wanted to die.

I covered my ears and squeezed my head.

I felt my mouth open. I felt the wind on my teeth.

Silence.

An old man plummeted from the sky, head-first, as if latched at the ankles to a bungee cord. He donned a parachute. For an instant I saw the world through his eyes—flat, vast, bright green, a geometric utopia…

When he pulled the chute, his body spun upwards on the axis of his armpits. He cut the strings before hitting the bed, fell, fell, fell, landed beside me, bounced off the bed, did a nimble somersault, and landed squarely, on both feet, knees locked, with the grace of a seasoned gymnast.

I knew him.

I had known him.

He was a stranger… but the face belied my instincts. Skin hung from the skull in loose knots. And yet, somehow, the face exhibited certain definition and contour. A rhytidectomy gone bad.

He shrugged off the parachute gear. He wore an intricate cape, a kind of frock coat, but more modern than standard Victorian fare, sharp and black and accented by fine blue cracks. An elastic fabric, although not Spandex. Oversized goggles concealed his eyes.

He smiled a warped smile.

The teeth were dark brown, possibly wooden, and they weren't all there. The longer the smile persisted, the more it seemed to blur, or smudge, or melt, as if it were a photograph of a smile beleaguered by a slow flame.

He pointed a gun at me. It had a giant barrel that curved down into a polished ligneous handle. The weapon was older than him.

We talked.

"How did you do that?" I asked.

He shrugged. "How does one disdain the tillage of thy husbandry?"

Confused, I pushed myself onto my elbows, squinting away sunlight. "No. That." I sat up straight and gestured at the sky.

He looked upwards and frowned, celluloid smile dissolving, congealing into a pained gash. A string of drool fell from the spigot of a cracked underlip.

It occurred to me that the bed had been situated on the front lawn, just a few feet from the sidewalk I had somehow managed to drag myself down. I looked behind me. No house. Only a gaping, excavated hole where the basement used to be. Even the foundation had been exhumed and taken away.

Worms fidgeted in the dirt.

"My home," I said, eyeballing the old man. He continued to hold the gun on me. "Put that thing away. You're not gonna do anything with that."

He shot me. Blew a hole in my arm. The musketball passed through my flesh like butter, singeing and flaying muscle. It missed the bone.

The neighbors poured out of their houses and stormed the yard.

I rolled off the bed and did a clumsy jig across the lawn, shrieking like a mad wraith.

The neighbors didn't know what to do. We had a loose acquaintance—wave perfunctorily at each other when passing in cars, nod coolly at each other when passing in riding mowers, etc.—and they treated me like a bonfire gone haywire, wanting to help but fearing the hard burn.

The old man reloaded the gun. He turned his attention to the neighbors and, without warning, unloaded on them, possessed, relentless, discharging an impossible fusillade of bullets, and the neighbors exploded into putrid flecks, piece by piece, the old man roaring and yipping in triumph above the slosh of hot gore.

It was over before it had begun. Steam hissed from the carnage.

I passed out… and awoke in the passenger's seat of a van.

It might have been a Dodge Sprinter. It certainly wasn't a minivan. But doubtless a luxury vehicle, at one point, long ago. Cigarette burns dotted an interior of cheap upholstery with a garish, obsolete pattern. Layer of dust on the dash. Pinetree deodorizer hanging from the rearview mirror.

Outside, a quick swath of landscape…

My arm had been treated and bandaged. I could almost feel the ointment speedhealing the wound. I touched my arm. It hurt.

We talked.

"Where are we going?" I asked.

"To eat the world's due, by the grave and thee," he replied.

There was nothing left to say.

We went on a murderous killing spree, through suburb after smalltown after suburb, robbing gas stations, blowing up strip malls, kidnapping children and selling them to black marketeers, fucking strippers and prostitutes in the dark, selling angel dust to teenagers, all the while chainsmoking and flicking our butts out the car window at unsuspecting pedestrians. At first, I resisted. It was wrong, what we were doing. Unethical and depraved. In time, though, I grew accustomed to it. I never took a life, but I witnessed interminable body horrors, gruesome slayings and unspeakable bloodbaths, and I did nothing to stop it, fearing for my safety, doing what I could to stay alive. For the most part, we were able to avoid the police, despite several would-be citations for "spreading hate," "chasing people with chainsaws," and so forth, but before the citations could be written up, the various minions of the Law typically found themselves spurting rich substances onto the canvas of Life. Once we picked up several young hitchhikers that turned out to be a team of upstart filmmakers. They bought permission to shoot footage and document our exploits for fifty dollars, plus royalties down the road. Inevitably the old man murdered them, one at a time, over a period of three or four weeks, consistently unsatisfied with their artistic vision. I actually liked what they were doing but was in no position to make a compelling argument on their behalf. I simply treaded water. Or rather, the water treaded me.

On numerous occasions—sometimes at night during periods of insomnia on some cot in some flophouse, sometimes in the heat of battle, although never between these emblematic sheets—I thought about the Experience. How I nearly escaped. How it transformed my perception, my selfhood… I wanted to go back. But the future denied me history at every turn. And then, suddenly, I couldn't remember it. The Experience was gone.

We talked.

"Some experiences aren't meant to be remembered, let alone spoken of," said the old man in a rare moment of clarity. "Life happens fast, young man. Even when it's going slow. Of course, we miss things. In the end, in retrospect, it's all a monstrous blur. Too many memories. The mind filters them out, discards the past and moves on, as fresh as it can be."

During my response, he produced a molten scream.

We pulled over.

"Get out," he said. "I want to show you something."

The desert sped to a horizon defined by the silhouettes of tall, off-kilter buttes. Clouds streaked across an auburn sky.

I stood on the roadside like a condemned man waiting patiently for his executioner to pop him in the head. Slouched over, defeated. Yet oddly content. I don't know why I had worried so much. About death. About the little things that culminated in death. Everybody dies. Nobody cares. And if they do care, one day they will die, too, along with their anxieties and memories. Eventually everything starts from scratch. History books are mere insignia of deleted and lost scenes.

The old man swung open the trunk doors of the van, retrieved something and brought it to me, cradling it like an ancient artifact.

A paper lunchbag. Crinkled. Aged.

"I am going to breathe in the content now," he croaked. "Carbonic acid. I do not know if I shall die."

He put the creased aperture to his lips and sucked deeply, repeatedly, the bulb of the lunchbag expanding and contracting… He removed his lips.

"It does not taste poorly," he wheezed. His cheeks turned purple. "In fact, I may not taste anything at all."

His knees buckled. He clutched his chest and the lunchbag fell from his hand.

"I believe I shall not die," he said in a voice like a deflating tire.

Staggering backwards a pace, then swaying from side to side, his skin shriveled, desiccated, as if timelapsing, and a webwork of sick, wriggling veins sprouted to attention.

"I believe I shall not die," he repeated in a weakened, distant voice.

He collapsed, head slamming against the pavement. Blood leaked from his mouth and flowed onto the highway.

"I believe I… I shall not… die," he gurgled, and went into convulsions, blood mixing with white froth…

I watched him writhe, squirm, lash out. For a moment I had to defend myself as, in a final burst of energy, he clutched my ankle and tried to bite it.

Shuddering, I kicked him squarely in the jaw. His teeth sprayed across the asphalt.

He said something before dying, something serious, a crumb of wisdom… but I had already begun collecting the teeth, and I had already plotted out everything, all of it, from beginning to end, if only in theory, in the space that precludes definable experience.

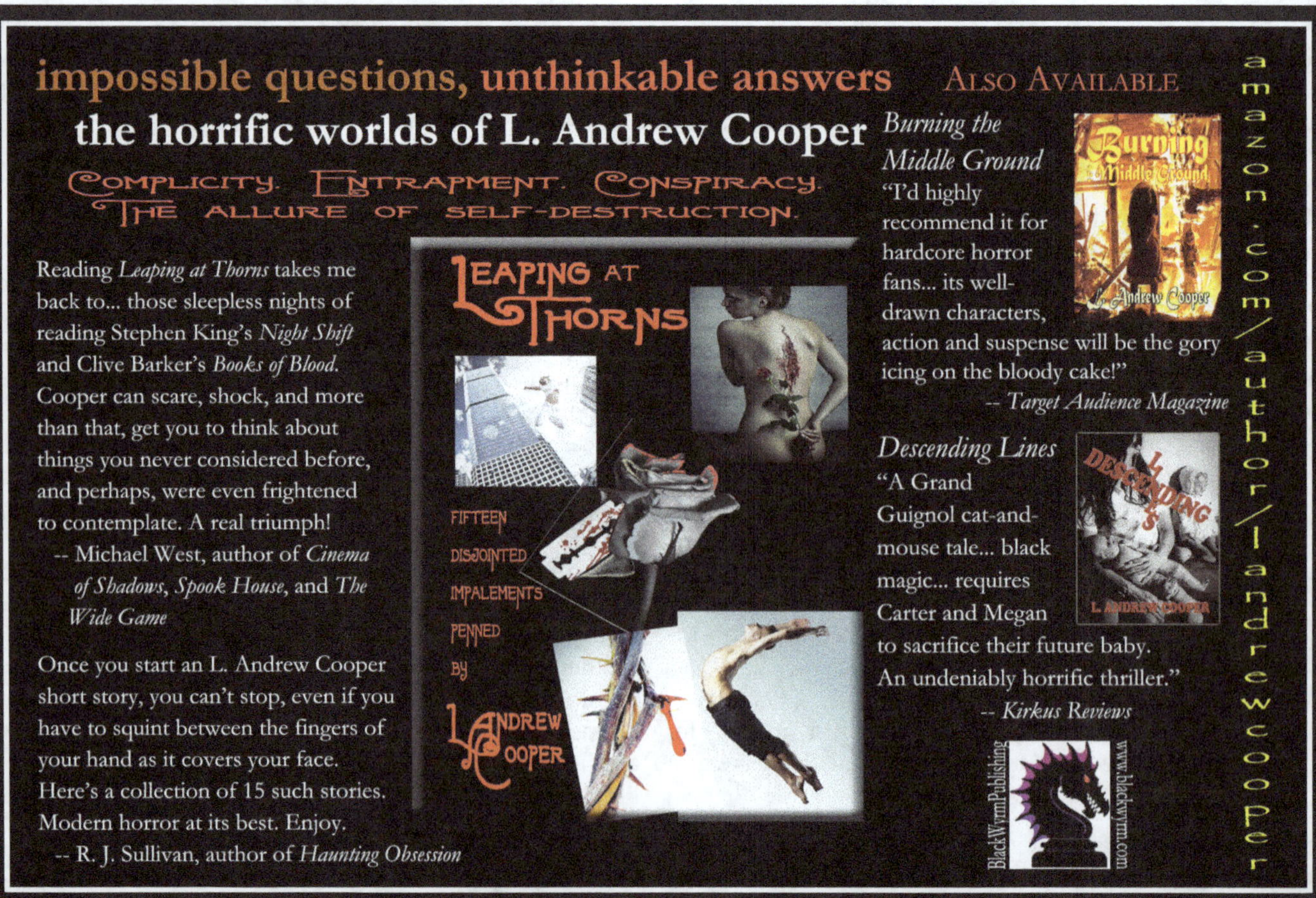

---

impossible questions, unthinkable answers   ALSO AVAILABLE

the horrific worlds of L. Andrew Cooper

COMPLICITY. ENTRAPMENT. CONSPIRACY. THE ALLURE OF SELF-DESTRUCTION.

Reading *Leaping at Thorns* takes me back to... those sleepless nights of reading Stephen King's *Night Shift* and Clive Barker's *Books of Blood*. Cooper can scare, shock, and more than that, get you to think about things you never considered before, and perhaps, were even frightened to contemplate. A real triumph!
-- Michael West, author of *Cinema of Shadows*, *Spook House*, and *The Wide Game*

Once you start an L. Andrew Cooper short story, you can't stop, even if you have to squint between the fingers of your hand as it covers your face. Here's a collection of 15 such stories. Modern horror at its best. Enjoy.
-- R. J. Sullivan, author of *Haunting Obsession*

LEAPING AT THORNS

FIFTEEN DISJOINTED IMPALEMENTS PENNED BY L ANDREW COOPER

Burning the Middle Ground
"I'd highly recommend it for hardcore horror fans... its well-drawn characters, action and suspense will be the gory icing on the bloody cake!"
-- *Target Audience Magazine*

Descending Lines
"A Grand Guignol cat-and-mouse tale... black magic... requires Carter and Megan to sacrifice their future baby. An undeniably horrific thriller."
-- *Kirkus Reviews*

amazon.com/author/landrewcooper

Driving into the Sun
SHRIEKFEST 2014

By John Palisano

Fade In

EXT. PACIFIC COAST HIGHWAY - DAY

Once you make it outside of Los Angeles and you cross into the north, where the highways get smaller, and the landscape stretches wider, and where the air turns blessedly cooler and cleaner, you may find a little Dutch town called Solvang. Several years back, my friend Alex Bram and I took a trip up there. We brainstormed a little film that was originally called *Run For Your Life*. The script grew, contracted, and grew again. Folks got attached. Folks got disattached. At one point, it sort of just faded away, as so many projects often do. Then? Several weeks back, there was a message that *New Breed*, the script's new name, had made it as a finalist for Shriekfest 2014.

INT. HOLLYWOOD HILLS HOUSE, BEDROOM - NIGHT

The day started with a panic attack. As the time for the first party neared, I found myself locked to my bed. Filmmaking has been such a large part of my life, and my self-imposed retirement was about to be lifted. Images raced through my head. Going to CBS in New York City with my Dad as a kid. He worked in graphics, and I often wandered the sets.

MONTAGE:

Fast forward to my early teens. Zombie movies in my garage. How I wish that old VHS would show up again one day with the super-8s we made. Then Emerson College. So many film projects. Watching *Good Will Hunting* shoot. PA'ing on Brad Anderson's first feature. I still have a scar. Philip Seymour Hoffman running lines around the corner from my house. He wasn't famous then. No one was. Shooting in alleys. Seth Grahame-Smith was headed to be the next great cinematographer. We all knew it. Denis Leary gave us advice and cracked us up. I worked every position on a set and off. My final film project proved popular enough that we had to have a second screening. The script won the *Latent Image Award*.

Fast forward. Los Angeles. Day one.

The first person I see is Madonna driving out from her company as I interview for my first job with Ridley Scott,

PHOTO COURTESY OF JOHN PALISANO

Back to square one. Commercials. Music Videos. Everyone famous and infamous passes through. Somehow, I get a job on a big budget feature as a Director's Assistant on a movie starring an Austrian weightlifter fighting the Devil. Learned and saw the inner workings. Sleep turned into a joke. Every second spoken for. I ran tasks while I slept. Years of this…

"What do you want to do?" says the producer, the same one that welcomed me on board at the Palms.

"I want to make movies, too," I say.

"Great," he says. "Go do it. You'll have to start all over again. Unless you want a career as a high-level assistant, that is."

There it began.

My descent.

Freelance gigs. Part-time jobs. Writing scripts. Filming shorts. First Panavision 35mm short film. Festivals don't care. My old contacts have moved on. Editing gigs. Answering phones. Anything. Rental houses. Corrupt keyboard manufacturers. Checking DVDs. Still dreaming. Writing constantly. There's got to be something. A *hit*.

The first feature. Produced by MasterCard and American Express. Two years shooting on weekends. Met with the worst fate: indifference. More shoots on smaller projects. A second feature, made with lessons from the first in mind. It, too, is met with a collective shrug.

Extra work to make ends meet. How am I on *Will & Grace* with cameras pointing at me? I'm not an actor. Or am I?

A boy comes, born as fireworks go over Dodger Stadium in the distance. Magic. A baby in Hollywood divides. Many flee. Many join together. His mother finds him work. Typecast as a baby. He's Melanie Lynskey's kid. Then a scene in a Robin Williams movie. I saw him back in Boston, filming with Spielberg right next to my apartment. Mandy Moore takes a picture of Robin holding Leo. Circles expand and contract.

Another feature film, shot in my hometown of Norwalk, Connecticut, is a success. Locally, we are given a full page spread. We sell out two theaters. No one will tell me what they think. Oddly, the Q&A at the end brings no questions.

Defeat.

Maybe this is just not meant to be.

Retreat.

Some who've seen the film tell me it's a fabulous thriller. They rave about it.

It makes no festivals, and does not get distribution.

I am Ed Wood. Worse. I am not even that good. The worst filmmaker of all time. Three bombs and you're out. I'm out. Sidelined.

Like so many other projects and people, I let it all go.

CUT TO:

A man reading a message.

New Breed has made it as a finalist.

FLASH CUT:

The lights dim. I'm back in that old familiar haunt—a

PHOTO COURTESY OF JOHN PALISANO

movie theater.

INT. BAR SINISTER - NIGHT

The party takes place at Bar Sinister, which takes me a bit to find, even though I've been there before. It took a lot for me to make it out the door. Returning to a world that brought with it such disappointment; this was not something I wanted to do.

I texted loved ones. They urged me to get over myself and just get the hell out there. So I did.

As soon as I got to Bar Sinister, my old friend and co-conspirator Alex greeted me with a bear hug. Damn right things were off to a good start.

He led me through the Lestat-like draperies and pummeling Goth metal music, toward the main room, where a DJ dressed like a muppet vampire was dancing away. "Our poster's going to be up there," Alex said, and I waited forever for it to appear on the slideshow. I grabbed a shot of it before we headed upstairs, past the huge, overstuffed red velvet chair thrones and suspiciously-eye-balling goths.

Me and Alex caught up; he filled my head with the several projects he's got in development. That was really interesting. In the filmmaking world, it seems you've really got to have a degree in juggling. You never know which way things are going to go.

What's the story? That's what they all ask.

Our script, *New Breed*, is an action/horror story about a secret government agency that's creating super-werewolf warriors. It's got a strong female lead, and is wall-to-wall action. It's something he and I, along with Christina Eliason, had written a few years back. Suddenly, with the Shriekfest finalist status, the project's gained heat.

When Alex first emailed me, I couldn't believe it. We'd been through a lot developing the script, and Alex had long since gone on to many other projects, the least of which was mounting the *Carnival of Darkness* film festival.

So this reinvigorated my screenwriting. I found myself thrust right back inside the strange world of filmmaking.

At the upstairs lounge, I found horror celebrity Robert "Corpsy" Rhine with his wonderful *Girls & Corpses* magazine. As always, he was surrounded by a posse of stunning women.

I also ran into old friend Rolfe Kanefsky, writer and director of cult classic *There's Nothing Out There* and the recent *The Hazing*. We caught up. The cool thing was that Rolfe was there to support his fellow filmmakers and screenwriters at the fest, and didn't have a horse in the race. Very cool of him. That's Shriekfest in a nutshell, too. He updated me on the great *Megafoot* project he's been developing. Hoping to see it one day. I'm sure I will. Rolfe said he'd rather wait and do it right, then shoot it on weekends. "That's not a way to make a movie like this," he said.

"I totally agree," I said. "Gotta do it right."

We watched a hypnotist knock out a pair of lovely young girls. "Do you have to be a hot chick for that to work?" Alex asked.

I said, "Yeah. I think it's got something to do with being malnourished and underweight."

I asked the gorgeous blonde in the red dress how it went after. "You just have to let it go," she said. "Like in *Frozen*."

Indeed. Let it go.

Alex took off. I found an issue of *Girls & Corpses*, read it for the articles, and quite enjoyed the gorgeous women posing with corpses new and old. A very fun and twisted magazine. Right up my alley. Or down.

***

On my way out, I ran into the charming Denise Gossett, the actress whose inspiration has given us Shriekfest all these years. We were off to a smashing beginning. Speaking of smashing, when I arrived at my car, there were two rival frat boy gangs about to go at it. Some were even pushing and shoving, and I saw a punch to the gut. There was a lot of yelling. A huge SUV barreled down Las Palmas, nearly taking us all out. Someone yelled something at me, I think, and I got in my car and hit the gas pedal without a word or a look. The Old Me might've said something smart, might've gotten into it, might've had a little trouble. Instead? I just wanted to enjoy the ride, man. Forget all the outside noise. There's always a fight if you go looking, after all. Ain't hard to find.

INT. DRAWING ROOM - DAY

The Screenwriter's Happy Hour

I've never met a happy screenwriter. Well, not a struggling one, at least. They're a pretty grumpy lot. Which makes sense. Most of them are tired of their day jobs, and the writing that once held so much promise can easily turn into a succeed-or-I'm-a-total-failure-why-the-hell-am-I-even-out-here existential crisis. I have that at least twice a year. So a Happy Hour seems appropriate. I'm sure us bitter curmudgeons could be happy for an hour. At least until we hear about the horrible writer we all hate getting the three picture deal with Warner Bros. That might sour the mood. Hopefully, then, no crappy writers got lucky.

When I get to the Drawing Room and open the door I see nothing but black. My fight or flight response kicks in, but thankfully, I am rescued by Christina Eliason, my co-writer of *New Breed*, who has spotted the stumbling man blinded by darkness. I sit, and Jeffrey is quick to get me all Newcastled up. The gang of writers is as eccentric and wonderful as I'd hoped. I get into some conversations, and it's nice to hear all these creatives enjoying themselves. Of course, having never met Christina after several years of online back-and-forth, it's amazing hearing her many stories. Her handsome British husband holds court at the bar. This is a pub, and as she says, he's in his natural element. We are, too.

TITLE CARD: INTO THE SUN

As I'm tailing Melanie and her husband down Melrose toward Raleigh Studios, the sun is setting perfectly. Even

though the sun hurts, the silhouettes of the cars, building, and palm trees, is worth it. Like the good man said when his mamma told him not to look into the sun, well, mamma, that's where the fun is.

Most of the screenwriters found dinner. I somehow missed that.

It's been a while since I've been on a back lot in any capacity, but the rhythm is like an old friend. The production trucks. The production types. Hi. Good to be back. It was neat walking past the stages. I'd always wanted to shoot something on a stage. Never got a chance. I ain't dead yet. Could happen.

EXT. RALEIGH STUDIOS - NIGHT

There's a crowd assembled outside. Lots of smiling people. Everyone's dressed up. I grab my passes and head inside.

INT. RALEIGH STUDIOS - NIGHT

There's a small concession stand. Water and a box of candy are dinner. I get a tech tour from the projectionist. He says they're down to only three or four showings on 35mm a year. And they're a studio. He also tells me film tops out at 2k and so the new 4k is even higher resolution. I always knew the day would come. And there you go.

There's a bomb inside the program. There are twenty screenplay finalists. Twenty. Jesus. I start doing the math. Does that give us a five percent chance? Well, there it is. We've already got a huge leg up on getting *New Breed* made, but it'd sure be nice to take home the gold. I get a text from my friend Deborah. After many years, she's got full financing on her feature. Good stuff is congealing all around. Her timing is perfect.

Then there's the festival intro from Denise Gossett, and the first films unroll. Not too shabby. The theater is full. The first one's a slow burn of a haunted house movie, with a sucker-punch ending.

My gut gets the best of me, and I slip out, onto Melrose, in search of chow. I find it, in the form of a taco truck. When in Rome. I dine next to a guy in a motorized wheelchair. He eyes my meatless tacos suspiciously. I wonder if his mountain of radish slices will come back to haunt him.

On the way back, a girl carrying a 40 ounce beer in a paper bag smokes a cigarette and chats me up. She wants to know what I'm doing down there. I admit to having something in the festival. The street is dark, and I'm convinced there's a gang of rejects waiting to pounce on me; she's the bait, and they'll trap me. I'm relieved when I see the studio. "You going that way?" she asks. Yup. I am. She looks mildly disappointed. I'm not ready to be the secret ingredient at a taco truck just yet.

Back inside, I run into Jeffery, who offers me a beer from his trunk. He's got enough convention survivalist stuff to keep Motley Crue drunk for a month. Now he reminds me of a young Christopher Lee. I'm not sure what I'm getting into. I see the actress I helped take a picture of on the carpet earlier, and wave her over. She waves back, but it's Christina again who appears, her man along with her. "They said John was having a beer with Jeffery over here," she says. How the hell do these people know? She's out for the night, and I am, too. We vow to get a shot with Alex when he joins us Sunday night. That'll be a great moment. That's one of my main missions.

On the way home, I'm grateful. There are no roving gangs of frat boys, I'm not hungry, and many new friends have been made.

SATURDAY & SUNDAY

And we're off. We do what we're here to do, which is promote one another, and watch a boatload of films. The days are filled with short films, and the nights are for features. There's also a good mix of science fiction and horror films, which is cool. The biggest throughline I notice is the quality of the films. Most of them are of extremely high production quality. This is amazing. Only a few years ago, there was really no easy or inexpensive way to make a decent picture. Technology has advanced tremendously. No one is making *Iron Man* or *Transformers* at this level, effects-wise. Most are people-centric, and thriller-centric. All exhibit professional class writing, directing, and performances. I loathe reviews where only a few are singled out—it disregards a lot of people's work—and I'd rather they all receive equal footing. They each deserve it. Shriekfest's main motto seems to be to help everyone in the festival, and not just a chosen few. I love that, and I'll carry that torch. There's plenty of room in the marketplace for excellent horror, be it books, short films, or feature films. Can we have too many great movies to watch? Not from this gang. I was not bored at any point during the many screenings, and they all seemed to end much too soon.

Between films, the crowds gather outside and talk. I meet some amazing people outside, especially the other filmmakers and screenwriters. Everyone's story behind their stories are so different. It's invigorating and inspiring to be around so much passionate creativity. Founder Denise Gossett states that the Shriekfest is meant to, "... lift you... not take you down," and she's absolutely right in that regard. Everyone's smiling. There's lots of happy faces—off the screen. Onscreen? Well, that's a different story. Lot s of terrified people up there.

It's all a blur. Many of the screenwriters in the competition meet up at a fancy-pants place called Lemonade, where they charge you a lot for a little. Ted Dewberry's paper plate had two little scoops on it, of two gourmet thing-a-ma-bobs, and his bill was over seven bucks. Zippity-Do-Dah. I choose carefully, and get out with an almost adequate plate for a ten spot. While we down our chow, Dewbury splashes Vodka inside my lemonade. It makes it worth it. There is a steady in-and-out of amazingly beautiful people, men, women, and everything else. The folks around me comment on it. "This is Los Angeles—the Larchmont district—it's everywhere out here. It's nuts. You never get used to it." Several people take pictures of us sitting at the table. I do my best to make the most erotic faces I can.

Near the end of the meal, the energy changes. People's energy gets weird. It's closing night, and there's only one movie between us and finding out who gets the Best Screenplay award. I'm not worried. As soon as I saw there were twenty finalists, I was pretty sure I'd be safe in my seat, and not having to stand up in front of a crowd and say anything profound. The others? Some had come far. Joe raised a GoFundMe to make it. Others came as far away as Connecticut, my old home state.

We made it back where we caught the fantastic *Berkshire County*, the closing film of the festival. It was tense, and genuinely scary, and looked great. I was in the mood for more films, but just as it began, it started to end.

Denise gave a heartfelt speech. We really did end up a family in the end. I made some amazing friends. I looked around and saw lots of awesome folks, and felt validation and comfort. These were my people. We were all together in this crazy undertaking of bringing our deepest fears to life.

We didn't win.

Only just the award.

We did win.

Camaraderie. Friendships, and the fact that our little script was amongst the top out of over four thousand entries. The fact that it's actually going into production also softened the blow. Considerably.

I gave out hugs, clowned on the carpet for pictures, said my goodbyes, and drove my car off the lot, passing the stages and active productions, and I heard the voices of all the actors and filmmakers and good people I've had the chance to work with, or who had a film in a festival alongside me... and they all spoke out to me. Welcome back, man, they said. And welcome home.

Fade Out

PHOTO COURTESY OF BRADLEY THORNBER

Exemplifying the Sinister: An Interview with Nofar Avigdor

BY LEAH JUNG

LJ: What accomplishments are you most proud of?

NA: I believe that each day of succeeding in something big or small is an accomplishment. My proudest moments are those hard physical ones which earned me the trophies I have from Soccer and other sports. It's nice to be appreciated for something you love doing. More recent accomplishments include working with Galia Lahav and Michael Costello, two absolutely amazing designers and individuals. I am forever grateful for those moments.

LJ: When we approached you about our "Sinister Appetite" concept, were you more confident about portraying the innocent exterior or the hidden desire? Why?

NA: I was very excited when I first heard about this concept. It was pretty cool to portray both sides of innocent and

"badass" and I can't wait to see how it came out! I definitely did enjoy portraying the hidden desire more because all your life you're expected to be good and innocent, so it's fun to let the bad out even for a few minutes on set. Plus "badass" women are hot.

LJ: During our shoot, we were discussing horror films and I remember you didn't like one of my all-time favorites, *Evil Dead*! I almost kicked you off set, hahaha, but then you redeemed yourself by admiring our photographer's vintage horror movie posters. Would you say you generally like classic and subdued horror over the more comedic in-your-face variety? What are some of your favorite horror or sci-fi flicks?

NA: OMG Bradley had the coolest place I've been to yet. Vintage and modern art that is so easily appreciated. My geek came out as soon as I walked in. Best collections, and once you meet him you know why the house is so awesome. But yeah…cheezy "ketchup blood everywhere" movies aren't my cup of tea. I do love scary movies that make me flinch rather than laugh. My favorite horror film is *The Exorcist* (1973) and sci-fi is of course every *Star Wars* movie even though I know it's an ongoing "SF or not" controversy.

LJ: You also told us about your desire to learn how to play the drums. Are you still fantasizing about that all-girl band?

NA: Girl bands are hot! I'm getting better and better daily on the drums and I know you play the Ukulele. BAM!!! All we need is a few more talented hot girls to rock'n'roll with us and we got a band. I honestly can't wait, I know it will happen. We could make the world happy with our music.

LJ: Sought-after model, natural ability as a musician, is there anything you've attempted to do that you ended up being TERRIBLE at?

NA: I suck at basketball! I try so hard, I'm naturally good at every sport but I can't seem to dribble and run at the

PHOTO COURTESY OF BRADLEY THORNBER

same time without accidently kicking the ball away. If it was just to stand and shoot, no problem, but I find it so hard. Props to those people who know how to run the court! Not an easy sport!

LJ: If you could magically transform all human blood to be any other color, what color would you choose?

NA: Hmm…I love all colors so it would be awesome if people had different color blood because then if two people mix they can create a new color of their own. Oh and girls under 21 should have sparkles in their blood 'cause it's just too cool to pass.

Interested in learning more about Nofar? Find her on Instagram @OMGitsNofar

PHOTO COURTESY OF BRADLEY THORNBER

53

Horror in a Hundred Stories

Night Train
By Rick Hipson

Random flashes of life rush by my window and quickly fade away. Clattering down these tracks, the skin of my past is ripped from my bones and is devoured beneath the flight of my night train.

A whistle screams, jolting me upright.

"Ticket please."

Digging through empty pockets, I search for a ticket I'll never find. I don't belong here.

Hand upon my shoulder I look up and become bathed in burning laughter. The train crumbles beneath me and gives way to the fiery depths of my sorrow below. Screams fill the void as I fall forever against them.

Pumpkin Chunker
By Joe Nazare

Gordie was crazy with the idea of visiting this rural patch ever since he found out it featured a launcher. Unfortunately, he had to wait almost all October until his support-extorting ex deigned to relinquish hold of their daughter.

Now, though, Gordie sports a rapt smile as he watches the giant trebuchet rid itself of its cargo with one violent sling. The projectile soars high and far through the night sky before finally capitulating to gravity with a splattery thud.

"Wowser! How'd you like that, pumpkin?" Gordie enthuses, but regardless of her drugging, his offspring's in no shape to respond.

No Rest for the Wicked
By Catherine Bader

He stumbled over everything. Half a face, no nose, no left ear.

I knew him from the building on Fifth.

He carried a severed arm covered in thick clotty blood.

Took an occasional lick.

I watched him from my open window on the 4th floor.

I sneezed.

Long hair flew from one spot to another as he snapped his head forward and up.

Coming my way.

Guess it's time for the 9mm.

I can never get an entire day of rest anymore....

I turned as the door to my apartment blew open.

Rest was no longer an issue.

Emily's Last Session

By
Ray Garton

During the buffer of ten minutes or so between sessions with clients, Dr. Sheila Marx takes a few deep breaths and does some stretching exercises. She keeps flats of bottled water stacked against the wall behind her desk and takes a bottle from the top, then seats herself and pulls up her next client's file on her tablet.

The wounded light of a rainy day comes through the windows and windblown rain spatters the glass and dribbles down in jagged, drooling sheets, distorting the world outside. The office, a room in a converted old Victorian, is comfortably warm and lightly scented with lavender.

Her next client is Emily Shaye, 37 years old, a married high school English teacher with two children, a boy, seven, and a girl, nine. By all appearances, she is a perfectly stable, healthy woman with a full and productive life and a happy family, and Emily works hard to hide the truth by maintaining that facade.

The truth is that Emily suffers from depression and anxiety and struggles with unresolved issues with her parents, an abusive, emotionally unavailable alcoholic father and an abused, distant mother. She fears that she will be no better at mothering than her own mother was and, as a result, has become distant from her children. She knows her husband is being unfaithful to her, but she has not confronted him about it because, for some time now, she has been considering a little infidelity of her own.

Emily seems to be exhausted by years of trying to be someone she is not, of presenting herself to her husband as "sexually vanilla," as she put it, when, in fact, her sexuality is quite colorful. She entertains dark fantasies that combine lust with pain, violence, brutality, and even death. For most of her life, she hid these desires from everyone but herself, huddled with them in isolated shame. As she grew older, however, she began to think they weren't so shameful after all.

"Have you been on the internet?" she said to Sheila months ago, early in her therapy. "It's made me wonder if maybe I'm not so horrible after all. Somehow, fantasizing about killing some guy as he comes inside me just doesn't seem nearly as sick and disgusting as getting off on vomiting, or on little animals being stomped to death."

Emily's fantasies—and, more recently, her comments suggesting she might attempt to act on some of them—were troubling for a few reasons, not the least of which was the fact that one of her underage male students lately has been their focus.

She mentioned Bobby Sanchez in passing once, and when she brought him up again in a flirty way during a later session, Sheila asked about him.

"This student of yours, Bobby—he's really gotten your attention, hasn't he?"

Emily's laugh filled the room. "We might as well drop the preliminary questions and cut to it. Do I have sexual feelings for him? Yes. I think about him sometimes when I… you know, when I'm alone. I guess—"

"When you masturbate?"

"Yes, when I… yes."

"You understand, of course, that it would be illegal for you to pursue any kind of relationship with him. He's underage."

She nodded. "I know that, and I haven't done anything. And I won't. Well, I *probably* won't. But I think… he likes me. He's beautiful, you know. And innocent. A clean slate."

"Does that appeal to you?"

"Of course. Doesn't it appeal to everyone? Someone who has no baggage, no sensitive buttons or sore spots."

"And no frame of reference. Nothing to compare you to, right?"

Another laugh. "I suppose so, sure. And what's wrong with that?"

She spoke of Bobby often after that and Sheila became more concerned that she might decide to act out one of her fantasies with him, any one of which could be harmful, or even fatal. The situation had catastrophic possibilities. So far, Emily has said nothing that would warrant calling the police, but now Sheila is hyper alert for such comments.

"His skin is the color of a mocha latte," she said of Bobby one day. "And his face is… I don't know. Like a painting." A big smile. "I'd like to play with him." There was something juvenile about the way she said it.

"This is very dangerous territory," Sheila said. "The boy is underage and you are his teacher."

"I didn't say that I was *going* to play with him, only that I'd *like* to. I know it would be… it would be…" All the girlishness left her face as her features twisted up for a moment, then relaxed. "…wrong."

It was Emily's inability to shed all of the guilt and shame stirred by her fantasies that moved her to find a therapist almost a year ago, when she came to Sheila. She's never missed a session and is always punctual. She seems to have a genuine desire to work out her problems, but is hobbled by the part of her that just doesn't give a damn anymore.

"In your fantasy," Sheila once said to her, "how do you kill your lover?"

"Always with a knife."

"Why always? Doesn't the fantasy have any variations?"

Emily shook her head. "Always a knife. I think it's important that there be penetration. You know what I mean?"

"Penetration? Are you referring to killing or to intercourse?"

"Both." She smiled. "It's only fair, right?"

Sheila checks the time and is surprised to see that it's seven minutes after the hour. Emily has always shown up a few minutes before her scheduled appointment.

At the end of last week's session, Emily said, "I think some things are starting to come together, Dr. Marx. Coming to a head, you know? If I can't make it next week, I'll call you." She hurried out before Sheila could ask her what that meant. Instead, she made a note to ask her at the beginning of the next session. Which should be underway.

She listens for signs of Emily's arrival. The converted Victorian house she shares with another therapist is so old that any movement made within it has a corresponding sound. The front door is heavy and creaky and always announces a new arrival, but Sheila hears nothing but the rain against the window and muscular gusts of wind slamming their shoulders against the side of the house. The receptionist, Angie, has not returned from lunch and the other therapist is out of town for the week, and Sheila is alone.

Crossing her legs beneath her gray wool skirt, she leans back in the chair with her tablet for a closer look at Emily's last few sessions. They are always unpredictable because Emily's thought processes are idiosyncratic, scattered, and take her from one topic to another with no perceptible connection between the two and no indication that the subject has changed, sometimes mid-sentence. She bounces around like a pinball darting off of bumpers, but Sheila has learned her rhythm and knows that, however erratically, Emily somehow will connect it all before the session is over.

But she has not yet connected her sexual fantasies to the bitter resentment she feels toward her father and the damage he did to the family in general and Emily in particular. He died of liver disease eighteen months ago, which Sheila believes had more to do with Emily's decision to see a therapist than her sexual fantasies, whether or not Emily is aware of it.

"I'm not bloodthirsty, Dr. Marx, I'm not a psycho, it's nothing like that," Emily said in a previous session after describing her murderous fantasy. "It's not like I'm a danger to anyone, I really don't *want* to kill anybody. The killing itself, that's not what the fantasy is about. It's the idea of being the last sight… the last sensation… the last fragrance he will ever experience. He will die with me filling up his vision. Because, you know, I'd be on top of him. And I wouldn't stop, I'd keep riding him so that would be the last thing he felt. Fucking me."

"You find that erotic?"

Emily considered the question, staring distantly for a moment at nothing in particular, then said in a tremulous whisper, "Yes, I do. I would be everything to him in those last minutes. The *last* everything. It would be… almost… like swallowing his life whole. I'm not sure *why* I find that erotic, but I do. I'm turned on by the complete *consumption* of him. I would be the world he leaves when he dies." She turned to Sheila with a dreamy smile and heavy-lidded eyes. "Does that mean I'm a sick, horrible person?"

"A fantasy is just that, a fantasy," Sheila said. "It says nothing about character or morality. As long as it remains a fantasy. You can engage in role playing games with someone you trust and act out the fantasy in a safe way. A lot of very stable, healthy people have sexual fantasies that are quite extreme, Emily. It doesn't mean you're a bad person."

Emily's smile faded and her eyes darkened with a worried frown. "But I don't feel stable. Or healthy. I wish I did, but I don't. But Bobby… his face makes me feel a lot better." The smile returned. "And when I think about what I'd like to do to him, I feel even better." She saw something in Sheila's eyes that made her quickly add, "Don't worry, Dr. Marx, I have no intention of acting on my fantasies. If it sounds like I do, that's only because part of my fantasy involves *acting* on my fantasies, so when I talk about them… well, it sounds like I'm planning to live them out."

After the abuse Emily endured at the hands of her drunken father while growing up, it made sense that she would make someone like Bobby the focus of her sexual fantasies. She has power over him, as her father had over

her, and he is still a person in the process of developing, forming, becoming, as malleable as she was when her father beat her and told her she was ugly and stupid. And he's as needy as she was when her father chose drunkenness over a healthy relationship with his daughter. It was her way of re-enacting and gaining control of what happened to her in the past.

Emily slyly evaded much discussion of her husband, so Sheila honed in on that subject in a session.

"You've said your husband is very vanilla," Sheila said, "but he believes the same about you. Have you considered discussing these things with him?"

"I've *considered* it, sure. But Joel was raised a Catholic, went to Catholic schools. And he never outgrew it. He only goes to church around the holidays now, but everything else stuck to him like glue. He thinks a man and his wife should have sex to reproduce, and then occasionally to maintain intimacy, as he puts it. Mostly missionary position, although he'll occasionally let me get on top. I guess he saves all the fun, kinky stuff for the waitress he's fucking."

"Does he know that you know?"

"Oh, no, he'd be mortified."

"Don't the two of you ever talk about… intimate things? What do you think would happen if you told him about your fantasies?"

She laughed. "It'd probably scare the hell out of him. I mean, his idea of pornography is *Playboy* magazine." She looked at the window and her smile grew, as if she were imagining Joel's reaction. Another laugh. "It might be fun to do it just to see him react. But, look, I don't want to give the wrong impression. Joel is a really sweet guy. He's very good to me, and he'd never deliberately do anything to hurt me."

"Doesn't his infidelity hurt you?"

"Not as much as I thought it would at first. But it works out pretty well, to be honest. Now I don't feel so bad about fuckin' around on him, you know? If I ever get around to doing it."

When Sheila checks the time again, it's sixteen minutes after the hour and she has heard none of the sounds that would accompany Emily's arrival. She places her tablet on the desk, stands, and leaves the office. The floor creaks and pops beneath her feet as she crosses the hall and enters the waiting room.

The receptionist's desk stands empty, the couches and chairs are unoccupied, and the magazines on the coffee table look abandoned. The growing storm outside rages against the house like a howling mob trying to break in.

Sheila goes to the front window and looks out at the street. The day is a gray smear through which hazy shapes move at dreamlike speeds: stationary cars pressing forward when the light turns green, two people hurrying down the sidewalk beneath umbrellas, a bus sidling up to the curb like a fat worm full of parasites. But she does not see Emily's red Honda Accord parked on the street.

She goes back to her office but leaves the door open as she returns to her desk and picks up the tablet.

"I've been thinking about talking to Joel," Emily said a few weeks after they discussed the possibility of telling her husband. "I've steered the conversation to sex a couple of times. Just to… test the waters, you know?" She was more relaxed than usual on the couch, one knee up on the cushion, leaning to one side against a couple of throw pillows. She looked comfortable, at ease. "I don't know, maybe he'll be more open than I think. Or maybe he'll kick me out of the house and never let me see the kids again."

"Is that a real concern?"

"Well, I don't know how likely it is, but it's a possibility. He may just decide I'm the Whore of Babylon and pack my things for me, who knows? I wouldn't run that risk with Bobby, though. I think he'd do just about anything I asked."

"Have you made Bobby aware of your sexual interest in him?"

"Not intentionally. But he's aware of it. He had an erection in class one day last week. He sat so that I could see it. So that *only* I could see it. I thought my knees were going to give out on me. I'm not sure how I got through that class, it's a blur. But I did. At lunch, I got in my car and drove to the back of the car wash across the street from the school and… well, I had to… I just couldn't take it any longer."

"You masturbated?"

Emily nodded.

She discussed the details of her necrophilic fantasy without difficulty, but she could not use the word "masturbate" in any form and apparently experienced great shame about it. That was odd, but Sheila was more concerned about Bobby and his safety.

"Have you spoken with Bobby about this?"

"Not with words," Emily said. "Just… you know, looks."

It was at that moment that Sheila considered, once again, alerting the authorities to this situation. But Emily was clear—even though she spoke as if she would, she had no intention of becoming sexually involved with her student or doing anything that would harm anyone.

Sheila hears the thump, rattle, and creak of the front door being pushed open and someone entering the waiting room. Either Emily has arrived or Angie has returned from lunch. She stands and leaves the office as the front door thumps closed. As Sheila crosses the hall, hurried footsteps clump over the wood floor in her direction.

Emily has not stopped to hang up her coat on the tree by the door or to put her umbrella in the stand beside it. She is barreling directly toward Sheila bundled in a long black coat with all four large red buttons fastened up the front, a dark wool cap pulled so low over her red hair that it covers her ears, umbrella clutched in a fist, purse strap slung over her left shoulder.

Upon seeing her, Sheila thinks she is hurrying to get into the office because she's late. As soon as she sees Emily's wide, frenzied eyes, however, she realizes that she is not hurrying toward anything but running away from something, and Sheila's insides become cold with dread. She steps aside and Emily rushes across the hall and into the office.

Sheila follows her in and closes the door. Emily goes to the window seat and stands with her back to Sheila, staring out at the storm.

"What's wrong, Emily?" Sheila asks.

She does not move or speak. Sheila stands a few feet behind her, waiting for a response. When one does not come, she steps forward, reaches out a hand, and places it on Emily's shoulder.

Emily's body jolts with a startled cry and she spins around to face Sheila. Her frightened eyes are puffy and red from crying and the freckles on her cheeks stand out vividly against her pale skin.

"Emily, what's happened?" Sheila says.

She drops her purse and umbrella to the floor and plops down heavily on the window seat. She presses her hands flat to the seat cushion, elbows locked at her sides. Her eyes seem to stare through Sheila at something troubling in the distance.

"Would you like some water?" Sheila asks. "Can I take your coat?"

"No, I, uh… no. Thank you."

She isn't sure which question Emily was answering. "Would you like to move over to the couch?"

Emily slowly turns her head from side to side.

Sheila notices that Emily's fingers are digging into the cushion, as if holding on for a rough ride. Rolling her chair over from behind her desk, she sits down facing Emily and leans forward.

"Talk to me, Emily. I can tell something has happened, you're very upset. Tell me why."

Emily takes in a deep breath and lets it out slowly. She is about to speak when she is startled by a sound.

The front door opens. Footsteps enter, the door closes again, and there are more footsteps. A moment later, Sheila hears the familiar jangle of keys.

"It's just Angie coming back from lunch," she says, smiling reassuringly. "Now, tell me, Emily, what's wrong?"

Her wide eyes look all around the room, as if to make sure they are alone, then she focuses on Sheila. She opens her mouth to speak, then frowns as she searches for words. Shaking her head with frustration, she says, "It's just… so… disappointing."

"What's disappointing?"

Her head continues to turn back and forth, but slowly now. "Wanting something so bad for so long… thinking about it all that time… thinking about it and thinking about it… and then… when it finally happens after… after all that anticipation…"

Sheila's chest feels tight as she waits for Emily to continue. But she says no more as her head turns slowly back and forth. "What are you talking about, Emily? Wanting what for so long?"

Her eyes meet Sheila's suddenly. "Nothing ever seems to work out… the way… you plan it. Does it? One way or another it just… it goes all wrong."

"What didn't work out, Emily? What went wrong?"

Her head keeps turning as tears flood her eyes and tumble down her cheeks. She no longer seems to be aware of Sheila sitting in front of her.

"Have you been with Bobby?" Sheila says, trying to keep the dread out of her voice.

Emily's eyes slowly narrow beneath a gradual frown and she looks at Sheila with confusion. "Whuh… what?"

She is about to repeat the question when she glances

briefly down at the floor and sees something that makes her do a double-take.

Emily is wearing blue booty slippers with soggy fur cuffs and splattered with dark mud. A pale band of bare ankle flashes between the fur and the elastic cuffs of her dark blue sweat pants.

"Let's get your coat off, Emily," she says as she slowly rises to her feet. "Come on, get up and let me take your coat."

"What?" she says again.

Sheila leans forward and tugs on her arm. Emily stands and Sheila rolls the first big red button through the buttonhole.

"Tell me what happened, Emily." She goes to work on the second button, exposing a red shirt underneath.

Emily speaks swiftly and rapidly but in a soft, breathy voice. "Well, I told you, remember, that I was considering telling Joel, um, well, you know, everything. About me. Remember?"

Sheila nods as she releases the third button, but her hands stop moving when she sees that the shirt under the coat—a typical cotton T-shirt—was white. *Splashed* with red. Sodden with it.

"Emily…"

"Well, I did. And it… it… it was so… *wonderful*, Dr. Marx, it was, oh my god, it was *wonderful*."

"Emily, please, tell me. Who were you with just now? Before you came here?"

Sheila is only vaguely aware of a distant explosion of sounds in another room.

"It was so wonderful, Dr. Marx. But…"

The boom of the front door bursting open…

"What was wonderful, Emily? Where *were* you?"

…heavy feet stomping over the creaky floor…

"…it went wrong."

…raised voices, shouting…

"Tell me, Emily, whose blood is on your shirt?"

Emily is turning her head back and forth again. "It all went so wrong."

Sheila thinks of Bobby Sanchez, the beautiful boy with the face like a painting, and imagines him lying in a bed somewhere, bleeding from several stab wounds, maybe a slashed throat.

"Dr. Marx! Dr. Marx!"

Sheila isn't sure how long Angie has been shouting her name but the alarm in her voice finally startles her out of her bloody vision of Emily's student. She turns as the office door bursts open.

Uniforms everywhere, rushing into the room like wasps flying out of the small opening of a hive.

Sheila's chest clogs with terror as she reflexively steps back and stumbles, and in that moment when she is falling blindly backward, breathing is impossible.

Hands clutch at her. Arms catch her. One arm, Emily's arm, the one on the left, wraps around Sheila's chest, pinning her own arm to her side as the uniformed men reach uselessly for her from too far away, shouting something at her. Emily's other hand places something cold and sharp to Sheila's throat.

The shouting stops and the room is crushed beneath a sudden silence. Guns are drawn but not aimed. Tense faces stare at Sheila.

Her mouth is dry, but she licks her lips and says, "You don't want to do this, Emily. Not to me. I've only tried to help you."

"I… I'm sorry, Dr. Marx, but—"

"I want to keep helping you, Emily, so put, just put, please, put the knife down, all right?"

"If I do, they'll take me."

"The police? Why? Why will they take you?"

Quiet sobs propel the hot breath that hits Sheila's left ear.

"Is it Bobby? Is that it, Emily? Did something happen to Bobby?"

The sobs stop and the left arm loosens, then falls away as Emily steps around Sheila, stands before her and says, "Why the hell do you keep asking about—"

A single gunshot fills Sheila's ears with a frenzy of ringing and Emily collapses to the floor, a marionette with snipped strings.

Sheila feels her fingernails cutting into her palms before she realizes that her fists are clenched, and she backs away from Emily's heaped form until her calves bump into the window seat. Her ass hits the cushion hard, sending a punch up her spine.

There is movement among the uniforms but Sheila can hear only the bellowing ringing left in her ears by the gunshot. One of them materializes in front of her, tall and beefy, and he puts a hand on her shoulder.

"…ambulance will be coming… make sure you're okay…"

She tilts her head back and sees his round, friendly face, frowning slightly with concern as he speaks.

"Was it Bobby?" she says, realizing she's probably shouting because of the damned ringing in her ears, but she doesn't care.

He looks baffled.

"Bobby, her student. At school. Did she… hurt him?"

Understanding softens his face as he nods, then he turns his head from side to side and says something.

"…her husband Joel… some kind of sex thing…"

As if hit with a bolt of electricity, Sheila stands as her hands sweep up to cover her mouth. She stares at the officer for a moment, then drops her hands and says, "She killed her *husband*?"

He nods and says something that's a garble of sound.

Sheila says, "I'm sorry, *what*?"

He leans toward her and raises his voice: "She killed her children, too! They walked in on them!"

Her legs melt beneath her and she finds herself sitting in the window seat again, remembering her own words to Emily:

What do you think would happen if you told him about your fantasies?

I TELL YOU IT'S LOVE

JOE R. LANSDALE

ADAPTED AND ILLUSTRATED BY DANIELE SERRA

CONTAINMENT

ERIC RED

ILLUSTRATED BY NICK STAKAL

INTRODUCTION BY WES CRAVEN

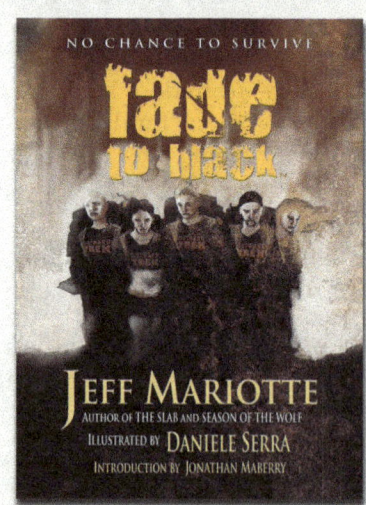

FADE TO BLACK

JEFF MARIOTTE

ILLUSTRATED BY DANIELE SERRA

FOREWORD BY JEFF MARIOTTE

INTRODUCTION BY JONATHAN MABERRY

WHY "SINISTER APPETITES" ARE *SINISTER*... AND WHY THEY AREN'T

By Michael R. Collings

When I read the theme for this issue of *Dark Discoveries*—"Sinister Appetites"—my first thought was to talk about the fact that monsters are frequently defined by their needs. In each of the classic monsters, for instance, one need becomes paramount; all others are forgotten, ignored, erased until the creature remaining *is* that need. Vampires need blood; for them, it alone ensures existence. Zombies need brains; it is as if, having no reason or will of their own, they seek the source of both in the uninfected and are compelled to destroy it—hence the recurrent cry, "Bra-a-i-i-n-n-s!" Werewolves need flesh; their flesh has turned against them, transforming them into something unspeakable, something that often they themselves cannot endure knowing about.

But the more I thought about it, the more I realized that I was concentrating on only the second portion of the theme, largely ignoring the first. True, drinking an innocent victim's blood is sinister—*evil*—as are most of the actions of most monsters (and thus they *are* monsters), but that raises what for me is a more intriguing question.

Most people, I think, automatically associate the word *sinister* with darkness, with evil. Common synonyms include *malevolent, ominous, perverse, threatening.* All of those are clearly, and etymologically, associated with evil. As far back as the word appears, *malevolent* has remained true to its roots, the Latin *male/mal,* 'evil,' coupled with *volentem,* 'wishing' or 'desiring.' Thus, 'desiring evil or ill-will toward someone.' *Perverse* literally meant 'turning the wrong way'; a modern cousin is 'pervert.'

But *sinister* is a bit different and requires some social

PHOTO COURTESY OF MICHAEL R. COLLINGS

engineering (to borrow a contemporary phrase) to turn it into *evil.*

In Roman augury, predictions for the future often depended upon directions. Those that appeared on the left side were considered unlucky, unpropitious. That is perhaps to be expected among a species that includes only about 10% left-handedness; like all minorities throughout history, those who deviated from the norm, especially by this small an amount, tend to get slighted. In a world in which most devices, from coffee mugs with handles to complex machinery ancient and modern, are designed by and for the right-handed, to be the odd man out, so to speak, runs the risk of stigmatization and marginalization. Or, in this case, of being considered unlucky.

(As a side note, lefties in the past have often been forced to train their right hands into dominance, to ensure that they would fit more comfortably into society. My grandfather, and most of his generation, learned to write with his left hand tied to the desk. As recently as four decades ago, while I was serving a Church mission in Germany, hosts often asked how I injured my right hand as soon as they saw me eating with my left—such a thing was simply not done.)

But back to Roman times. *Sinister* made the transition from being simply denotative or descriptive to suggesting moral connotations. If a thing was associated with the left side of the body, it was also associated with being unfortunate, inauspicious. And over time, the second meaning came to overshadow the first, so that throughout much of the Dark Ages, *sinister* remained primarily negative, although not overtly connected with *evil.*

Around the fifteenth century, however, the word

underwent a subtle but crucial shift.

One of my language professors explained what happened like this: Imagine, he said, that you are a lone knight knight-erranting through the forest and you come upon another knight, a stranger, fully-armed (as you are) and possibly belligerent. How do you best communicate your intentions since, as humankind has long since discovered, one may say one thing and mean another?

Since most weapons were designed for right-handed proficiency, the simplest expedient would be to raise your right hand, to show that it is empty and that you have no hostile intentions toward the stranger—a greeting, incidentally, that rapidly became a cliché in Westerns.

The stranger sees that you are unarmed, in your stronger hand, at least, and responds with a similar open-handed gesture.

You come closer, and suddenly you recognize the face of the man who, years before, killed your brother in battle. You thirst for revenge, but he is taller, stronger. In a fair fight, you would not stand a chance. He does not recognize you, however, and now holds his right hand out, again empty. You grasp it and shake it….

And at the same moment, with your left hand, until now possibly hidden beneath a cloak, you slide a dagger between his ribs, thus paying once for all.

The act is literally *sinestral*, 'having to do with the left hand' and 'inauspicious or unlucky.' But more than that, it breaks all of the laws of then-civilized behavior. It ceases to suggest negative connotations and becomes actively associated with viciousness, with villainy, with outright *evil*.

From the mid-1400s on, textual references to *sinister* and its associated forms move farther and farther from the morally neutral 'of or pertaining to the left side' and become increasingly pejorative. That trend parallels—whether coincidentally or not—the decreasing influence of Latin on written and spoken English, until within several centuries the original, descriptive definition is all but lost, and what remains is a word fraught with darkness. With evil.

Now the word almost immediately conjures stereotypical imagery. The villain of melodramas cackling and twirling his stage moustache. The mad scientist arching an eyebrow as he pulls the oversized master-switch that will end the world. The murderer—human or non—skulking in the nighttime. The crooked shadow ascending the stairs.

And only a few pedants, most of us left-handed, remember that once, long ago and far away, *sinister* had an entirely different meaning.

***

To be fair, I should also note what happened over time to *sinister*'s companion, the Latin word for right-handedness: *dexter*. Unlike its unfortunate counterpart, right-handedness represented the norm. It was the ideal state. Thus, its modern descendants have avoided most hints of sigma. In fact, *dexterity* is a state much to be desired. *Deftness, adroitness, skill, agility*—all positives, all reinforcing the idea that right-handedness is good, noble, wholesome.

The only common use of *dexter* that carries a negative connotation is a bit of twentieth-century slang. *Poindexter* stems initially from a character in a 1950s television cartoon series, *Felix the Cat*—the stereotypical scientist nephew of the primary antagonist. Poindexter wears the requisite lab coat and thick-lensed glasses, and, as if those were not enough to identify him, he consistently wears an academic mortarboard. The name crossed into popular culture with 'Arnold Poindexter' in the 1984 film, *Revenge of the Nerds*. From that point, the name became essentially a common noun: a *poindexter*, a highly intelligent, overly intellectualized but socially inept person, almost always used comically, satirically, or mockingly.

The joke, of course, is that such a person is considered a *poindexter* precisely because he (rarely she) is highly accomplished, deft, adroit, skilled—all of the things that make *dexter* positive. In this case, however, those accomplishments are exaggerated until they become the entirety of the person; there is nothing left *except* intellectuality. Now simply using the word *dexter* can communicate most of the negativity implicit in the longer form.

Horror, Science Fiction, Fantasy

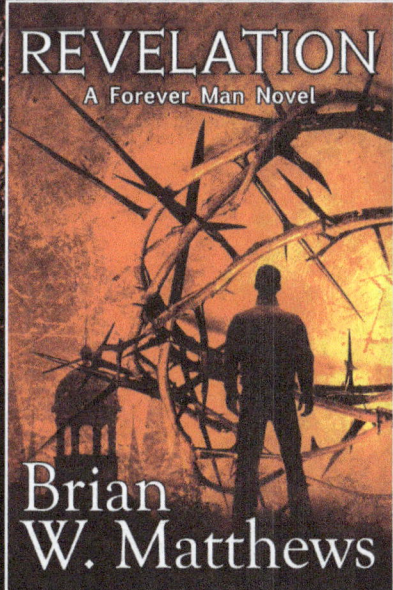

COMING FEBRUARY 2015

JANUARY 2015

COMING APRIL 2015

DECEMBER 2014

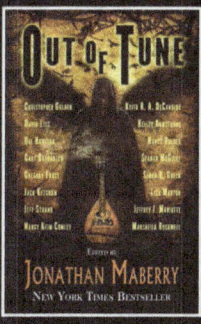

NOVEMBER 2014

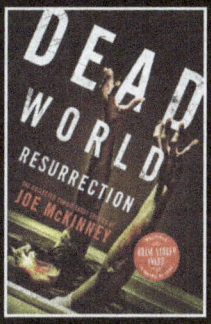

NOVEMBER 2014

NOVEMBER 2014

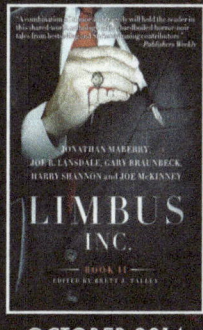

OCTOBER 2014

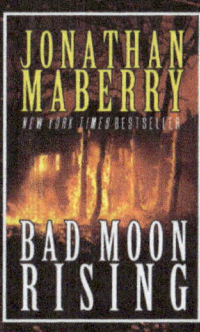

SEPTEMBER 2014

SEPTEMBER 2014

DOUBLE DOWN V
AUGUST 2014

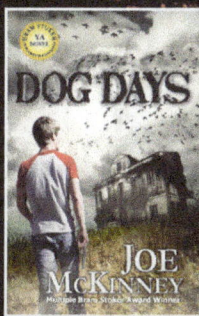

AUGUST 2014

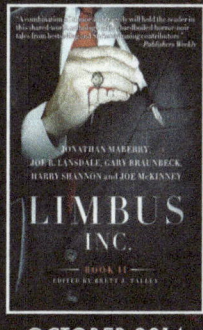

Special Edition
JULY 2014

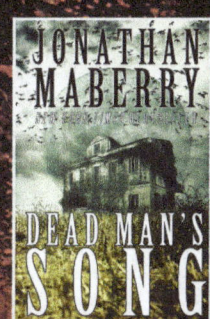

JULY 2014

DOUBLE DOWN IV
APRIL 2014

JOURNALSTONE
YOUR LINK TO ARTISTIC TALENT

WWW.JOURNALSTONE.COM

MAY 2014

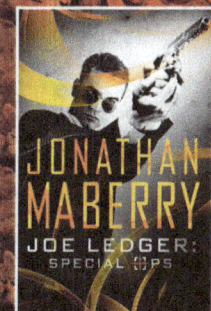

APRIL 2014

EPISODE FOUR: HEARTS ON FIRE

Original Story by Patrick Freivald
Adaptation by Patrick Freivald and Joe McKinney
Art and Lettering by B. Mack

NO! TED, NO!

WOK

THUD

DO IT NOW!

WHOOSH

BRING YOUR CAMERA OVER HERE. I KNOW THIS ONE.

THIS GUY IS ONE OF JANE'S MUTTS.

WHAT'S A MAKO KING DOING WITH THE SIX DEVILS? THESE GUYS DON'T RUN TOGETHER.

STAY WITH ME, TED YOU CAN DO THIS YOU CAN...

I DON'T KNOW. BUT I KNOW HE PLANNED THE ORIGINAL ATTACK. HE SHOULDN'T BE HERE.

OH, TED, NO. NO, PLEASE, NO.

WHACK

SQUELCH

KEVIN, DON'T!

NOT ANYMORE.

HE...HE'S MY BROTHER.

ratatat

AS JANE PLAYED THE CITY'S TWO BIGGEST GANGS AGAINST EACH OTHER, SHE HAD TO HAVE SOMETHING TO TAKE THEIR PLACE. WHAT WAS IT? AND HOW MANY MORE PEOPLE WOULD HAVE TO DIE BEFORE SHE'D STOP?

I DON'T LIKE THIS, BOSS.

YOU DON'T HAVE TO DO THIS ALONE. WE'RE A TEAM, REMEMBER?

I SAID I GOT IT.

WHERE'D YOU GO, BABY?

MANDARIN BUFFET

HEY BABY, ¿QUE QUIERES? YOU SEE ANYTHING YOU WANT?

NO, BUT THANKS. WE JUST WANT SOME DINNER

TRUST ME, YOU DON'T WANT TO EAT HERE.

AIMEE, THAT'S ENOUGH. THE BOSS IS WAITING FOR THESE TWO.

YOU COME BACK IF YOU WANT SOMETHING MORE THAN DINNER, OKAY? WE CAN EVEN LET YOUR GIRLFRIEND PLAY, IF SHE WANTS.

YEAH. YOU KNOW, I JUST MIGHT TAKE YOU UP ON THAT.

I HOPE SO.

YOU'RE WASTING YOUR TIME. WE DON'T WORK WITH PIGS.

IT'S NOT YOUR DECISION TO MAKE. JANE'S MADE IT FOR YOU. SHE'S USING US TO KILL YOU.

WE STILL DON'T WORK WITH PIGS

AGAIN.

WHAT DO YOU WANT TO KNOW?

WHERE IS SHE?

JANE'S NOT IN THE PICTURE, I TOLD YOU. YOU'LL NEVER TRACE THIS BACK TO HER. SHE'S SET THE PAPER TRAILS TO GO RIGHT BACK TO THE SIX DEVILS AND THE MAKOS. THAT'S ALL YOU'LL FIND.

THE MEETING WAS SUPPOSED TO START AT EIGHT...

...BUT BY MIDNIGHT SHE STILL HADN'T SHOWN.

WE HAD TO CHANGE TACTICS.

click

BAM

cough

P-TAFF

NO! LET HIM GO.

YOU'RE CRAZY. THAT BASTARD'S MINE!

I SAID NO. WE NEED HIM TO RUN.

YOU GOT HIM?

YEP. HEADED WEST, JUST LIKE MIKE SAID HE WOULD.

DID THEY FOLLOW YOU?

NO WAY. I WAS CAREFUL.

MY GOD.

FOR SOME, YES.

BOSS, I SWEAR, I...

IT'S OKAY.

wrrrroooooooooo

BOSS...

NO WORRIES, OLD FRIEND.

squelch

THIS IS ALL WRONG...

YEAH, THAT'S EXACTLY WHAT I WAS THINKING. TOO EASY...

HEY GUYS...

RUN!

beep beep

BOOOOM

YOU KNEW IT WAS A TRAP?

NO.

YOU KNEW TO LOOK FOR THE BOMB.

BECAUSE I KNOW JANE.

SHE'S ON THE MOVE.

SHE'S GOING TO THE WATERFRON'

HOW DO YOU KNOW?

I TOLD YOU. I KNOW JANE. SHE'LL WANT TO GET OUT TO INTERNATIONA' WATERS, WHERE WE CAN'T TOUCH HER.

A WORD WITH YOU.

YEAH.

IF YOU KNOW SOMETHING...

I DON'T. JUST A HUNCH.

GUYS, WE GOT HER!

MIKE, SHE KILLED TED.

I KNOW, ALICE. I KNOW IT.

ANGELIS IMPERATORI

YOUR GIRLFRIEND REALLY KNOWS HOW TO DO IT UP RIGHT.

SHE'S NOT MY GIRL. NOT ANYMORE.

COVER! WE'RE GOING EXPLOSIVE!

BOOOOM

SO MUCH FOR STEALTH MODE.

BAM

HOW'S THAT FOR STEALTH MODE?

THIS IS A BUST. SHE'S NOT HERE.

SHE'S HERE.

I KNOW IT.

whack

BAM

POW

I GUESS YOUR BROTHER COULDN'T MAKE IT, HUH?

BAM

whoosh

POW

CRACK

SNAP

WHAM

UHHHH!

RUN.

IT'S TOO LATE. LET HER DO IT.

RUN!

SO, THAT'S IT? SHE GOT AWAY?

YUP. WE WON'T SEE HER AGAIN AROUND HERE.

YOU'RE SURE OF THAT?

IT WAS A GOOD BUST, BOSS. WE CRUSHED HER ORGANIZATION. SHUT DOWN THE MAKOS AND THE SIX DEVILS TOO.

NOTHING ELSE YOU WANT TO TELL ME?

NOPE.

BYE, BABY.

END.

Inner Demons: Desire and Conflict in Horror

K. H. Vaughan

"I dunno. Do you always know why you do things, Leo?"
"Sure I do."
—From *Miller's Crossing* (1990), written and directed by Joel and Ethan Coen.

When introspective gangster Tom Reagan poses this question to crime boss Leo O'Bannion in *Miller's Crossing* (1990), Leo is confused. As far as he's concerned, his motivations are transparent. Earlier in the film, Leo states that he doesn't like to think. He does what he wants, or what he feels is right, without worrying much about the odds or the angles. The idea of hidden motives is fundamentally alien to him. In contrast, Tom questions the motivations of everyone. "Nobody knows anybody. Not that well," he says on more than one occasion, and he includes himself in that thinking.

The idea that we do not understand our own motivations, or that our motives may be in conflict with one another, is a common one in horror. Carrie's confusion about her psychic powers and growing sexuality (Carrie, 1976), Father Karras' lack of faith and reluctance to participate in the exorcism of Regan (The Exorcist, 1973) and Henry's strange ambivalence about fatherhood in Eraserhead (1977) are critical to these films. There are many stories in which the characters' internal ducks are all in a row and their motives are a pure straight line, but they don't really have the same emotional resonance for me. In addition to adding character depth and dramatic tension, the presence of unclear or conflicting motives allows even the smartest and capable characters to make bad decisions. It can be fun to yell at the

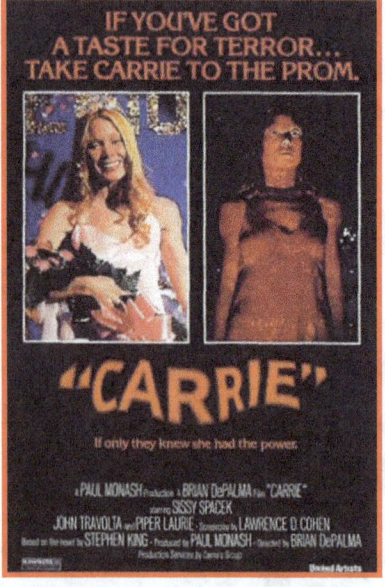

idiots running to the basement or attic instead of the front door once in a while, but it isn't scary, a point perfectly made by a recent GEICO commercial in which kids flee to the barn filled with chainsaws instead of escaping in the running car. ("If you're in a horror movie you make poor decisions. It's what you do.") Personally, nothing pulls me out of a story faster than characters acting stupid just so the plot can continue. Hey, everyone makes bad choices, and I'm not saying I'll keep my wits about me in the midst of the zombie apocalypse, but if the writers can't provide a subtext or justification for doing stupid things, I start rooting for the monsters. On the other hand, if the bad decisions of the characters reflects internal conflict, I can get right on board.

You cannot talk about hidden motivation in art and literature without talking about the father of psychoanalysis, Sigmund Freud. More than any writer, Freud popularized the idea that we cannot truly know ourselves. Freud's ideas were unscientific and in many cases just plain wrong, but his influence on Western civilization is profound. People use Freudian ideas and language in everyday life without any awareness of their origins. Ever call someone anal retentive, accuse someone of being in denial, or of just being an asshole? Yeah, you've been talking Freud. Because his ideas have been so thoroughly absorbed and propagated, it doesn't even matter that he was so often incorrect. We know the language and the tropes, and recognize them when they appear in literature and film.

Freud championed the idea that there is an unconscious mind that lies outside of our awareness. Deep within the unconscious, hidden from us, lies the Id ("It"). The Id is the primitive core of the mind, filled with nothing but appetites and rage: drives so powerful and perverse, that we would go insane if we had real knowledge of what lies beneath the surface. Life, in Freud's view, is about internal conflict. The conscious part of the mind (the Ego) is constantly driven by the instincts of the Id, and must bring to bear a range of defense mechanisms in order to keep these impulses out of awareness and out of reality. No matter how bizarre, alien, and horrific an idea is, if you can imagine it, your Id knows things far, far stranger and more dangerous. It is infinitely perverse. Our sometimes-ally in this fight is the Superego, which is the part of the mind that contains our sense of morality. You've seen this represented in cartoons as the angel and devil on a character's shoulders, each trying to persuade, cajole, or threaten the individual to behave a certain way. We live in a constant state of anxiety that we will give into the desires of the Id, which will bring madness and destruction.

I'm not going to spend much time on academic arguments about the best or right or even the possibility of psychodynamic interpretation of art and literature. There's a lot of it out there, none of it can be proven, and an awful lot of it is nonsense. There is a great deal of literary and film criticism that is explicitly Freudian, that generally tries to strip away the superficial surface content of the text and reveal the covert or latent meaning, which is almost always sexual in nature. Simply, every book or film is a place where we process, indulge, or confront our inner psychological demons. If you don't believe that Freudian ideas permeate a lot of horror material, you need look no further than Norman Bates' Oedipal Complex in *Psycho* (1960), the sexualy charge set and creature designs of Alien (1979) or the enormous phallic power drill on the poster for *The Slumber Party Massacre* (1982) for examples. Much horror can been seen as narrative around losing control of

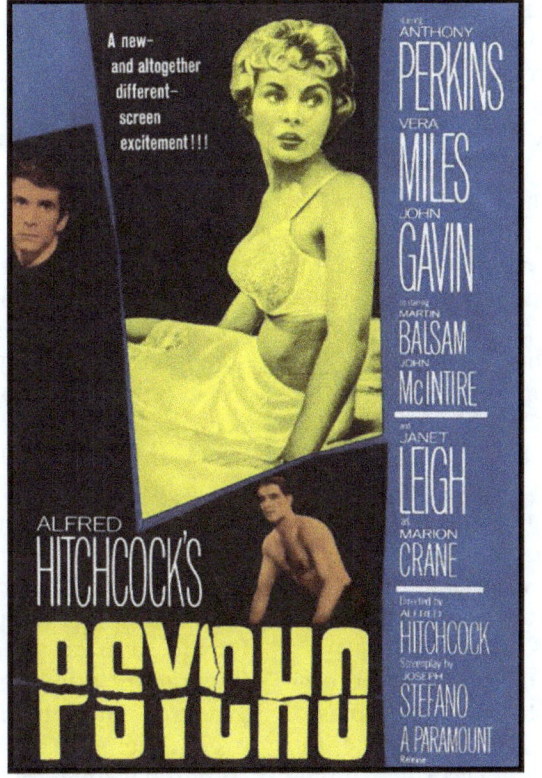

our impulses in one way or another, either directly or in displaced symbolic form. Tony, the lead character in the low budget drive-in classic *I was Teenage Werewolf* (1957) transforms into a beast when he becomes sexually aroused and then murders the object of his desires in an atavistic frenzy. Many of the classic slasher films of the 1980s can be read as morality plays in which teen rebelliousness and sexual behavior is met with supernatural punishment. The kids who indulge in their desires are killed, while the

virginal final girl survives (*Men, Women, and Chainsaws: Gender in the Modern Horror Film* by Clover is a good read on this subject). Freud himself was mildly interested in horror literature and lays our appetite for horror and the uncanny in anxieties that most people have. He would probably have described most modern horror as regressive, and indulging in it as an unhealthy pastime, unless that interest were explored in depth on the couch. (And remember, he was often wrong, but that is another column.)

When confronted with our deepest, darkest desires, the Ego must protect itself. This is done by employing a series of defense mechanisms that help reduce the anxiety we feel when the Id wants us to do something horrible. To be fair, the Id constantly wants us to do something horrible, but there are times when it is harder to resist it. When we are fatigued, sick, distracted, stressed, drunk, or situations remind us a little too much of our childhood complexes, the Ego has to get creative. Most of this happens outside of our awareness. It is a constant battle between parts of the mind that we only get glimpses of.

Not all defense mechanisms are created equal, either. For example, you could express your rage against your father with a complex revenge scheme that would make Danny Ocean proud, or you could just take a dump in his shoes. As our first line defenses fail, we rely on increasingly primitive strategies that reflect more immature or childish ways of dealing with conflict and anxiety. They are the last ditch defense of an ego under stress and trying not to break down, as ugly and unfocused as the fight for the football at the bottom of a scrum after a fumble. What follows is a discussion of some of the more common defense mechanisms that are relevant to horror and dark fantasy. The ones grouped at the beginning of the list are more primitive and those at the end more mature.

Denial is a distortion of reality so severe that people do not acknowledge or accept the truth that is right in front of them. This includes alcoholics who claim that they are in control of their drinking or the parents in a horror movie who insist that their bad-seed demon child is innocent despite the all the evidence. Horror narratives generally require a lot of denial, as otherwise people would not stay in the increasingly dangerous situations that are the core of the plot. Monsters do not exist and there is a rational explanation for everything and it will all work out in the end, right? It is also a common feature of ghost stories, as many ghosts are spirits who simply do not realize that they are dead. Dr. Malcolm Crowe, the child psychologist in *The Sixth Sense* (1999) and Grace Stewart in *The Others* (2001) are two examples of this type of spirit.

Regression occurs when a person reverts to behavior or

thought patterns typical of earlier stages of development. We become more child-like in response to anxiety. Like all defense mechanisms, everybody does it to some degree some of the time. You have a miserable day, and instead of cooking dinner you want someone else to make you your favorite comfort food and clean up after you. Just like mom or dad did when you were a child. I was never a fan of *The Blair Witch Project* (1999) and there's a moment of absolute stupidity in the film that never made sense to me. Mike reveals

that he has kicked their only map into the lake, essentially sealing their fate. It isn't well-explained in the film. Is he simply frustrated, or is the witch affecting his mind? I had no idea. Looking back and seeing this an example of regression allows the moment to make more sense. Mike has taken out his fear and frustration out on the map, like a child who throws a toy that won't do what he wants. It is also a passive-aggressive attack on Josh and Heather. In support of this interpretation is the fact that Mike is last seen standing in the corner like a punished child. Many monsters can be seen as living in regressed states. Zombies and werewolves are essentially the Id unleashed: humans with all reason stripped away, leaving nothing but violence and bestial appetites.

Acting Out refers to just that: acting out a conflict in symbolic form rather than verbalizing it. Because the defense mechanism does not directly address the underlying conflict, the behavior will tend to repeat compulsively. Here again, many ghost stories are based on the idea that ghosts have unfinished business, and are compelled to haunt based on some underlying regret that they cannot communicate directly. Once their concern is heard, they are often able to cross over or vanish. Samara in *The Ring* (2002) communicates her trauma symbolically again and again: she wishes to be heard, but cannot speak directly. Jason (and his mother) in the *Friday the Thirteenth* series could be taken as a symbolic representation of this defense: a hidden crime is revenged again and again by a killer who cannot speak.

In *dissociation*, different aspects of the mind become separated from each other. The most radical examples of dissociation include fugue states and Dissociative Identity Disorder (formerly Multiple Personality Disorder), which frequently appear in horror film and literature. Norman Bates in *Psycho* (1960), Teddy Daniels in *Shutter Island* (2010), Malcolm Rivers in Identity (2003), and Mort Rainey in *Secret Window* (2004) all have fractured identities, with different selves, or aspects of self, operating independently. Stevenson's Strange Case of Doctor Jekyll and Mr. Hyde (1886) is a classic literary example. Hypnosis and other markedly altered states of consciousness are also dissociative in nature and are featured prominently in

horror. *The Cabinet of Dr. Caligari* (1920), *The Hypnotic Eye* (1960), and *Cure* (1997) all feature hypnosis as a central element. In real life, some theorists have suggested that cases of demonic or spirit possession may reflect dissociative processes as opposed to supernatural activity.

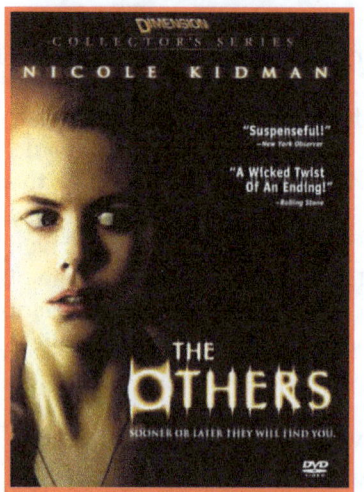

Projection occurs when an individual takes their own feelings or impulses and attributes them to someone else. Note again, that to truly describe these as defense mechanisms, the person should have limited insight into the process. Imagine you are at a party chatting up an attractive stranger and getting a little excited about it. Your boyfriend or girlfriend notices and comments on it later. You say "Oh no, I wasn't interested in them at all. They were really hitting on me pretty hard though!" If you know that you were flirting and found it a little exciting, then that isn't projection; the technical term for that sort of thing is "lying." However, if your actual experience is that you had no attraction, then projection may have occurred. The Ego has become threatened by an inappropriate desire, and has used a defense mechanism to pretend it did not occur. The ventriloquist Corky cannot express his own desires, but his dummy Fats can, in Richard Attenborough's film *Magic* (1978). Although there is a psychic or supernatural element involved, the rats of *Willard* (1971) express the titular character's impulses in ways that he cannot. In each case, the impulse does not "belong" to the person who has it; it is passed off to someone else.

Reaction Formation occurs when a person harbors some impulse that they find so threatening that they must publically express the opposite. If you have ever been to Mardi Gras, you may have seen street preachers in the midst of all the debauchery telling everyone they are going to hell unless they repent at once. Perhaps they are sincere, but Freud would point out that they have found a way to participate in the party and soak up all the nudity while denying that they have any interest in such things. Although not a horror example, Colonel Fitts in *American Beauty* (1999) presents a perfect fictional illustration: a hypermasculine individual who expresses virulent homophobic beliefs, but harbors homosexual urges. There is some interesting research in this area using subliminal imagery and a penile plesmograph, which is like a blood pressure cuff, but worn further south. Men who express the strongest and vitriolic anti-gay beliefs on surveys tend to demonstrate more arousal to subliminal homoerotic images than men who identify as heterosexual but describe themselves as being comfortable with the sexuality of gay men.

Repression is a universal defense mechanism by which dangerous thoughts, feelings, and impulses are forced out of consciousness. Freud presumed that we are all constantly repressing various unacceptable desires, and that this happens without our knowledge. We may also repress the memory of events that are too painful to cope with. Alfred Hitchcock based the film Spellbound (1945) on repressed memory of trauma. Repression sounds a lot like dissociation, and it is a dissociative process, in that some aspect of memory or experience is cut off from consciousness. The difference is one of degree. Dissociation as a primary defense mechanism involves a significant breakdown of personality as a whole, while repression allows people to function pretty well for the most part. In the *Halloween* franchise, Laurie uncovers repressed memories of her adoption by the Strodes and early relationship with Michael Myers. Freddy Kreuger's victims in *A Nightmare on Elm Street* (1984) have no memory of their abuse as children, but are otherwise fine. Their personalities are not as fragmented as the characters described in the paragraph on dissociation, above.

Rationalization is the use of argument to convince ourselves that our desires or actions are acceptable when, in our heart of hearts, we know better. You might take some office supplies home from work, but then, you are underpaid. Your boss made you work through lunch last week, and the ream of printer paper you brought home was not stealing, but a form of compensation for your extra effort. You really were owed that. Besides, everyone else steals more than you do, so you are one of the good guys. Dexter Morgan (*Dexter*, 2006 - 2013) is a master of this defense.

These are only some of the defense mechanisms Freud proposed, and subsequent research hasn't supported many of his ideas. However, even if they are not literally true, his ideas have been so thoroughly absorbed into Western culture that film and literature make use of them and audiences respond strongly to these themes even if they do not know the ultimate source. Likewise, it isn't fair to assume that the creators of film and literature are unaware of the Freudian concepts they employ. Hitchcock played with Freudian ideas frequently and consciously,

even though he did not seem to believe in the theories themselves. The viability of a Freudian interpretation of a movie doesn't mean that it reflects the unconscious conflicts and wishes of the writers and directors. They may be fully aware of the potential interpretations they have incorporated into their work, much in the way the writer and director of *Scream* (1996) were fully aware of the conventions of classic slasher films and allowed their characters to discuss them openly.

Subsequent theorists approached internal conflict in different ways, tending to downplay sexuality and the fantasy life of the Id and placing greater emphasis on actual conflicts and the need to maintain a coherent stable sense of self. Karen Horney, for example, thought that children developed coping strategies to deal with parental abuse and neglect. The child is defenseless and dependent on their parents, no matter how horrible the relationship, and has only three options when parents are abusive. They can express their rage (which risks punishment), they can try to sooth and placate their parents by being good (which risks rejection), or they can try to escape by withdrawing emotionally (which results in isolation). Everyone has the capacity to attack, to make nice, and to run away, but some people become overly invested in one style at the expense of the others. It colors their perceptions of everything, and they are ever alert to potential threats. Situations that remind them in any way of how they once felt vulnerable and hurt provoke reactions that are out of proportion and not appropriate. A character with an aggressive style will use it whether or not the fight is necessary, or winnable, and without regard to the cost, even if another strategy would produce better results. The most basic human needs for many post-Freudian theorists are not sexual, but for safety and love. In either case, there are plenty of ways for our desires to lead to darkness.

ADVERTISE IN DARK DISCOVERIES MAGAZINE

Get your product or service to thousands of horror and dark fantasy fans!

E-mail christophercpayne@journalstone.com for rates and more information

"Dark Discoveries is a high quality mag... and it keeps getting better..."
--Horror Fiction Review

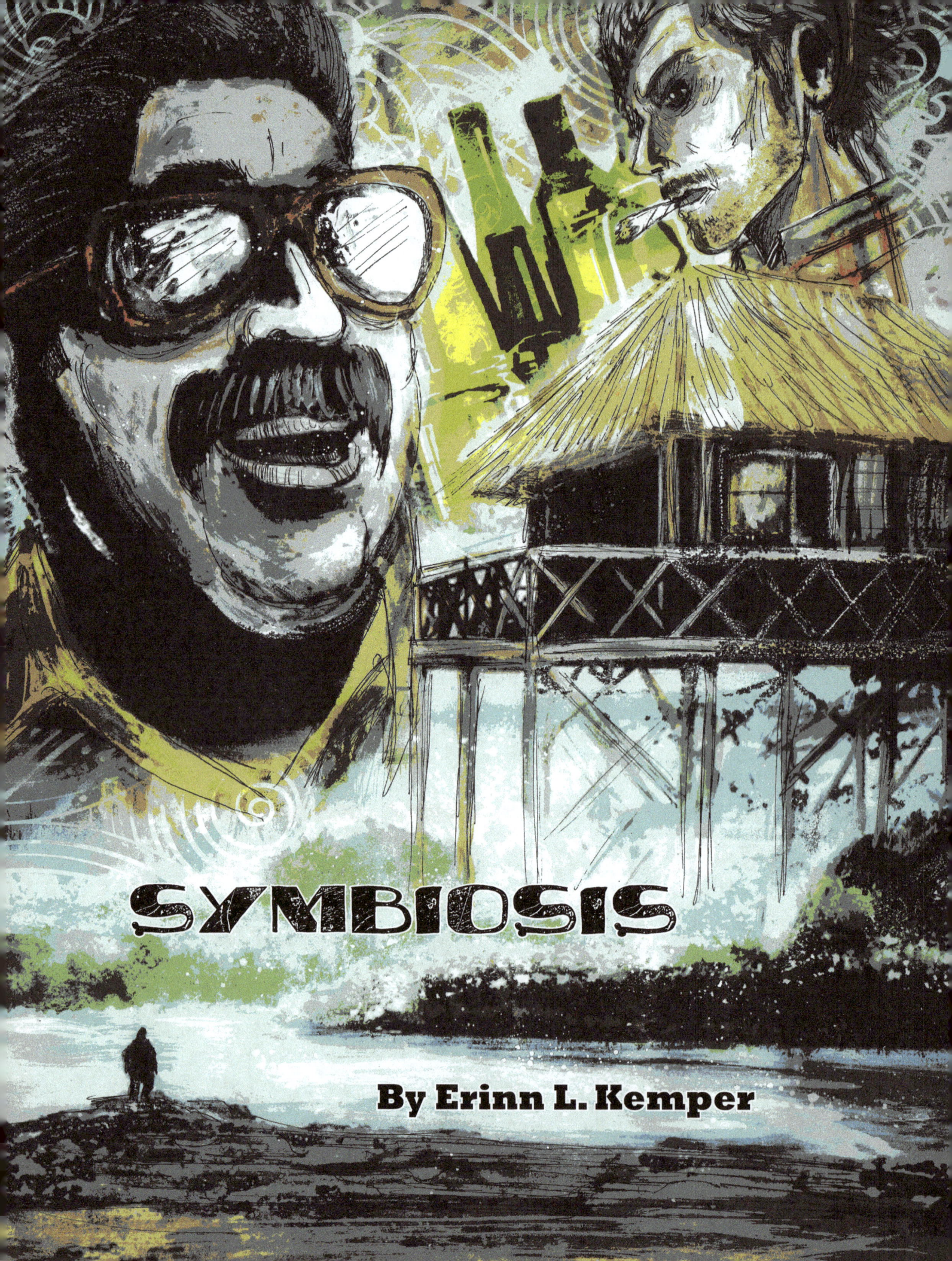

SYMBIOSIS

By Erinn L. Kemper

The laugh was the first thing that caught Les Morley's attention.

Loud and wheezing with a lot of belly to it—and this guy had one serious belly on him. Les looked over and recognized the guy right away. It was his new best friend.

Only useful piece of advice his grandma ever gave—if you're down to your last five dollars, spend it at the bar. When Les had woken up that morning and emptied his pockets he knew he had a choice. Used to be easy—head for the beach to catch lobster or to surf. Things were different now. He had child support to pay and the cops at his door if he was even a day late. So he could stand on the corner with the boys and hope some goof came along looking for diggers or cutters to pretty up their yards. That had panned out into some good grabbings in the past. Or he could go into town and hustle.

At the bar, he'd ordered a beer and sat street-side. The barefoot black kids playing kickball across the street looked up when he sat, but went right back to their game. From his shaded stool he could see the bright turquoise of the Caribbean beyond the row of trinket vendors, the taxi parade on one side, and the bus stop on the other. Most tourists in town would pass by, giving him good opportunity to suss out their attitude; loose and easy, or wary and tight.

"*Una mas*?" The girl stopped by his stool to collect his empty. Time to make his move.

"*Una* for me and one for the fat dude down the way." Les dropped two dollars on her tray. Three down, two to go.

When his beer came, running with rivulets of condensation, he raised the bottle to his new friend, then turned back to the street.

"Thanks fellah." A massive hand clubbed him on the back, sending beer out his nostrils. The stool next to his groaned.

"It's nothing." Les wiped his nose. "You look like a man with a thirst is all."

"That I do." The guy stuck out his hand, small black curls decorated the wide fingers. "Name's Gordon Trump, no relation."

"Lester Morley." Les grasped the hand, soft and gummy, in his. "Here's to living in paradise."

Gordon's bottle slid through a handlebar curtain of black bristles; he drank to their meeting with a long sucking pull.

"So what do you think?" Les asked, tipping his beer at the road and the bikini-clad *touristas*, Hispanics peddling empanadas, high-breasted black girls with their long legs and braids swinging. "A man could sure get used to this."

"Sure could. Been here only a few days, but I see myself finding it real hard to leave." Gordon dabbed his forehead with a napkin.

"I came to Costa Rica twenty-eight years ago. Sat down on this very stool and said to myself, here's where I want to die." Les gave the polished wood counter an affectionate rub. "Haven't gone anywhere since, 'cept the bathroom."

Gordon laughed appreciatively.

"Hey Walter," Les called to the back where the proprietor stood watch. "Two more cold ones and some of that chicken. Put it on my tab."

He turned back to his new friend. Ball was in Walter's court now. He could hold to his policy on Les running a tab, or he could bring the damn chicken.

The kickball match across the way was breaking up. Big Rasta's kid, Donald, noted Les and the new arrival, and dragged his snot-nosed brother over.

"All right, Donnie," Les shook the boy's hand. "How's your Pappa?"

"He's good, sir. At home now with Mamma. She's not so good today." Donald stood straight with his hands behind his back, the little one held onto the bottom of big brother's shorts.

"Here, little man, go get yourselves a soda." Les offered up his last two dollars. Donald grabbed and ran before Les could change his mind.

"I'm like an uncle to these kids." Les shook his head in sorrow. "Things are hard down here for these people. That family—I met Big Rasta first day I got here. Man was happy, had money in his pockets and a hotel full of good people. He let me stay free, gave me a room and a hot shower. That's how people are here. When you have, you share."

The chicken and beers arrived, they dug in, and Gordon ordered another round.

"This sure is a great place. Dollar beers, beautiful women." Gordon licked bits of crumb and grease from his fingers. "You know, I've been wondering about getting myself a little piece of this, having a getaway. I've been lots of places, but this one has them all beat."

Les leaned back in his stool with his hands in the air. "You won't find anyone who knows more about the place, Gordo. I know all the land available, even spots that aren't on the market. I could take you around if you like. Like the girls always say about Lester Morley. Les is More."

They toasted to business, and Les drained his beer as another plate of chicken landed.

***

The old pickup rattled down the road, the beach on one side, waves breaking against the lightly toasted sand, shacks and restaurants lining the other. Les waved at two housekeeping gals working their beat of beach house rentals. They glanced his way, bundles of linens tottering on their heads like massive turbans. He wiped muck off the dash of the truck, then leaned back, arm slung out the window.

Danny hadn't liked lending his truck out when Les first started working for Gordon. Every time Les showed up they had to negotiate. Danny wanted money, wanted a full tank, wanted weed. When Les showed with a wad of bills—a few lighter for the Lester Morley beer and bud fund—Danny handed over the keys and registration quick enough.

Les played it cool with his new buddy, but Gordon liked dipping into his wallet so Les could keep things happening. From the first night, when Les told Gordon he'd left his wallet at home and couldn't cover their beer and chicken, Gordon had kept his wallet fat and flowing.

It was the best hustle of Les's life.

Coming to a gravel-cracking stop at the river bank, Les

surveyed the site. A few nods and waves in his direction told him the big man was in. The boys were putting on a good show, no shovel leaning, no scowls or dirty looks. Abel spat on the ground as Les walked the plank across the river toward him, and turned his back to hide the sneer that twisted his sun-creased face. That boy'd recover quick enough when the wad came his way, Les figured. It was payday. Money in your pocket always made the sun shine brighter.

It was a huff up to the main house. Gordon had claimed a real out-of-the-way spot. There was beach-front and town-side to look at, but Gordon had been particular about location. He wanted something remote, up where the air was cooler and hosted fewer bugs. He wanted a big piece with no neighbors in sight. It took some doing, but Les got a local Auntie to carve a chunk off her Mamma's farm with an old house on it, and sell it at the price that Les suggested. A little on the side covered Les's *chorizo*.

Twenty-eight hectares of pristine jungle surrounded the *Casa*—banana trees, monstrous tangle-limbed hardwoods, streams slicing channels on all sides. The house rose from stilts off the side of the mountain. Two stories of dark wood and a *palapa* grass roof. Les tried to persuade Gordon that he needed something less rustic, but the big man liked the local jungle style with the open kitchen on the main floor balcony, the hammocks swaying in the breeze, the shuttered windows painted bright pink and green.

So there'd be no new house, but the rest was good. Les suggested a bridge over the river and a massive locking gate, and Gordon said sure. Then Les said he needed a water tower; Gordon agreed. The well, *ranchero*-style gazebo, guest *cabina*, swimming pool and covered parking area all were okay'd and the money paid. Materials and tools were stacked in the shipping container already on site, and Hugo, a local one-eyed drunk, got paid to pass out in a hammock by the container and make sure nothing walked. At least until Les said it could.

"Beautiful day, Lester, my boy," Gordon said from behind him on the balcony.

"Shit, man, didn't see you there."

For a big guy, Gordon had a way of sneaking up, Les thought. Even in flip flops on those creaky old boards he managed to catch Les by surprise time and again. You could learn a lot from waiting on the other side of a door. But no matter how hard he tried, he could never get the drop on the boss-man.

"Payday today. Boys are all looking forward to a nice weekend off."

Gordon handed down a wad of cash he pulled from a pocket in the tie-dyed muumuu he wore around the house. It gave his expanding belly room to breathe, he said.

"I trust you can handle divvying this out."

Les clicked his heels and saluted. "Aye, aye, Capitan." Before heading down the hill, he added, "Haven't seen Elias today. You want I should keep his part?"

Gordon's head rocked in a slow nod as he surveyed the workers. "I'm sure you can see it to the right hands."

***

The air hung thick and wet over the jungle. Most nights the sun slammed down and things started to cool. Not tonight. The steady insect buzz and the bellowed rasp of a frog were the only things that cut through the smothering heat.

In his hammock, Les took puffs from the joint he pinched between thumb and index finger and watched geckos rummage through the grass roof. Sweat tickled down his sides and the worn string of the hammock dug fishnet grooves into his bare back. He reached up to the post and tapped the ember from the tip of the pea-sized roach before setting it in a tin to cool. A weekend of beer and babes splayed out before him, and he deserved it.

On the way home he'd been distracted by a troop of Nordic beauties, their white-blonde hair streaming, their flesh blasted brown and red by the sun. They pedalled by in bikinis, backs straight, breasts jiggling. That was the moment Elias's wife had approached, getting between him and the store that sold Les's beer.

"*Tienne la plata para Elias.*" It wasn't really a question.

"Sure, sure, Rosa. I have his money right here." Les dug in his pocket, surfacing with the remainder of the roll that Gordon had given. "But since he missed a couple days, it's not a lot. *No mucho, senora*. Okay. *Que pasa? Infirmo?*" He peeled off a few bills and handed them over.

Her nod confirmed that Elias was sick, the sway of her backside a sweet sight as she waded off through the dripping heat. Another worker gone on a bender, or just plain tired of getting up in the morning, Les told himself.

As if that weren't enough, when he'd reached home his ex was waiting, baby suctioned to her breast. Could she smell the money coming? Tamara only showed up at his house on payday. Any other day, if he wanted to see his baby, he had to go begging around her place or the restaurant where she worked.

"The money's late, Lester." She started in. "You got a week to pay it before I call the cops."

"No need for that, now." She knew he had an expired visa and trouble waiting for him back in the States, and she used it against him every time. Les leaned in to the baby, giving her a kiss on the cheek. "Hey, sweetness. You having a good dinner there?" The baby never looked at him wrong, with eyes full of accusation. Not yet, anyways.

Tamara pointed with her chin at the chilled case of beer he'd set by his feet. "I see you have enough to drink on, but your baby needs formula. I can't be feeding her like this at the restaurant."

He'd peeled off another few bills for formula and diapers. The rest of the child support he'd have to get from the boss-man as an advance. That left him with enough for a nice bag of the sticky green and a few nights out on the town.

Silence dropped on the night, the insects still and alert. Les looked out into the darkness. Some creature stalked the jungle and every animal held its breath. Les

leaned his head back, closed his eyes, and listened for a scuff or crack of something creeping through the dark. Maybe a cat padding through the underbrush, or an owl perched overhead, moon-reflecting eyes scanning for a kill. He couldn't hear anything, but he could feel something watching, waiting. He held his breath, certain that whatever lurked out there would use the moment he exhaled to make its approach.

The electric hum and rattle of the jungle resumed, like a fridge kicking in. Danger had passed by. Fireflies drifted, embers igniting the dark with their cool light, and the loud brap of a toad interjected once more.

Les scratched at a lump on his shoulder. It was botfly for sure—hibernating under his skin, waiting to hatch. The tick of its quickening was only noticeable when he was still, like a worry he couldn't pinpoint. But his worries were real and easy to name.

Workers were bailing every week. The pay was good,

probably too good. Make enough for a few weeks, and then why work? When the rice is gone and the baby needs some medicine, then it was time to go back to the grind. There was always someone with an empty bag of rice. This was true, but there was not always someone willing to jump on the Les Morley gravy train. It wasn't enough that he always saw the guys paid. Just because he was a *gringo* didn't mean they shouldn't give him his due for getting them a job. It was only a few bucks here and there, after all. He'd been living here forever, but they still treated him like an outsider, handing over his *chorizo* with a curse and a scowl.

Gotta work the angles, Les thought. He took a cleansing swig of beer. There were still materials to buy. Most of the sawmills weren't calling back, but there would be someone with wood to sell who'd do business. Always was. The night chirped and whirred around him, full of possibility.

***

Palms cut criss-cross shadows on the ground like scissor blades. Les watched the workers straggle off for the day. Elias was back, which was good because they'd lost another guy to a bender. He was back, but he didn't look good. His left arm hung at his side, and his rubber boots dragged when he walked. The boys had put him on water duty, filling the cement mixer by hose. A pat on the back from Abel sent limbs wobbling. No, he did not look good at all, Les thought.

"Hey, Abel." Les beckoned.

Shifting his gaze to the side, Abel spat and headed toward him. Les knew the boys respected this old-timer. At fifty, Abel still worked the shovel better than anyone. When the days got long he'd let some cocky youngster challenge him, and they'd dig, the youngster dipping and flinging at lightning speed and getting nowhere fast. Abel plowed on steady—the trench opening below his feet with ease. The boys called Abel *patron*, even though it was Les got them the job.

"*Que pasa, Gringo*?" Abel spat again and looked over Les's shoulder.

"You seen Hugo, man?" Les decided to let the *gringo* thing slide. "He wasn't here this morning when I reached. You see him in town last night?"

Abel shook his head.

"That's the third guy this week. What's the deal? Can't keep your men working?"

Abel grunted and looked back at the crew. "Don't think it's the work they mind."

"Well, how about you get them back here, at least Chicho and Rigo, or find some new blood to finish up the gig. There's something at the end for you, old man, if you do me proud."

"I've been by looking for Chicho, and Rigo. Both their women say they're gone. Didn't come home Friday. Don't think they're coming back, *Gringo*."

On the drive home, windows down to let in the breeze and the swirling bits of road that lodged in his eyes and teeth, Les considered his angles. He couldn't lose any more workers. He'd have to start bringing them beer every couple of days, on the boss-man's dime. Gordon would appreciate that. He was a man who enjoyed the simple pleasures. Les could find another guard to keep an eye. The other option was to take advantage of the reprieve. Share information with the boys on the other side of the hill. Bring his buddy Carlos in for a few days' work so Carlos could get the lay of the land, then pick a night to do the deed. Les'd get a cut for the taking and then another cut for the replacing. Gordon would understand these things happen in the jungle. It was the frontier after all. Cowboys and Indians.

***

And that's how Les found himself hunkered in the rain in the middle of the night, keeping watch on the house. Carlos had set it up, spent a few days running buckets of cement and checking things out. When the time came to make a move, Les found Carlos collapsed in his bed, blinking in the darkened interior of his wooden shack. No amount of cajoling could motivate him. His slurred refusal muffled by his swollen slug of a tongue.

Maybe the boys were right, Les thought. Maybe the water was the problem. Couldn't hurt to have it tested—the well, the river—who knew what could be living there, corrupting the supply.

The rain continued to fall—on the jungle, the roofs, the ground—its thundering descent obliterating all other sound. Les strained to see through the wall of water. He spotted the lithe shadows of his crew as they slipped into the storage container. One figure remained outside the door, watching Les, who in turn watched both the container and the house. If Les saw movement in the house, a wave would alert the guy at the container and the whole crew would dissolve into the jungle.

He had to concentrate, but his mind kept returning to what he'd seen as they slipped in through the trees at the back of the house. A light had shone from beneath the house. It couldn't have been the moon reflecting from the groundwater. The moon wasn't out tonight. Maybe a loose floorboard in the house was throwing light down? But what it had really looked like was a faint glow tunnelling up from deep in the earth.

A wave and a flick of flashlight from the lookout at the storage container signaled it was time to move. The boys each took a different route back to their meeting place, scattering to be swallowed by the surrounding foliage. Les's route took him back behind the house. One last look for the light he'd seen earlier. There it was all right. But not the luminous pool he'd seen before. A sparse halo of light shone around a bloated shadow, crouched in wait between the wooden stilts of the house.

***

Gordon took it very well—didn't even bother calling the police. Some of the tools would need to be replaced right away, and he handed over the funds. Les put on a show of interrogating the boys, asking if they knew anything, had seen anything. Once the big boss was satisfied they'd been hit by outsiders—forces beyond their control—he'd been happy to discuss new projects.

They sat in the shade at the bar where they'd first met. Plate after plate of chicken was set in front of them, along with bottle after bottle of beer.

"Here's the deal, *Patron*." Les sat back on his stool and crossed his arms. "People are worried that they might get sick if they come up the hill for work. There's crazy things in the jungle. We got flies that make babies under your skin, mosquitos carry all kinds'a plague, bacteria that eats your flesh, caterpillars with stingers'll paralyze half your body. And that's on top of the usual scorpions, spiders and snakes. Silvia, that little honey that was cleaning your house, she's been sick. I hear she's better now, but she won't come back up the hill. People here, they can be superstitious. And really, everyone is thinking the problem is one thing, when likely it's really another. There's lots of other possibilities."

Gordon nodded through Les's whole speech, the folds of fat on his neck bunching and spreading. "I hear you, Lester-boy. But short of napalm and baptism for the whole bloody jungle, how can we put these people at ease?"

Les puckered his lips and scratched his shoulder. "Water's the most likely culprit, I figure."

And so getting the water tested and installing filtration systems moved to highest priority, and they got back to the more serious business of getting good and drunk.

***

The sun shone high and white, blazing through the bustling canopy. Toucans plunged from limb to limb. An iguana the size of a surfboard squatted on a bare branch, fanning its neck flap out as it basked.

Les moved about the lot, following the drift of a plate-sized blue butterfly. He took inventory, but was also focused on face time with the boys as they packed up for the day. Things were slowing down. He needed to get in good with as many of the laborers as possible so they'd be willing next time Les found a hustle.

He also needed some alone time on the lot so he could check around back. The more he thought about it the more he was sure there was something under that house. Gordon had a stash, and Les needed to know what it was.

The boys were moving slow, lingering over their Friday afternoon beers, and by the time the last of the crew hopped on his bicycle and coasted down to the road, the sun was starting to sink. Gordon had gone to town with Abel, for a quick dip in the ocean and to grab a bite, he'd said.

Les had the place to himself. Only the birds and a sloth that grinned as it clawed its treacherous progress along the new power line. Chucking back the last gulp of beer, he got up from where he lounged under the umbrella of the water apple tree, its confetti of pink petals carpeting the ground. He started toward the house, wiping his mouth.

Les rounded the corner to the spot where he'd seen that strange light. Kicking at the shrapnel of fallen palm and coconut husks he found a large section of debris that moved all together. Clever fucker had woven himself a trap door. Les pulled the door back, turned on the flashlight on his phone and cast the beam down the throat of the tunnel. It twisted and sloped and he skidded down, half on his heels, half on his butt, pausing to pull the woven screen of dead foliage back over the opening.

It had taken too long to get rid of the crew, so he'd have to take stock and scoot before the boss-man got tired of the beach and headed home. A quick slide and Les hit the bottom of the tunnel in a slop of water. He could stand now; it was some kind of cellar. The bottom was solid, gravel and rock rising in continents from rain water that had yet to be sucked into the ground. He shone his light at the ceiling, and found a string of bulbs dangling. Tracing the line with his beam he saw the cord went back up the tunnel, no switch down here.

And then the lights went on all at once. Les threw his hand up to shield his eyes, lowering it slowly to confront the thing swaying in front of him. Hugo was barely recognizable. His eye patch was gone, exposing the scarred flesh where his lid had been sewn shut. The other eye was wide and swiveled side to side in a desperate plea. A glugging came from his chest, the only sound he could emit. Some thick, glutinous gel was stuffed in Hugo's mouth and sealed across his lips. He was tied, and hung like a grotesque larva. Scabbed-over wounds pocked his naked torso, the larger ones sealed with the same cloudy goo.

Les stumbled back, taking short sucking breaths. Hugo wasn't the only one hanging from the timber beams that shored up the cavern's dripping ceiling. The new girl he'd brought in to clean was there, head lolling in semi-consciousness. Another worker, the kid who'd ridden an hour from the other side of the mountain for a few dollars a day, blinked a frantic message as he wriggled against the ropes that bound him. Both bore similar wounds to Hugo's, their cries choked by the same pus-like substance.

A noise from topside stopped Les's breath. The lights coming on could only mean the boss-man was home, and he was on his way down. Les had to hide. A pile of tarps slouched in a corner, and he lunged for them. Pulling a loose flap of the crinkling blue material, he dug and wrestled his way under its resisting burden, a moan seeping from his lips as a cold arm flopped across his chest. He squeezed his eyes shut, but the truth seeped in. Bodies. This moldering pile of rolled-up tarp housed the bodies.

Gordon ducked into the cellar, another tarp rasping along the ground behind him. On this one splayed the unconscious Abel, a fresh gash gleaming on his forehead.

Les sank deeper into the spongy pile of putrefying flesh. A cool thick fluid slid down his arm; the accompanying stench rose to gag him, but Les didn't move.

The man was strong. He bound Abel with fingers that operated with a delicate precision, rolling and knotting as he hummed a cheerful melody. He draped the line over a beam and pulled his victim up to join the others. Their bodies swayed and bumped against each other.

Abel moaned, and his eyes began to blink their way open. Gordon placed one hand companionably on Abel's shoulder and dropped his head. A shudder started as Gordon's sides worked like a bellows, a retching coming from deep in his guts. With his free hand he caught the thick phlegm that boiled from his mouth and crammed it in Abel's mouth to stifle his cries. He smoothed the excess that hung from Abel's lips over cheek and chin to form a

seal. Abel gagged and shook his head from side to side, but the only sounds were his muffled pleas and the creak of the beam from which he hung.

Through a rough tear in the tarp Les watched, mouthing a mute prayer. He realized he was shivering and he clenched his teeth with the effort to keep still.

The boss-man pulled off his shirt. Blubbery rolls of fat terraced his abdomen, every move quaked through those folds, the fleshy aftershocks never quite fading to stillness. Gordon stood in front of his latest catch. The vibrations in his stomach quickened with a wet smacking sound, and from between those dimpled folds he disgorged streams of black, rat-sized beetles. Like mechanized vermin they clacked across the bridge of Gordon's arm where it rested on Abel's shoulder. Each took a position—on Abel's spine, his chest, his head. Abel's muted screams intensified and his body arched and swung as he tried to shake the creatures loose.

Gordon stroked Abel's cheek, catching the tears that flowed over his pallid skin, and licked his fingers with a slow lapping tongue, savouring the flavor of that desperate water.

Once in position, the insects reared their heads, revealing shafts that peeled back to unsheathe a beak-like probe. They struck, burrowing deep into Abel's skin. His whole body clenched in rigid seizure, then went limp as he lost consciousness.

The burrowing continued. A buzzing gray cloud descended over Les. The liquid crunch, the humming, the rotten meaty stench of the corpses, the humming… Metallic chittering seeped through the fog, bringing Les back to full consciousness, to the cellar and the cold trickle of guts and sweat that ran down his chest, to the horror unfolding.

Once the creatures had consumed, their bodies bulging, they dropped to the floor and began the slow crawl up Gordon's legs, over his Bermuda shorts, and back into the recesses from which they'd emerged. It was over. Numb from shock, Les waited. It had to be over. But the quiver in Gordon's stomach intensified. It wasn't over at all.

Gordon continued to hum, a calm smile spreading his lips wide. With slow, languorous ease, worm-like appendages slid from the folds that had just closed behind those insectile monstrosities. Swaying, gray and eyeless, they were drawn toward Abel, toward the call of the seeping bloody tunnels made by their predecessors. With easy contractions they slid into the body, and Abel twitched and shivered, but remained unconscious.

***

Les didn't even taste the beer, just gulped it down and cracked open another. He was a dead man. He knew it. Could feel it in his bones.

The door was locked, but he checked it again. He'd left his truck, afraid to start it up and draw Gordon's attention. He had run, stumbling down the hill to the road where he flagged down a ride to take him home. But not to safety.

He would not be safe from the boss-man. Les shivered, crouching in the corner by the door. Then he paced. Then he started to pack, before he realized he had nothing to take. Nowhere to go.

Back in the cellar under Gordon's house, while those horrible worms sucked the life from Abel, Gordon's head had turned. Heavy and sluggish with a glutton's euphoria, his eyes mere slits, glinting. And when he faced Les, where he lay among the dead, the boss-man had smiled a slow, satisfied smile.

Les was a dead man.

But Gordon couldn't have seen him or he wouldn't be here. No way he could have escaped if that *thing* knew what he'd seen.

The jungle went still. The buzz and hum silenced, and Les tensed.

A light knock at his door broke the silence. Just three gentle raps.

"Les, m'boy. We need to have a chat." Gordon's friendly voice came from outside followed by the clink of bottles. "Come have a cold one. We've got some business to discuss."

There was no avoiding, no hiding, no running. Les knew it as he pulled back the bolt and opened the door, not even feeling the floor under his feet as he walked the boards toward his death.

"Don't look so glum, Lester. Things can go a lot of different ways." Gordon thrust a bottle of beer at Les. "We don't have to shoot for a tragic ending here."

Reflexively, Les cracked the bottle and took a swig, keeping his eyes open and on Gordon.

"I knew it was going to come to this." Gordon sat on the stairs and patted the spot next to him. "No fooling a fella like you for long."

Les sat, eyeing Gordon's middle for movement.

With a laugh, Gordon rubbed his stomach and waved off Les's concern. "Fed now. I was so hungry. Been looking for a place like this for a while. Too long, really. I was near starving, but the hunger isn't on me like it was."

Whatever he was, Les was afraid to ask. Didn't really want to know.

Gordon continued, "It was easier before, when folk'd just bring me food. Girls, babies they didn't want, the old, their enemies, I didn't always have to scrounge around like I do now."

"So you're…" Les started, but his voice failed him, getting stuck somewhere in his quivering guts.

"I am what I am." Gordon laughed. "But what people decide I am changes. These days I'm a monster. In the old days, well, everyone has stories about the good old days."

The jungle had come alive again, chirping, prowling. The two men sat and listened, Gordon leaned back with his eyes closed, Les stared out into the dark.

"What are you going to do?" Les asked, forcing his knee to stop its bouncing.

"That's just it, Les. Nothing." Gordon smiled without opening his eyes. "You just keep on like you've been doing. You get things going, bring in the workers, the cleaning girls, the salesmen, the tourists. You'll get what you need, guy like you always gets what he needs, doesn't he?"

"You want me to bring you people so you can…" He couldn't continue. The image of those snaking things sucking, feeding, it stopped him.

"Like I said, I've had a good run. Filled up. Things'll

settle down now. It's amazing how much you can take and the human body just keeps on going. Kidney, liver, intestines, tonsils, spleen, that useless appendices, anything for making a baby." Gordon snapped his fingers like he'd made a uterus vanish. "Man, you don't need the stuff in your bones, some nerves, parts of the brain, thyroid, lymph nodes, lung tissue, it goes on. There don't have to be bodies. Not many, anyways. Just some people feeling a little peaked for a while."

"But," Les took another swallow of beer to clear his throat, "people here are gonna talk, they're simple, but they're not stupid."

"Stupid? Never said they were." Gordon licked his lips.

"Those guys getting sick… you," Les shuddered, "you took something from them? And they don't know it?"

"A convenient side-effect." Gordon nodded. "Look, Lester, this can be good for both of us, or it can be really bad for you. You and your little baby." Gordon licked his lips again and stroked the bristles of his greasy mustache.

Les tipped his head back, swallowing the rest of his beer in one long gulp. Gordon smiled wide as he handed over another, cracked and ready to drink.

***

Sun glinted off bike fenders as people pedalled by, going slow, laden with beach towels and surfboards. The sun also caught on the diamond ring the blond-haired Rasta-girl wore on her wedding finger.

It was a hot one today. Les appreciated the fan Walter had hung over the street-side bar. Dance hall music pulsed from the restaurant above, and Ronald and his kick ball buddies rehearsed their goal-celebrating dances, stomping clouds of street up into the air.

"Hey, man, thanks for the beer." The Rasta-girl leaned against the counter next to him, her skinny, sunburnt fiancé standing behind, engulfed by a bulging backpack.

"No worries, *chica*. I overheard your predicament, thought you kids could use a cold one." Les clinked bottles with both of them and they drank.

The fiancé blew a damp lock of hair up off his forehead and pressed the cold bottle against his skin. "Shit, man. This blows. We hit Panama right in the middle of Carnival, ended up sleeping on the beach. Sandflies took us to town. Looks like the same gig here."

"Yeah," Les nodded in sympathy, "busy time of year. This week it's the surfing contest, next week they got a music festival. Lots a fun stuff going on. Hope you kids stick around for it. Best reggae on the coast."

The fan whisked back and forth, curling the napkins up from the counter as it passed.

"Maybe I can help you kids out. Hook you up with a quiet place in the hills you can stay. You won't find anyone knows more about this place. Like the girls always say about Lester Morley, Les is More."

Les took another look at that big diamond ring, then out at the road. The sizzle of street meat smoked the air as the vendors fired up their grills, preparing for the night's trade.

What the Hell Ever Happened to...
Jeff Connor and Scream/Press

PHOTO COURTESY OF JEFF CONNER

By Robert Morrish

Small-press horror publishing can be traced back to at least the 1930s, when publishers such as Visionary Publishing Company and Arkham House (which, of course, still exists to this day) produced horror titles in small print runs. But the horror small press never truly took off until the 1980s, when a surge in the mass-market popularity of horror fiction—spearheaded by the likes of Stephen King and Dean Koontz—led to an explosion of interest in signed, limited editions.

At the bleeding edge of that '80s movement were a small handful of publishers, including Dark Harvest, Donald Grant, and Whispers Press, but the publishing revolution was perhaps best exemplified by Scream/Press, which published its debut collection, Dennis Etchison's *The Dark Country*, in 1982 and went on to publish 20 more titles (including those published under the companion Dream/Press imprint) before shutting its doors.

Scream/Press was the brainchild of Jeff Conner, who's spent much of his life working in the horror and speculative genres, or at least on their fringes. Conner was born in Pasadena and now lives with his wife of 27 years in the Highland Park neighborhood just west of there, in

a 100-year-old house (with, appropriately enough for a former small press owner, a garage full of unsold books). His son is a freshman in college and his wife teaches high school English and film in East LA. I caught up with him recently to talk about the life and death of Scream/Press.

Tell us a bit about what you did prior to Scream/Press…

Not much in terms of publishing, aside from school newspapers and yearbook stuff. I'd always been interested in how those things worked, even back in grammar school. Go figure. But I hadn't done anything like Scream/Press prior to actually doing it. I was just enjoying an extended adolescence as a small business owner in sunny Santa Cruz. I had gone to UCSC for a year and really liked the town, and just couldn't see living in Los Angeles because of all the smog.

What prompted you to launch Scream/Press?

It was purely a fan impulse. At the time I was a co-owner of a record store in Santa Cruz, which I'd help start back in

1974, the same year I graduated college. The store was very active in the local music scene (we co-produced the first Talking Heads show in town, and hosted in-stores with bands like The B-52's and The Buzzcocks) and I was quite imbued with the DIY ethos of first-wave punk.

Also at that time I was reading mainly genre short stories, SF by the likes of PKD, Farmer, Zelazny, Varley, R.R. Martin, and Gibson, and horror/dark fantasy as found in Charlie Grant's *Shadows* anthologies, Schiff's *Whispers* collections, Wagner's *Year's Best* series, Kirby McCauley's *Dark Forces*, etc. For some reason, I just responded to the short story format more than most long-form. This wasn't my only reading diet of course (I really liked Gore Vidal's historical novels), but short fiction was definitely the blue plate special.

After seeing a notice about it in *Locus*, I attended the 1981 WFC in Oakland and had a great time. I had never encountered the small press scene before, and it really intrigued me. But I couldn't understand was why some of my favorite authors didn't have their own books out. WTF, right?

So as I said, starting Scream/Press was simply a way to get to know some of the writers that I admired, and to right a terrible wrong, of course—namely, no Dennis Etchison collection.

How did you choose which authors to approach initially? Especially Etchison, given that he hadn't previously had a book published?

Well, for me, Etchison was the shit; I still remember reading the opening to "The Dead Line." I knew he had enough material for a solid collection and it just seemed wrong that he didn't have one, so that was what got me started, plain and simple. Country rube that I was, as far as I could tell the mechanics of putting a book together was not rocket surgery; seemed like anyone could do it, so why not me? Hell, I had an MFA from CalArts in graphic design, which obviously qualified me to take on something I had no practical experience with. Learn by doing!

Anyway, after talking to Etchison at the convention, I looked him up in Los Angeles and somehow ~~tricked~~ convinced him that I knew what I was doing (or he thought that even if I utterly failed it wouldn't destroy

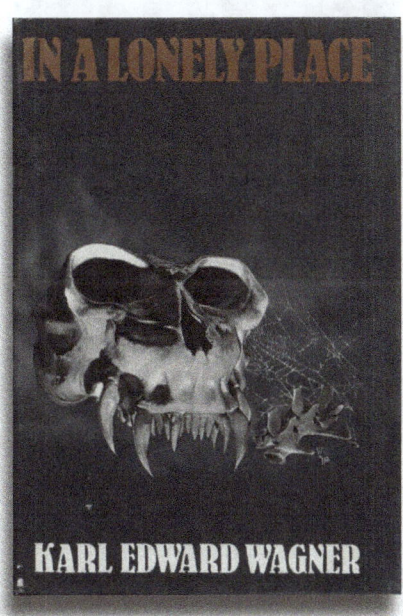

his career). Then I contacted artist JK Potter; Dennis and I were both big fans, having admired his work for publisher Donald M. Grant. After that, I got with a typesetter in Santa Cruz, a print rep in San Francisco recommended by Tim Underwood, and away we went, ready to put all that prior yearbook experience to good use.

I thought this would be a one-off project, something new to try, and hopefully make a meaningful contribution to that community I had met at the WFC in Oakland. Thus I was blissfully unencumbered by any long-term planning, figuring that if I liked a certain thing, then simple statistics dictated there must be at least 500 other people who also liked that same thing, even a Dennis Etchison collection. I was still busy full-time at the record store and had started writing weekly reviews and articles for the local papers, so I wasn't looking to start a whole new business, just have some fun and learn by doing.

Any interesting anecdotes to tell in how you eventually acquired the rights to publish titles by some of the bigger names of the era, such as Stephen King, Clive Barker, and Ramsey Campbell?

At that time super-agent Kirby McCauley pretty much had the horror market all sewn up, repping King and Straub, and just about anyone else who mattered, such as Dennis Etchison and Ramsey Campbell. *The Dark Country* was a great calling card and Dennis introduced me around. I found out that Ramsey was interested in an unexpurgated edition of his *The Face That Must Die* novel, which sounded pretty good to me, especially as JK Potter was a big Campbell fan as well. So, another no-brainer.

As for Stephen King, he was still going to conventions back then and had seen my first two books. So doing a book with him came together pretty easily as well, which I'm sure Kirby McCauley had a lot to do with. As for Barker, Ramsey Campbell introduced me to him. I believe the actual deal was a sub-license from his American publisher, who was only going to release the *Books of Blood* series only as mass-market paperbacks. (We set our type from the UK paperbacks and did our own line edits, with Barker's cooperation.) Scream's Karl Edgar Wagner collection, *In A Lonely Place,* was also a sub-license of a paperback edition. Karl added a new story, "More Sinned Against," which was a very strong piece that I think had been rejected from the mainstream outlets due its graphic nature (a sign of those simpler times). For me, having added content justified the hardcover incarnation of an easily-available title.

Eventually I was able to simply contact writers directly and he or she would tell their agent or publisher to make the deal. The so-called selection process was just my personal taste, suggestions from writers or editors (like David Hartwell and Ellen Datlow), or happenstance, like seeing Michael McDowell on a panel and talking to him afterwards. Remember, this was still just a hobby for me, and the workload, at least in terms of publicity and shipping orders, was fairly minimal at that point.

What was your fastest-selling title? Slowest?

It's not a competition, but I hope you won't be shocked to learn that the bigger "the name," the faster the sales. And while one likes to believe that quality is always rewarded in the marketplace, that is simply not the case. So forgive me if I won't identify my "slow sellers" as I would hate to have them judged as "lacking" somehow.

Do you have a personal favorite among the Scream/Press titles? If so, which one and why?

You have to remember that back when I started it was pre-digital. I worked with a typesetter in Santa Cruz, getting these long rolls of photographic type that I'd cut up, wax, and position onto special paste-up paper using a light-table with the book's books layout on a clear sheet of acetate (with registration pins to keep it all lined up). The body text and running heads were separate pieces and each had to be placed by hand, so it was a meticulous process putting even the most simple book together. Oddly, I very much enjoyed "building" the books in this way, like they were handcrafted somehow.

The point is, having such an intimate relationship with book creates certain expectations about the final results, which rarely lived up to the imagined ideal. So many of my personal favorites are the ones that caused the least "shock" when I unwrapped the advance copy. (Sorry for the jargon, but even with "blue lines" and unbound "f&g's," there could still be some big surprises.)

At any rate, our edition of Stephen King's *Skeleton Crew* accomplished everything I set out to do, on several

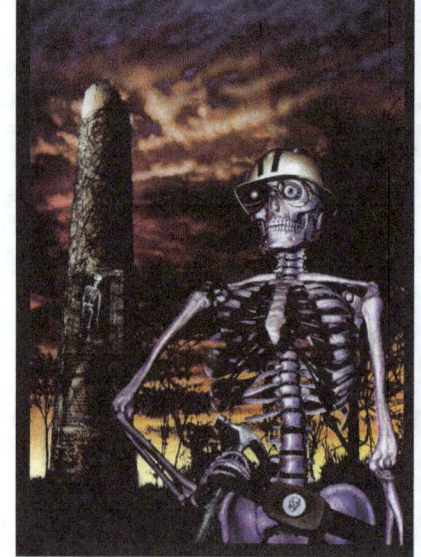

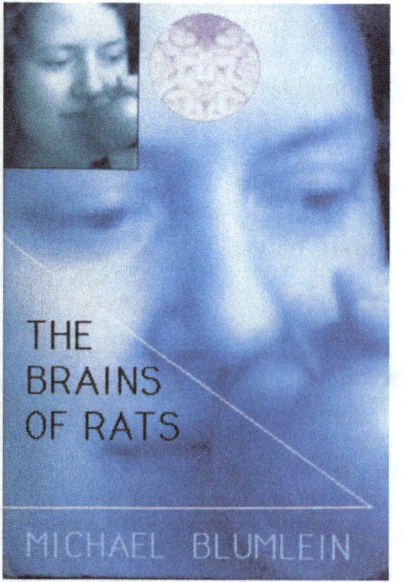

levels. (My biggest mistake was underpricing the book so egregiously; I just had no concept of how to work on that scale financially.) Thanks to the rabid King collectors, limited editions in general were taking off in our little neck of the woods (the notion of special limited editions dates back to Dickens), and it bothered me that people would pay premium prices for what was essentially just a trade hardcover with a signature page, a slipcase, and number. (Oh, the power of numbers.) I felt that these editions should truly be as "special" as possible.

As the book's design, I used Harry Clarke's 1923 edition of Poe's *Tales of Mystery and Imagination* as a touchstone, having picked up a vintage copy the WFC in Montreal. JK Potter really exceeded himself on the project, with Harry O. Morris helping him out on some of the title treatments. As with the Wagner collection, it was important to me to feature expanded content, so I was really pleased that King allowed us to include an additional story. I think that was his first limited to have distinctly different core content from any other edition. The text we used was generated from a set of over-sized floppy discs supplied by King directly; his own digital manuscripts, unedited by Putnam, who was issuing the trade version. I just corrected the spelling and put it out, which I like to think makes our text "purer" somehow.

As for my other "favorite" editions, I do have real fondness for the two Ramsey Campbell collections, namely *Cold Print,* which gathered his Lovecraft-inspired tales, and *Scared Stiff,* an early entrant in the so-called "erotic horror" trend. (I was criticized for that cheeky title, but I think it still holds its own.) JK Potter's illustrations were fantastic and the stories were all so great; putting those two books together was a pleasure and they turned out the way I conceived them.

I also liked *Toplin,* Michael McDowell's surrealist novel of urban dislocation. The text hit a real chord with artist Harry O. Morris, who produced some of his best work for it—one of the reasons I printed the entire run on coated stock. I also spent a bit more time on the design and layout, but unfortunately the title wasn't as popular as it should have been. I can't help thinking that its outré square format had something to do with that. A mild bummer.

Of the books I produced in Los Angeles, Michael Blumlein's *The Brains of Rats* stands out. Tim Caldwell's Surreal collages really complemented the stories, which are quite strong. Seek that book out, folks!

Scream/Press titles were notable for their artwork and design... how did you go about choosing the artists

that you worked with, such as J.K. Potter and Harry O. Morris? Were they simply personal favorites of yours?

I always tried to elevate the book design, though I was by no means a trained designer, or even particularly knowledgeable about it; again, learning by doing. I enjoyed the creative aspect of book production and simply did what appealed to me at the time, not trying to over-think it. For me, the two presses putting out the best product at the time were Don Grant and Underwood/Miller, so I copied them when I started out. Tim Underwood was based in the Bay Area and was very generous about sharing information and production tips. Without his advice and guidance, I doubt I would have gotten my first book out, and we became very good friends.

As I noted, Etchison and I both liked artist JK Potter, so that getting him signed up was a no-brainer, and he introduced me to Harry O. Morris. I had gone to high school with artist Glen Iwasaki, so that's how he came to design and illustrate Chelsea Quinn Yarbro's *Signs & Portents*. I think I met Ron & Val Lakey-Lindahn at a convention and got them for Wagner's *In A Lonely Place.*

Were/are you a small press collector yourself? If so, any particular publishers whose work you've admired?

Back in the day I would see what the other presses were doing, but I certainly couldn't afford limited editions. My collection has been around meeting authors I like and having them sign their books for me. The personal connection was what made it special. Or I might pick up older books as art objects or for inspiration, like the Harry Clarke book. I ended up liquidating my collection of signed first editions many years ago.

These days I'll sometimes pick up a particular edition for its design or construction elements, or if it has Potter artwork. On the small press side, I think what Bill Schaefer is doing with Subterranean Press is really impressive, Jerad Walters has really turned Centipede Press into a powerhouse, and Cemetery Dance continues to be relevant. I also like Clarke's World. I do actively collect film tie-in editions from the silent era through the Forties, as well as popular fiction from those eras, especially if the book was the basis for a film. I'm a geek for old movies so having a small library of "vintage fiction" is part of that ~~addiction~~ interest.

You also established a companion imprint, Dream/Press, under which you published three titles... how did the publishing philosophy/goals of Dream/Press differ?

I didn't want to be constrained by the Scream/Press name, so the Dream/Press imprint was a convenient way to do less abrasive material. The Matheson books would not have been appropriate as Scream/Press titles.

What led to the demise of Scream/Press and Dream/Press after the publication of the Richard Matheson omnibus *Somewhere in Time / What Dreams May Come* **in 1992?**

The short answer is "money," as in "ran out of it." The old cliché about making a small fortune in publishing by starting with a large one is pretty much true. (Just look at the state of mainstream publishing today; it's swirling around the bowl.) Scream was always a one-man operation and never had appropriate backing to take it from being a casual hobby to a real business. Also, one learns more from failure than from success, and since my initial books were pretty successful, I was not learning very much, which is a shame as I could have really used some practical knowledge when times got tough.

Frankly, I should have taken on a partner who had some money and worked the press a serious endeavor if I had wanted Scream to be more than a weekend hobby. There had been a lot of painful drama in my life with various business partners and artistic collaborators, so I had vowed not to go down that road again anytime soon.

After moving to Los Angeles, what had been a hobby became my sole income, and I was too distracted with other things to properly adapt. If I'd stayed in Santa Cruz then things would've been different, I'm sure, but I was getting fed up with the place and wanted to explore other avenues. There were big changes in the marketplace as well, such as a national recession and the library market drying up (almost half of my retail sales were libraries). So while I still enjoyed making books, the business side was becoming very unpleasant, and there was little hope of improvement, which burned me out. That's basically it.

I have to say that my edition of *Somewhere in Time / What Dreams May Come* was more of a tie-in for that hotel on Mackinac Island where they shot *Somewhere In Time*. I don't know if they still do this, but at the time the hotel hosted an annual convention, sort of a cos-play thing based on the film. Our edition was basically just for them to sell at the hotel store. As both titles were then out of print from the mainstream pubs, folks who wouldn't normally contact us sent in orders, often with very heartfelt notes. I was a big Matheson fan for sure, but I hadn't realized the profound impact these two novels had with his readers; they really loved him.

There were some announced titles that were never published, such as an illustrated edition of Anne Rice's *Interview With a Vampire,* **the Richard Matheson collection** *Darker,* **and William Relling's** *The Infinite Man,* **for which an Advance Review Copy was issued... besides the Relling book, was there a lot of work put into some of those unpublished titles?**

It's a stone against my heart that I couldn't get those books out, as well as Campbell's *The Nameless*. I really tried, and I regret taking advance orders for them, though it seemed like a good idea at the time. I did put quite a bit of effort into them, most being fully produced. The Rice project would have been great. Jeff Jones, an artist I absolutely adored, did pen-and-ink illustrations which were to be turned into full-color serigraphs, but it just got so expensive and time-consuming that I ran out of pier to fish on, as the saying goes. If I'd scaled that one back, maybe...

An even earlier still-born project was an edition of *Divine Endurance* by Gwyneth A. Jones, a novel that enjoyed. I started production on it, even had the signature sheets done, but ultimately I thought it wasn't right for what I was doing at the time and abandoned it. At least we hadn't taken any pre-orders.

Another factor in non-published books was my refusal to go "desktop" for typesetting, instead leasing a very expensive and complex Compugraphic system. It was the first "portable" version of this technology (meaning only two teamsters were needed to move it), and required writing long strings of code. You could print galleys on a laser printer, but the actual finished type had to output by a real photo-type shop. Slow learner that I am, I did manage to typeset the Matheson books on it, plus *Heatseeker*, *The Brains of Rats*, and the Relling book, as well as *Darker* and *Interview*. The idea was to save the cost of typesetting by doing it myself, and have more control over book production, thus yielding a superior product.

Now, I have come to accept that I have the time management skills of a distracted teenager, but back then I thought I could just start banging out these books and everything would magically work out—not a very good business plan as it turns out. The cold reality was that the monthly expenses of leasing the machine was too great to overcome. And honestly, only a trained professional could tell the difference between a book done on the Compugraphic and one using WordPerfect; so while I enjoyed a period of personal satisfaction, the end result was another nail in Scream's coffin. Again, if I had learned more early on, like not making the perfect the enemy of the good and just getting on with things then perhaps my half-assed plans might have worked out better.

I felt really bad about not getting the Relling book out, except in galley form. He was a really great guy and we socialized regularly at that time as we were both living in the Fairfax area just south of Hollywood. Later he moved out to Pasadena, but I did see him at a book signing at Dark Delicacies just a month or two before he died. As for *Darker*, those were three paperback originals from early in Matheson's career and I was glad that those were later re-published in the small press.

What other unfinished projects can you tell us about?

I already noted Campbell's *The Nameless*. We were going to use the original text, with Potter illustrations, but it never came together correctly. I can't remember why exactly, but I messed it up somehow. And I was also going to do a cool edition of *The Night of the Hunter* by Davis Grubb, with some added material. Great book; my brush with real American literature.

Another project that most don't know about is the complete Philip K. Dick short stories. I was such a PKD fan (I still have a complete set of his paperbacks, and some later hardcovers) that I wasn't thinking straight when I started that one. This was while still in Santa Cruz, and after digitizing several collections (namely having the stories manually entered into a word processor and then proofed), it became obvious that this one was going to be too much for me. I passed the project along to Underwood/Miller, who had the resources to get it done correctly.

Is there any other author that you really wish you'd had

the opportunity to publish?

I got into publishing as fan, and I pretty much got to fulfill those fan desires, at least in terms of meeting people and doing something creative in a field I loved. It would have been nice to do a project with Peter Straub, like *The General's Wife* that Don Grant put out, or Underwood/Miller's *The Throat*. That would've been pretty sweet.

What did you do after Scream/Press closed its doors?

Well, back the early '80s, just before starting Scream, I started writing weekly reviews and articles for the local papers in Santa Cruz. Being with the local daily paper meant free tickets to shows and screenings, even ones in the Bay area, so that was cool. Aside from the perks, it also taught me how to collaborate with an editor, interview celebrities (or at least musicians like Joey Ramone, Joan Jett, and Danny Elfman), and to generate different kinds of copy as needed. Having worked as a club and radio DJ, performed on stage, and been in retail for so long, I had gradually become comfortable with public speaking. Remarkably I was able to leverage these assets and interests into genre film promotion and specialized marketing, starting with *The Crow*. Paramount originally hired me, followed by Miramax after they picked up the film, which eventually led to working for the film's producer, Pressman Film, for ten years. While there, I set up Top Dollar Comics as an in-house mechanism for co-publishing licensed material, mainly with The Crow franchise.

My own editorial skills (such as they were), came into play when we did a six-book slate of original Crow novels with HarperCollins; a media tie-in deal made possible by the Crow television series from Polygram Filmed Entertainment (the show ran for one year). There had also been a novelization of the first Crow sequel, *City of Angels*, which got our feet wet in the prose end of things. As Pressman's in-house editor, I worked primarily with John Douglas at HarperCollins, which was great fun and very educational. Each novel featured a different Crow, and I intended the series to be a way to develop new material for the film side, which had two sequels already. This is why Norman Partridge's *The Crow: Wicked Prayer* became *Crow IV*.

After leaving Pressman, I worked with Conan Properties for a bit on their publishing program, which included new Conan comics with Dark Horse and a media tie-in prose package for *The Age of Conan* MMORPG, in the form of a series of original trilogies, released by Ace/Berkley as paperback originals.

You recently worked at IDW for a while, I believe. Tell our readers about some of the projects you worked on for IDW...

I headed up an original prose program at IDW for four-and-a-half years, working with a large group of talented authors and artists from all over the world. (Shout outs to Ellen Datlow and Paula Guran, who were very generous in recommending writers and supplying contact info early on.)

The bulk of the titles reflected IDW's various properties or licenses, such as *Zombies vs. Robots, GI Joe,* and *The Rocketeer,* or created new ones, like Jonathan Maberry's *V-Wars* series. My editorial work was mainly "developmental" in nature, done before the writer started working in earnest.

Truth be told, the Scream books are mostly all reprints; not much real editorial work required, save for normal production needs. With the IDW titles I was actively commissioning stories (for *Zombies vs. Robots,* we contracted over 500,000 words) and occasionally coming up with themes and concepts. The interaction with writers was much more involved. I also endeavored to educate myself more formally about typography and book design.

For a good overview of my IDW resume, check out *Classics Mutilated, Zombies Vs. Robots: This Means War!, V-Wars,* and *Rocketeer: Jet-Pack Adventures.* I loved working with all the writers and artists, putting the books together, and especially not having to contend with the retail part of the equation. The IDW situation was a perfect fit for my rigorous couch-based lifestyle, so if anyone wants to back me in a similar manner, please get in touch.

So you're interested in getting back into publishing?

I feel like I still am in publishing, though I don't see reviving Scream/Press. No one is clamoring for it and there are a lot of smart new players now, like JournalStone. I do like how Kickstarter has proven to be a reliable venue for funding original short story collections, as demonstrated by presses like Silence in the Library. Alternative ways of backing projects really interest me, but I'd need some patient and friendly teenager to handle the social media component; I'm still not on Facebook.

Up from Soil Fresh

A Collection of Zombie Stories
by Aaron J. French

"Aaron J. French is a writer to watch, and his collection Up From Soil Fresh is a great place to see the range of his talent."
Joe McKinney,
Stoker Award-winning author

With his new collection, Up From Soil Fresh, he shows everybody he's also a great up-and-coming writer. Highly recommended!"-
James R. Beach, Editor-in-Chief,
Dark Discoveries magazine

www.HazardousPress.com
Read at your own risk...

CARRION HOUSE

ILLUSTRATION/FINE ART/DESIGN
www.carrionhouse.com

ALEISTER CROWLEY'S MAGICAL CHILD

By Donald Tyson

Aleister Crowley was obsessed with the Antichrist. It is a theme that ran through his entire life. When he was a misbehaving young boy, his strict Plymouth Brethren mother accused him of being the Great Beast of Revelation 13:1. Crowley accepted her words as prophetic. But what was the Beast? He was the herald of the Antichrist. Crowley got it into his head at an early age that in some way he was to cause the manifestation of the Antichrist.

While he was at Trinity College, Cambridge, corrupting the morals of English youth, he began to study occult texts such as A. E. Waite's *Book of Black Magic and Pacts*. Four months after leaving the university, he was initiated into a secret society called the Hermetic Order of the Golden Dawn that taught its members a system of ritual magic. The Golden Dawn had been founded in 1888 by three Freemasons. The formal grade ceremonies and lavish grade robes of this secret order of magicians delighted him. Crowley embraced its teachings joyously, without a trace of scepticism. It offered everything he loved—ritual, ceremony, costume, secrecy, and the promise of power over others.

Perhaps the most important aspect of the Golden Dawn teachings, from Crowley's point of view, is that they gave him a way to realize his destiny, which he believed to be the ushering into the world of the Antichrist. Ritual magic would be the method by which the Antichrist would be created, and he, the Great Beast of Revelation, was the magician who would do it. Indeed, he was the only magician who could perform this Great Work, because it was his True Will, and no one else's.

In 1904 Crowley went to Cairo, Egypt, where the spirit Aiwass, whom Crowley believed to be his Holy Guardian Angel, channelled through him the seminal document of Thelema by the process of spirit writing. On three consecutive days the spirit took partial control of Crowley's body and used his hand to write the three brief chapters of *Liber AL vel Legis*, which is usually known by its English title, the *Book of the Law*.

Thelema is Crowley's system of spiritual development

and ethical conduct. It is a Greek word meaning "will."

The concept of will, or rather, of the True Will, is central to Crowley's teachings. By "True Will," Crowley understood that primal intention or purpose that lies at the heart of every human being—the thing which a person is born to accomplish in life, along with every act that contributes to or enables the accomplishment of this ultimate purpose. What is understood as "will" by the average man, the common will or mere willfulness, Crowley held in disdain. Wilfulness was an impediment to the accomplishment of the True Will.

The primary expression of Crowley's True Will, which he had recognized from childhood, was the bringing forth of the Antichrist, and the ushering in of the time of chaos and destruction commonly known as the Apocalypse. This was to be done by magic—that much Crowley knew. But how?

Crowley decided that the Antichrist must be his own son. It made the best sense to him that the Antichrist would come forth from him organically, and be trained by him during childhood in his ultimate role as the scourge of Christianity. It was Crowley's intention to use a very carefully crafted set of rituals during the conception and birth of his son that would channel the child's natural destiny or true will toward realization.

He knew the child was to be his son and not his daughter by the words of the *Book of the Law*, where it is written to Crowley, who is called the Prophet, "The child of thy bowels, he shall behold [the mysteries of the book]. Expect him not from the East nor from the West, for from no expected house cometh that child."[1]

In 1915 Crowley undertook a great magical working with Jeanne Foster, who was known in Crowley's occult order of the Silver Star as Soror Hilarion. She was the third in Crowley's series of Scarlet Women. The working involved sex magic, and was designed to bring forth his son, the Antichrist. It was unsuccessful. Crowley remarked of it in his diary, "I did not know that I was attempting a physical impossibility."[2] It may be that Hilarion was barren.

We can guess something about the nature of this ritual working from a novel Crowley wrote in 1917 titled *Moonchild* (not published until 1929). It contains Crowley's occult detective character, Simon Iff, around whom Crowley wrote 23 stories. Crowley cast himself in the novel as the hero, Cyril Grey, a disciple of Simon Iff and a magician of white magic who attempts to created a magical child with lunar properties in the womb of the character Lisa la Giuffria.

Cyril Grey intends to conceive this magical child in the womb of Lisa la Giuffria in the usual way, but he then plans to exclude the coming into the embryo of a normal human soul through the use of occult wards to prevent its entry into the house where la Giuffria is kept, so that a lunar entity of great wisdom and power can be induced to inhabit her unborn child. This lunar spirit is to be called into the embryo by saturating la Giuffria's living quarters with lunar symbolism, thereby attracting it.

The principles Crowley gives in his novel can also be applied to the creation of the Antichrist, who was

understood by Crowley to be a living incarnation of Horus, the Egyptian god of war. It was Crowley's view that the Christian age was the age of Osiris, coincident with the astrological age of Pisces, and that it would be succeeded by the age of Horus, which would coincide with the astrological age of Aquarius. The Antichrist as Horus, the conquering child, would usher in this new age. All this he believed had been predicted by the *Book of the Law*.

Simon Iff tells Lisa la Giuffria in *Moonchild*, "the idea has been almost universal in one form or another; the wish has always been for a Messiah or Superman, and the method some attempt to produce man by artificial or at least abnormal means."[3]

The notion of endowing a child with supernormal abilities is very ancient. Crowley mentions rites used by the priests of Egypt at the conception of a Pharaoh.[4] The time of birth of Alexander the Great was said to have been delayed in order that he be born at precisely the moment that was astrologically most auspicious. Even the fairy stories of the Brothers Grimm that talk about the gifts given to a child on its christening by its fairy godmother are an expression of this idea that magic can channel and release divine, or at least otherworldly, talents in the newborn.

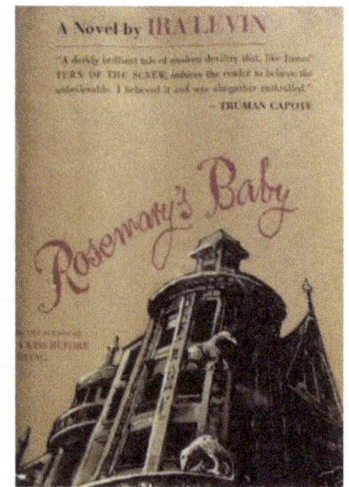

The concept of creating a magical child by ritual during conception was used to good effect by Ira Levin in his 1967 novel, *Rosemary's Baby*. In this novel, which was made into an excellent film

by Roman Polanski, we see Crowley's entire agenda laid forth in a slightly modified way—in Levin's novel the Antichrist is not the son of the magician, Roman Castevet, who leads the Manhattan witch coven that conducts the ritual, but is the child of the actual Devil, summoned by ritual magic to impregnate Rosemary.

Yet, when you think about it, how could a noncorporeal entity impregnate a mortal woman? Only by becoming corporeal in some way. The obvious way would be to possess the magician and use his body as an instrument to achieve its purpose. So perhaps Rosemary was impregnated by Castevet while he was possessed by the Devil. This is left ambiguous in the book and the film. Anton LaVey, the founder of the Church of Satan, is said to have acted as an advisor on the film version, but the character of Castevet in the novel is an obvious homage to Aleister Crowley.

There are other examples of the Devil's child in popular culture, although none are as perfect as Levin's novel. The writer Dennis Wheatley suggested something akin to the process in his 1953 novel, *To the Devil, A Daughter*, which enjoyed great popularity when it was published. In that novel a young nun, Catherine Beddows, is ritually prepared by a group of Satanists to become the avatar of the demon Ashtaroth when she turns eighteenth.

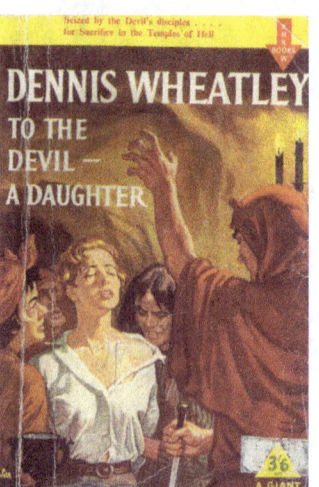

The 1976 movie *The Omen* extends the theme by imagining what would happen after the Antichrist was born into the world and began to live in it as a child. The American diplomat in Rome, Robert Thorn, is persuaded to adopt an infant boy as his own son after his wife loses their child in labor. The child has already been transformed by occult means into the Antichrist before Thorn adopts him. This film echoes the folklore of the Changeling—an unnatural fairy child that is substituted in the crib for a human infant whom the fairies steal away and raise as their own.

And what of Crowley's own dream of fathering the Antichrist? Alas, his various Scarlet Women either suffered miscarriages or gave birth only to girls throughout most of his life. Crowley was baffled and became disheartened, but he never doubted that he was destined to herald the Antichrist. After all, was it not prophesied in the *Book of the Law* that only the child of his bowels would grasp its secrets?[5]

He decided that the Antichrist must be a student that he would mentor and teach in the ways of Thelema. For a time he believed it might be a man named Raoul Loveday, who came to Crowley's Abbey of Thelema, as he called his small villa in Cefalù, in November of 1922. Crowley wrote of Loveday, "I designed him from the first interview to be my Magical heir."[6]

Unfortunately for Crowley, Loveday died at the Abbey from a lingering disease in February of 1923. For a while, Crowley was convinced that the one who "cometh after him,"[7] as the *Book of the Law* put it, must be a magician named Charles Stansfeld Jones, who called himself Frater Achad, but ultimately he disagreed with some of Achad's teachings on the Tree of Life and fell out with him. Jones became a Roman Catholic in 1928.

Perhaps Crowley should have paid more attention to the exact text of his *Book of the Law*, which specifically states that the glories of Thelema will belong, not to Crowley himself, but to one who "cometh after" him. If we take this literally, as we are intended to do by the angel Aiwass and by the Great Beast himself, then the successor to Crowley would be someone who would only arise after Crowley's demise in 1947.

It is worth noting that Crowley did have a son, or at least, so it is claimed. Randall Gair Doherty was born on May 2, 1937, to a woman named Deidre Patricia O'Doherty, with whom Crowley had formed a friendship the previous year. Crowley was 61 at the time of conception. Only a DNA test could prove that Doherty was actually Crowley's child, and to my knowledge no such test was ever done. Doherty died in 2002.

Dishonorable mention must be made of a man who called himself Amado Crowley, and asserted himself to be Crowley's illegitimate son and heir. His real name was Andrew Standish (1930-2010). He made the claim that Crowley was his father in 1971, and declared that the *Book of the Law* was a fraud. Biographers of Crowley say that it is Standish who was the fraud. It may be that Crowley's magical child has yet to reveal himself to the public at large.

Notes

1. Crowley. *The Book of the Law.* Quebec: 93 Publishing, 1975, pp. 24-5.

2. Crowley. *The Confessions of Aleister Crowley.* London: Arkana, Penguin Books, 1989, p. 801.

3. Crowley. *Moonchild.* New York: Samuel Weiser Inc., 1973, page 109.

4. Ibid.

5. *Book of the Law*, pp. 24-5.

6. Symonds. *The Great Beast.* London: Ryder and Company, 1951, p. 198.

7. *Book of the Law*, p. 72.

Field of Flesh

By John Everson

*E*veryone knows the saying: only the good die young. But the corollary is, only the bad live forever. And to crib from another really well-known pop song, forever is a really long time.

I'm a neutral party. Or at least, that's what I always said. Call me a voyeur if you want. I call me a private dick. And I don't mean in the sense you're probably thinking. My dick *is* private, but I meant that in the parlance of 1950's noir movies.

I watch people.

I find out their dirty secrets, and bring them out of the closet and home to roost. And no, I'm not normally the purveyor of a cavalcade of clichés, but those timeworn phrases are perfect to illustrate my profession. I make money by watching people… usually people involved in nefarious activities.

The people who will live forever.

So I didn't blink when the woman in front of my desk said she wanted to pay me a retainer to go to a sex club, find her husband and bring him home. It was not *exactly* something I'd done before, but I'd been asked to do stranger things. And been paid well for it.

In this instance, the setup was intriguing. I was to be a "white knight" in the dark cellars of kink. Apparently the client—who introduced herself as Patricia Delacruiz—had been attending a super exclusive bondage club called NightWhere for the past few months. Every month, she and her husband Lucas would receive an invite delivered to their home a couple hours before a session was to occur, with instructions on how to find the secret club. Because NightWhere, apparently, was never held in the same location twice.

Smart setup, I thought. Keep the lookie-loos out and the local constabulary off your back. Before any of the locals knew any wiser the club would have come and gone. So to speak.

"Here's the thing," Mrs. D informed me, with fingers entwined nervously on her lap. She was wearing a short black dress, and I could see the top of a garter belt holding up the black pantyhose she wore. I suspected I was meant to see that, so I ignored it. "They have a room where they torture people, and never let them leave. They have my husband Lucas locked up there, and now I don't receive any invitations to come back to NightWhere, so I don't know where they are. I can't get back to the club to find him and get him out."

"Well, if you can't get back there, how am I supposed to?" I asked. Yeah, I know I'm a private eye, but… that doesn't mean I always want to do things the hard way. I wanted her to help me out a little. One thing I've noticed—people are usually more resourceful than they give themselves credit for. I never pass up help.

"That part's easy," she said. My ears perked up at the word *easy*. It's a word I like. Eggs over-easy, The Big Easy, women who are… you get the picture.

"I know a couple who go to NightWhere every month," Mrs. D said. "If you stake out their place at the right time, you could get their invitation, and use it to get in."

"Well," I said, thinking this one through. "That seems like a sound plan. But why couldn't you just ask them to take you? Or stake out their place yourself and snag their invite? It would be cheaper than hiring me."

"Because the doorman at NightWhere would recognize me. He'd know not to let me in. With you? You'd be a newbie, and they always have a few new recruits every month. He won't recognize you, but you'll have an invitation, so he'll think you're one of the newbies. So you could get in, find your way to the Field of Flesh, and set Lucas free. They'd never suspect what you were there for, until it was too late."

"Field of Flesh?" I asked. I wasn't sure I liked the sound of that. I tapped my Bic pen impatiently on the notepad. So far I hadn't written anything beyond a sketchy list:

sexy dame
easy
bondage club
find NightWhere
Call Tommy to see if bowling is still on for Friday night

I needed to fill in the blanks on this assignment and then hustle it over to the bank to make sure her check cleared.

"Yes," Mrs. D said. "The Field is the place where they take people to torture inside NightWhere. You'll have to look for it, but carefully."

She chewed her lip before continuing. "The Field of Flesh is kind of the last resting place in NightWhere for voyeurs."

"So Lucas was a voyeur?"

Mrs. D uncrossed her legs, and then crossed them again, with her opposite foot now on top. She made sure to give me a long look at the shadow above her garters before settling back in the chair. She smiled, two cherry red lips moist and full of promise.

But whatever she was promising, I didn't want. Except as it applied to money. As enticing as it may have been, payment in cooch didn't pay my rent.

"He liked to watch," she admitted, dipping her head a little. I could almost imagine that she blushed. "He *really* liked to watch me."

"Hmmm," I said. "And now they've locked him up in the voyeur's prison? What's he watching now?"

"He can see everything that goes on in NightWhere," Mrs. D said.

"From what you've described, that sounds pretty good for him. What's the downside?"

"He can't ever leave."

"Maybe he doesn't want to."

"I've seen him in my dreams," Mrs. D said. "I know he wants to come home. They're milking him dry."

I chose to ignore the dream comment. I could have found a few choice barbs to puncture that. But somehow the picture of a guy watching scads of people doing all manner of sexual things and the phrase "milking him dry" struck me as too funny to pass up.

"A guy's gotta rest between milkings," I said, trying to keep my lips serious. My face betrayed me.

"It's not funny," she said. "If you can't get him out of there, I'll never see my husband alive again."

I slapped myself mentally, scribbled a note to myself, and then told her my price. She didn't blink, and handed me my upfront money—$500—in crisp Benjamin Franklins. She provided photos of her husband, the address of her kinky friends, and the knowledge that invitations seemed to come mid-month and usually mid-week. Since it was a Monday and the 13th of this month, I figured I should start a stakeout at the friends' house in about 30 minutes. They may already have gotten an invite… but chances were, it would be turning up over the next couple nights. I was already mentally making a list of things I'd need to keep me occupied in the car for the next few evenings, as I watched their mailbox. I had a *Victoria's Secret* catalogue already stashed in my glove box, but I had a feeling that this case was going to need something stronger. A bag of Doritos and a stack of *Busty Babes In Naked Peril* magazine (I was a lifetime subscriber) was going to be more like it.

The invitation came on Thursday. I never saw who delivered it. It was around 5:30 p.m. and I knew that within the next 30 minutes one of the two would get home from work, so just to be safe I got out of my car (parked halfway down the block) and took a walk to wake myself up for the next couple hours of stakeout. If they didn't receive an invite by 8 p.m., Mrs. D had said, there wouldn't be one.

On a whim, I reached out and unobtrusively opened their mailbox. I'd checked earlier, after the post office truck had swung by, and all they'd had was an advertising circular for a chimney sweep and what looked to be a credit card bill. I hadn't seen anybody walking around the block for the last couple hours.

Still…

My impatience was rewarded because on top of the junk mail was a bright red envelope. I slipped a finger between the loose end of the back flap and slit it open. An invitation was inside, as I'd suspected. It said very little, though every letter appeared to have been fingerpainted in bloody red on white paper. The text was obscure, but I knew what it meant.

You asked for it.
You have this chance to get it.
Come to 69 Angle Ave. in Riverside tonight at 9 p.m.
Be there.
—NightWhere.

I folded and pocketed it after making sure nobody was out and about and watching. Then I got the hell out of Dodge.

More clichés. Sorry. I watch a lot of old movies when I'm not watching philanderers, perves and perps.

What does a guy wear to a sex club? Especially when he doesn't intend to have sex? I pondered that quandary for several minutes, and finally decided on a pair of faded bluejeans that looked weathered but not ragged, and a black button-down shirt. Part of me considered opening the shirt buttons extra low and donning a gold necklace. But honestly, I don't have the thick black chest hair to pull off the disco stud gimmick, and I hadn't been able to stomach *Saturday Night Fever* even when it was hip.

I pulled on my favorite pair of leather boots and slipped my secret weapon into the custom scabbard on the top of the left one. I didn't know what I was walking into, and I sure wasn't going to go there unarmed. Since I wore my black shirt untucked, I was able to easily hide my little Kimber Solo in the back pocket of my jeans. If they patted

me down at the door, they *might* find the little handgun, but I was betting on not.

Booted and armed, I stood before the bathroom mirror for a moment. I didn't hate what I saw. A little weathered maybe, but I hadn't let too much beer go to the gut. And there was still a feathering of dark hair across the dome. The furrows that hundreds of nights on stakeout had helped carve gave me a man-of-the-world look, I thought.

I'd probably get hit-on tonight, I mused. Although, from what Mrs. D had told me, I wasn't sure I wanted the attention. Whips and chains looked great in glossy, tawdry magazine photoshoots, but I had no desire to feel the reality of their painful welts on my couch-conditioned skin.

Still, before I left the bedroom I stopped at my nightstand and pulled out a small square foil package with a rubber raincoat inside, and slipped it into my front right pocket.

Be prepared, the boy scouts had taught me.

I had a gun, a knife and a condom. What else could I possibly need?

I had a pretty good idea of where my destination was based on the address. Angle Ave. ran along the railroad tracks on the outside of town. There was a long stretch of small businesses, from auto mechanics to glass shops to lumberyards there. I guessed that 69 Angle (I had to give them credit for their sense of numerical irony) was on the far side of the lake, on the seediest outskirts of Riverside. That would make the most sense. And Google Maps agreed with me.

I backed out of my drive at 8 p.m. It was going to take me close to 45 minutes to get over there, and I didn't want to be a latecomer.

Not that I expected (despite my right pocket preparation) to be a *comer* at all, in club parlance.

But I didn't want to be noticed as the guy who walked in last. I planned to get there on time, stake out my place on the wall, and then watch the flowers shuffle in. I'd do a little reconnoitering, get some hints as to the location of the Field of Flesh, and then slip out of the main club in the direction of that hidden room when the festivities were getting, shall we say, boisterous.

I noticed I was being followed about a half hour into the trip.

The headlights had been tailing me for some time… maybe all the way back to my apartment. I realized after three or four turns that the same lights had consistently sat there in my rearview mirror.

I was being followed? Wasn't that supposed to be *my* job?

Just to prove that I wasn't being paranoid thanks to my profession, I pulled off on an abrupt right turn into a small subdivision of beat-up old ranch homes. At the first stop sign, I turned left, circled the block and then exited back to the highway at the same spot I'd entered.

The lights stayed with me through every turn… though I noticed they faded back quite a bit. When I pulled back on the main road, it was only a few seconds later when the beams flipped out of the subdivision and resumed their path behind me.

Hmmm.

Who would follow me? Well, I supposed there were any number of potential "whos" out there. Open any file in my wide three-drawer file tower and you could find a couple people in every manila folder who had a reason to stalk me back.

Strange thing was, none of them ever *had*. Before now.

Hmmm, indeed.

The highway turned left and began to follow the edge of the bay. The businesses and buildings along the route dropped away until there was only one about every 30 seconds or so.

I watched the address signs as they slowly slipped down from 1500 Angle to 900, to 330, to 102 and then, just ahead, on the Bay side of the road, I saw a lone outpost.

The mailbox at the edge of its driveway read 69. Luckily, I'd already slowed down.

The lights behind me did as well.

Interesting. I shifted on the seat to feel the hard shape of the concealed handgun in my back pocket. Had the owners of the invitation witnessed my mail theft? Had the inviters?

I pulled into a long gravel drive that led back to a Quonset hut. It looked as if a giant coffee can had fallen on its side in the middle of an overgrown prairie. But despite the remote location, I was definitely not alone. There were at least three dozen cars scattered around the building.

My intent was to be unobtrusive, so I turned left before reaching the front of the metallic structure, and drove past several parked cars before pulling into an impromptu parking space. The tall grass scratched against my already tortured muffler as I slowed to a halt. I felt a twinge of concern over the beating my car was taking on gravel roads and weedy parking lots, but it was the lights in my rearview mirror that held my attention. My follower hadn't slowed when I pulled into the drive on 69 Angle. If anything, my pursuer pulled closer, and followed me right down the weedy path to pull in alongside me. A silver Lexus. Nice—quietly confident money on wheels.

I popped my door open and stepped out; I wasn't going to be caught sitting down.

The door to the other car sprung almost before I was on my feet, and I saw the black lace of fancy, impractical headgear rise above the silver roof. And a cascade of equally impractical black locks flowed around it.

The head turned and I knew those dark eyes, even at three yards away in the dark.

"Patricia Delacroix," I said. "You are following *me*?"

"Shhhh!" she implored, a finger to her lips. She darted around the car, and I saw that she was very definitely dressed for the occasion. Black silk dress slit up past her hip, it seemed, thin shoulder straps that only got thinner on their way down, leaving plenty of room for her more-than-adequate, um, assets, to be displayed.

Her legs were spidered in fishnet, and as she moved closer, I realized that her heels had to have been six inches long. She was looking down on me, the moon shining cold over her right ear.

She slipped an arm around my shoulder and leaned in to whisper. "If anyone sees us, we're together," she said.

"I thought you can't go in?"

"I can't," she said. "Not through the front door."

She reached into her tiny leopard-skin handbag and pulled out a small business card. "But when you find him... I want you to call me. You might be able to let me in through a back entrance or something. And if not, I'll be out here, waiting."

"You followed me," I noted again. This time, she acknowledged it with a curt nod. "You might need me," she said. "I had to be here."

"I keep thinking that you don't really need me. You could handle this all on your own," I said. But Patricia Delacroix only pulled me close, pressing my face into the soft crook of her neck and forcing my eyes into the open invite of her cleavage.

"No," she whispered, pressing my face lower into that softness. As if smothering me with the thing she knew I wanted. "I absolutely *do* need you for this."

With that, she pushed me away, and put a finger under my chin, forcing me to look up into her eyes, not down the line of her neck.

"Call me when you find Lucas. If you can find a way to let me in, I'll be out here waiting. Now... just... get *in* there," she said, pointing at the steel door of the Quonset hut. "Go find my husband." She sniffed, and closed her eyes for a moment, taking a deep breath, as if steeling herself, forcing the emotion at bay. "I want my Lucas back."

"I'll see what I can do," I told her. "But from what you've described, it's going to be tough picking him out in a 'field' of people."

"Field of Flesh," she corrected. "And you have his picture. Plus, they will likely have stripped him, so you'll be able to see his tattoo. I'm pretty sure that nobody else is going to have a tattoo of a man in chains stretched across his chest. It might take you a while, but you'll find him."

She had given me a photo of Lucas's tattoo in my office. I had to agree with her. The tattoo of the chained man on his chest was striking. Especially since the detail work put the droop of the tattoo man's penis right onto the O of Lucas's bellybutton. I'm sure it looked better when he was younger, but now? That bellybutton was sagging. I guess that worked in the favor of the man in chains, but...

"Stay out of sight," I warned and stepped back from her. Then I walked toward the front of the giant coffee can. My fingers stroked the invitation in my pocket and I felt increasingly nervous that they would identify me as an imposter as soon as I presented it.

When I reached the door, it was closed. A steel rectangle set in a steel half-oval... it was easy to think at first that it was not even an entrance. But I knocked; I could see the outline of the opening, even if there was no handle.

A moment later my confidence was rewarded. The door cracked open. "Invitation?" a low male voice said from the slit of darkness beyond.

I held my red slip of paper out, and it disappeared inside the chasm.

The door opened, and a pale face peered out. "Come in, and sin," the man said.

I had no intention of the latter, but I was happy for the invitation in the former. I'm sure I grinned a sappy grin and nodded, as I wholeheartedly, and yet falsely, agreed:

"Yes, I will!"

But I was here for one reason and one reason only. To discover the room where Mrs. D's husband was being held naked, captive, and presumably without his wishes (though I, frankly, had begun to doubt the latter point). All I wanted was for this job to be over and my payment to be propping up the balance in my checkbook.

At least… that's what I wanted until I stepped into what was known as The Blue Room of a club called NightWhere. Then, I have to admit, I began to want the job to last a while longer.

The first thing that struck me once I was inside was the music.

It was pulsing throughout the black-walled rooms. I mean *pulsing*. I could feel the low end of the bass shivering the cuffs of my pants. I think my thighs shook. Not an altogether bad sensation… but weird. A band played some kind of dirgey, throbbing anthem up on the dark stage, and all around the room along the ceiling, tiny lights blasted blue glare onto the floor and walls of the place. But it wasn't the light or the sound that held my attention, I'll be honest.

It was the breasts.

Lots of them.

Without any attempt at concealment.

Beautiful, bouncing breasts. There were women all around the main lounge area of the club dancing and disrobing… or disrobing and dancing… I couldn't look away. I was here to find a man, but all I could do was look at…

Mentally, I slapped myself.

Boobs wouldn't pay the bills. Even really bouncy ones, with tattoos of flowers or skulls or Betty Boop on them.

I walked past the bar and the dance floor and found myself in the super kinky zone, where a dozen men and women brandished whips upon people bound in chains, laid back on racks. I watched one woman, clad only in a black leather corset, twirl a wand with a half dozen leather straps on its end. She brought the tips of those straps in contact with an overweight balding guy's painfully white ass again and again, just barely lingering before pulling the straps away. With each stroke of the leather, he moaned as if in ecstasy instead of pain. Then her hand moved in an easy figure eight, quickly teasing away before returning to slap again with six separate tongues a second later.

I leaned back against a black pillar and smiled. The air around me reverberated with the techno sounds of the darkwave band (they were playing on a small stage near the bar), but it was also colored by the moans of dozens of people in the throes of various carnal pursuits. I felt as if I was standing on the set of a really dark, kinky porn film. In fact, I would never have guessed that a place like this existed outside of a prefabricated, calculated movie set.

As titillating as the show was, I couldn't spend too much time enjoying it. The night was short, and somehow, I needed to strike up a conversation with someone who would know what and where this "Field of Flesh" was. But Mrs. D. had warned me to be careful. The Field was not something that the general populace of the club had any knowledge of, and those that did might be suspicious of some newbie asking about it.

It was like a poker game where I had some cards but they had not been dealt in an easy straight. More like an almost full-house that needed the Jack of Hearts in the next deal or I'd have to fold and go home penniless.

There I go with the bad analogies again.

I forced myself to look away from the woman wearing a Saran Wrap bikini (the plastic made her nipples stretch unnaturally wide, like a pair of lips pressed hard to a window). She was kneeling and bobbing her head at the waist of a man in a pinstriped suit (who wears Armani to a sex club?). I walked back toward the bar. A good investigator listens, before talking. Observes before diving into action.

I needed to hear some of the patrons—and I don't mean their moans of passion. The bar seemed the most likely place to pick up some easy information without having to probe. People talk at bars. Though I had to wonder why anyone in a place like this would be sitting at the bar for very long. There were definitely more interesting places to be.

"Well, hello stranger!" The bartender was on me before I'd fully gotten my ass on the stool. I looked up and saw two astonishingly round but proud breasts jutting over the bar in my direction. Twin Xs of masking tape covered her nipples, but aside from that, all the woman was wearing was a cascade of startlingly blonde hair and a skirt made solely of threaded beads. She tantalized the male eye with what shown briefly behind those beads with every step or bend she made.

"My name's Sin-D," she continued. "I'll be your server for the evening. What can I get for you? Cock-tail, or cock-tease?"

"Are they mutually exclusive?" I asked.

That brought a smile from between cherry red lips. Sin-D nodded. "We're going to get along just fine."

I ordered a whiskey on the rocks and when she returned with the glass, her lips were swollen in an exaggerated pout. She set the glass down, ice clinking and threatening to slosh over at the top. Then she pointed at a trail of liquid that was dripping down the side of one creamy, perfectly complected breast. "I spilled some of your booze on my boob," she complained. "Could you lick it off? I hate to waste good liquor. Or the chance for a good licker."

She leaned over the bar, and suddenly I had that beautiful boob right in my face. What could I do but kiss it? So I did. Her skin tasted like booze and vanilla, and I felt my concentration swoon. I could get lost here, I thought, still tracing the curve of her femininity with my tongue. Sin-D pulled away and winked. "You wanted both, so you got it," she said. "'Tail and Tease."

"I think I ordered the wrong kind of tail," I mumbled.

She leaned forward and licked the tip of my nose. "Bad boy," she said. "If you want that kind of cock-tail, you'd better finish that drink and get out on the dance floor. This is the waiting zone, stud."

I nodded, but she was already moving away to help another customer. I could see the bare cleft of her ass revealed, twin globes shaking between the beads of her skirt as she walked down the bar.

Something stirred at my left, and I turned to see a cloud of black hair bending down over the stool next to me. A woman. She was setting a handbag on the ground, and when she straightened up and slid onto the seat, I realized she was a striking if painfully thin woman. She might have been 10 years older than me, or not. It was hard to tell. While her facial skin color was pure above the faded leather dog collar she wore around her neck, the skin of her arms and shoulders, and of the part of her back that I could see where her thin black dress dipped low, were crisscrossed with chicken-scratch scars. She looked weathered, though still desirable.

"Hey," I said as she settled in.

She raised an eyebrow and brushed back a strand of kinked raven hair from her forehead. "Hey," she answered. Her tone didn't invite further discussion. Her breath sounded rushed, as if she'd been running.

"Who won?" I asked.

She gave me a blank stare, and I thought the brown of her eyes held deeper mysteries than I ever wanted to plumb.

"The race," I added to clarify. "You sound like you've been running."

"Just wanted to get in here before they locked the doors," she said.

"They lock people out?"

Her eyes brightened, and she looked me over more carefully. "You're a virgin, aren't you!?"

I shook my head adamantly. "Not since I was 27."

"Didn't you read your invitation?" she asked. "If you don't make it here by 10, you're SOL. Everyone gets in, they throw away the key, and…"

"…then somebody yells 'Let's party like it's 1999,'" I finished for her.

She gave me a piqued look. "Something like that."

A chipmunk-cheery voice and two bouncing breasts suddenly were back on our side of the bar. Sin-D leaned down, elbows on the bar with her hand on her chin. "What are ya havin'?" she asked my new friend. "Bloody Mary… or just blood?"

The thin woman gave her a "you can't be serious" look and then finally answered. "Alcohol first, blood later. Tequila Sunrise?"

When Sin-D turned away to mix the drink, the woman turned to me. "How are you with a flogger?"

"Inexperienced," I said. "I'm more of an observer."

"Figured," she said. There was an element of disgust to her tone that I couldn't miss. She downed half of the Sunrise as soon as Sin-D set it in front of her.

"Just remember," she warned. "If you spend your life watching, your life will pass you by, unlived."

"Is that from *Famous Quotes, Volume Two*?" I asked. My sarcasm was not appreciated. She cracked the glass down on the bar and stood up. "People who refuse to learn are doomed to remain dumb."

Part of me wanted to laugh at the ridiculousness of that declaration, but instead, I saw an entry here.

"I am not refusing to learn, but I don't have a teacher," I said. "This is my first time here… would you show me the ropes? Can you teach me *something*? I know there is more to this place than just this bar and the band and the whips-and-chains club over there." I pointed to the far corner of the room where the floggers were busily eliciting twisted

moans of pain and pleasure. "Can you show me the secret side of NightWhere?"

I knew I was probably pushing it there, but what the hell. She looked like a woman who knew the score here, and she was challenging me… so I used it. If she believed what she said, then she should live by her words and show me the ropes. Although, preferably, without putting any of them around my wrists.

I saw the change in her eye. The spark of a challenge. She saw in me someone she could break in. She couldn't know that I intended simply to hitchhike on her good (bad) nature to get where I needed to go.

"Come with me," she said, and held out a long, thin hand. I pressed her fingers in mine, and slid off my stool. Her fingers were warm. And firm.

She led me past the goth band, who, I noted with amused disinterest, seemed dressed exclusively in fishnets, even though they were all men.

The blue and red lights reflected strangely off the scars on her back, illuminating and accentuating them as if she were white cotton in a field of black light. When we reached the wall of racks, she was greeted warmly. Obviously she was no stranger to this section of the club. Two of the male floggers offered her their whips, but she put up her free hand and turned them down. "I have a date," she said.

I wasn't sure I liked the way they grinned when she said that. It made me fear for the wholeness of my skin.

We stopped in front of a large wooden door. It looked like the entryway to some medieval castle, all rough-hewn wood with iron straps inlaid, fastened by fat bolts. There was a guard there, or maybe a ghoul. Certainly he looked more like the latter. His skin was a sickly gray and he was bald and emaciated, his face lined with a dozen rivers of age. But when my guide nodded at him, he didn't balk. He stepped to the side and opened the cavernous door for us.

When we stepped through, it felt as if we'd walked into another world.

While outside in the club it felt modern, if dungeon-influenced, here the medieval wasn't an influence, but a fact. We *were* in a dungeon. A long stone hallway led away from the antechamber, its walls occasionally lit by the flickering orange light of a low-burning torch attached to the walls.

And the walls… they looked freshly painted… as if the painter had been dipping his brush into a recently gored carcass. The hallway smelled dank and metallic. But it wasn't empty, not completely. While there was nobody in sight, the echoes of screams and moans, and even faint cheers, reverberated out of the surrounding darkness.

I was suddenly both anxious, and afraid, to see what lay ahead.

"Let's start here," she said. Her voice was cool, soft and distant, as she held my hand.

She stepped into the doorway of a sideroom, and I followed. Inside, torches lit the dark gray rock-hewn walls with shifting shadows, but it was the floor that instantly held my attention.

A man lay naked there, in the center of the room. A ring of people surrounded him, though they were not lying down, but on their feet. They too were nude, and ranged from fat dumpy old women to hot, skinny chicks who looked like someone had just panty-raided them and dragged them here from their sororities. Most of the younger women had the kind of full-body tans that said they were not strangers to tanning beds or beaches.

Oh, there were a few cocks dangling around that circle too, but I wasn't looking in their direction.

My eyes were on the taut belly that writhed and jolted on the floor.

And the weird colors that covered it.

Because the circle of bodies surrounding her were not just *holding* candles.

They were diligently pouring the byproduct of those candles in a molten stream onto the girl's nipples and belly and lower...

Hot wax dripped in a kaleidoscope of colors onto the nude girl's most sensitive parts, dyeing her in red and orange and yellow. With each drip of hot liquid, she twisted and groaned on the floor, whether in ecstasy or pain it was hard to tell, but she didn't get up.

When one guy tipped his blood-red candle to rain over her pubes, and a trail of scarlet drops drew a line from her bellybutton to the swollen lips that opened below, I shook my head.

No way was anyone going to dribble hot wax on my Johnson. Not on your life. That said, I had to admit that I enjoyed the colorful view. And my guide knew it. She stood very close behind me, and after we'd watched the waxing for a couple minutes, her hand brushed across the front of my Dockers, lingering on the thickness that had grown there.

"You like the wax room?" she whispered into my ear. "I could arrange for you to stay here a while if you like."

I wanted to say yes, but I shook my head. "No, I would rather see more."

"As you wish," she said, and drew away from my shoulder, pulling my hand until I turned and followed.

We stepped back into the shadows of the long stone hallway and moved silently toward the next door on the right side of the hall. I could see the glint of flames escaping the room like skittering shadows on the opposite wall. We stopped just before entering, and my guide looked up at my eyes with a smile that was as cruel as it was amused. "It's warm in here," she said. "You're probably overdressed, so if you want to get more comfortable once we're inside...?"

"I'll be fine," I promised, but a moment later, I began to wonder as the sweat began to slip down the back of my neck. It beaded under my arms and instantly showed through in dark patches on my polo shirt.

"You saw 'wax' in the other room, but this is the NightWhere version of waxing," my guide told me. It only took me a moment to understand her meaning.

In the center of the room was a stone-bordered pit, with a heaping mass of glowing orange coals. Tongues of flame jumped in the air periodically from the incendiary heat, but it was the view beyond the heat that drew and held my eyes. Along the wall, a dozen men and women, stripped nude, were arranged side-by-side in a row against a stone wall, hands locked in cuffs and held up by chains bolted into the stone above their heads.

A ghoulish man wearing what looked like a black, tattered loincloth paced between the imprisoned, waving

a long iron pole to and fro, seemingly idly. But then he turned suddenly and pointed the iron at one of the men in the midst of the chain-line. He thrust the iron rod at the man's chest and rolled it up across his nipples.

The sulfurous smell of singing hair filled the room almost instantly. The man shook and trembled beneath the rod, but didn't cry out. In fact, his penis grew visibly hard as the burning hot rod rolled back and forth across his chest, smoke rising in its wake.

Now *that's* a pervert, I thought. Getting hard from being burnt!

"There are many things that can excite the human animal," the woman at my side whispered, as if reading my thoughts. "Watch."

I did.

I watched as the ghoulishly pale and bony man dipped his iron rod into the glowing pit, until the edge came out electric orange. He waved that fiery rod around in the air a moment, and then brought it down to touch the pubic hair of the woman next to the man who no longer sported any chest hair.

In moments (and after a brief tortured scream), that black thatch of hair above her sex was nothing but char.

If I hadn't known better, I would have thought her screams of complaint were actually moans of arousal—her nipples hardened, and her hips bucked rhythmically as the molten metal burned the hair from her pudendum. I imagined that she came in part just to get wet—so that her orgasm could put out the fire above the lips of her sex. Part of me anticipated her torturer pressing the tip of that poker lower, and opening her up to the "heat" even more... but then I mentally slapped myself. What kind of sick ass would think of sticking a red-hot poker up a woman's....

The question was answered before I even finished asking it.

Apparently a sick ass like the ghoulish gray-skinned guy in front of me.

Because that's exactly what he did to the next girl.

Damn.

Ouch.

But I had to admit, he was an equal opportunity impaler. He sterilized his tool in the red hot coals, burnt off the pubic hair of a fat pasty man on the end of the line, and then slapped the man repeatedly until he turned, showing us the prodigious white ass that he'd probably spent the past twenty years sitting on behind a dark wood desk. And then the ghoulish guy stabbed that cooling, but still orange-glowing poker right up the man's rectum with a none-too-gentle, well-aimed thrust.

I'll be honest? I didn't look away. I should have. But I didn't.

A hand cupped my testicles, and I looked guiltily to my left, only to meet the dark, amused eyes of my guide.

"What's your name?" I asked. Generally I knew the names of women before they cupped my balls.

"Why do you care?"

"Because I hate to call girls, "Hey bitch?""

"Good point," she admitted, "sometimes we get irritable if you say that."

She stopped kneading my crotch to consider.

"My name is Andreisa," she said, tilting her head

toward my obviously aroused cock with a raised eyebrow. "And I can tell that you are enjoying what I'm showing you."

I shrugged. "I've always enjoyed watching," I admitted. "But you all take it to a bit of an extreme here."

She grinned. "That's really kind of the point, isn't it?"

Andreisa took my hand in hers once more. Her skin was cool and smooth, and I have to admit, I enjoyed its touch. She pulled me from the room and back out into the hall. We walked further away from the main room of the club, and passed several rooms without stopping. The sounds of whips and the clank of chains echoed from within the shadows of a couple of them, but Andreisa only shook her head. "Passé," she said. "I want to show you truly interesting places. With people who will haunt your dreams, doing things that will taunt your passions."

In my head, I rather thought that a simple bit of nudity with the occasional slap of a leather strap would do me just fine. But I went along with her. What else could I do… she was my guide in the strangest, seediest place I'd ever been in my life. I was not fearful of what she would show me next. I was anxious. Filled with undeniable desire.

"This will be good," she said presently, stopping outside of another room. "I want to show you what they do in here. I think you'll like it."

I followed her in, and instantly the air grew thicker, humid with the scents of sex, and something else.

Maybe blood. Maybe something more grotesque.

The room was dark, and until my eyes adjusted, I couldn't tell what was going on in the murk. From the sounds, it was both brutal and ecstatic.

When I saw what they were doing, my initial reaction was utter shock and denial. Nobody would agree to do that. Nobody would bend over, and bend backwards, to accept such a thing.

And yet…

In the shadow room, people did. They writhed and moaned and screamed and allowed the worst defiling I have ever imagined to happen.

Through it all, I watched.

I almost didn't even notice Andreisa's fingers on my crotch, stroking me to a pathetic climax as I viewed and grew painfully aroused by the defilements celebrated in the room.

"I knew you were right for The Red," Andreisa whispered in my ear, as I gave in almost unconsciously to grind myself against her skilled and agile fingers.

"I don't know what you mean," I breathed, not even really caring what words I said.

"You are a man who understands the pure joy of watching pleasure, in all its forms," Andreisa said. "You were meant to be the audience to the perverse."

I nodded in uncontested agreement. I did know how to watch.

Later, when the sex in the room had subsided, and my pants were uncomfortably stained, Andreisa gently led me out of the room and down the hall again to the next point on her agenda.

"You like to watch," Andreisa whispered at me in the darkness.

"It's my job," I answered.

"But you *like* it," she pressed.

I nodded. "Yes."

I can't deny that I do.

She led me down an incline of black floors and glistening red walls until I found myself in the midst of a disturbingly visceral scene. All around the room, a ring of people stood, watching. Looking down at the black center of the floor. Where seven men thrust into the torsos of seven men and women. They were not fucking the sex of their mates, but rather various holes carved into the bellies and sides of their partners… and in one case, a head.

Blood streamed and flowed in vicious visibility across the midnight floor, blooming in rhythmic beats around the fatal fucking…

"They're screwing them to death!" I said.

Andreisa nodded. "The ultimate rape fantasy," she agreed. Then she reached a hand around my middle and dropped her fingers below my belt buckle.

"Don't pretend to be offended," she said, kneading the thickness she found there.

I didn't say another word, but watched as the victims screamed, orgasmed (yes, I saw some visible evidence!) and bled out on the floor, fingernails clutching and marking the backs of their lovers/killers.

It was obscene and horrible and hideously erotic.

My pants were damper than before when we finally left.

"There are so many rooms I think you will enjoy here," Andreisa said. Her voice was smooth but I heard the edge in it. Like a blade poised eagerly over a vein.

I took my chance.

"Is one of those rooms called the Field of Flesh?" I asked.

Andreisa was silent. I could almost feel her draw away from me. I knew instantly that she knew what I was searching for. And she didn't want to talk about it.

"What do you know about the Field?" she whispered. "Virgins aren't supposed to see the rooms I'm showing you, let alone…"

"I heard someone talking about it," I dodged. "Voyeurs, the Field… it all seemed to go together."

Andreisa nodded. Her hair bobbed with the shakes of her head, but her eyes never really left mine. They were beacons, no, searchlights, honing in on me. Measuring. Considering.

"I can show you where it is," she said. "But I wouldn't go there if I were you. It's forbidden. And they say that people who enter the Field never come out."

"Well," I said, "Maybe that's just because they don't want to leave!"

The expression on her face said otherwise.

"I can show you some other things that you might be more interested in," she suggested. I could tell that she was still hoping that I'd change my mind. Maybe I'd finally get horny enough to strip her down and give her a good flogging in one of the other rooms with hooks and chains and the heavy smells of leather and wax and oils and sex. But I shook my head. "I really want to see the Field," I said.

"They say it is the ultimate place for voyeurs," she said. "But we'll have to be quick. If any of the Watchers saw me take you to the Field…"

"I understand," I said. "I won't be a problem. But I can't stop thinking about it."

"You're never going to hold a whip for me, are you?" she asked.

I sensed the question was rhetorical, from the sadness in her voice.

"I had hoped that maybe, once you saw a bit of The Red…"

"That I'd want to bend you over?" I finished. I shook my head. "No, you have the wrong guy for that. I might watch some other guy bend you over… but it ain't gonna be me!"

Andreisa nodded. "I'm beginning to understand that." She looked around, and then took my arm and pulled me back to the bloody hallway. "Alright, c'mon, let me give you a glimpse of a place that almost nobody ever sees. At least, nobody who comes back to chat about it. Most people in NightWhere never come here… but I'm told a lot of people do end up there. The Watchers take them."

When she said that, a chill shot through my gut. It didn't sound like the place I wanted to go, given every other enticing perversion I'd seen so far. But it was why I was here.

"Who are the Watchers?" I asked.

Andreisa laughed. "You *are* a virgin aren't you? Haven't you seen those men here who are pale and bony… almost ghoulish? They walk the club and make sure that everyone is having a good time. They call the shots here. They're known as the Watchers, because they never take part in any of the fun, they just encourage it."

I followed her quick and quiet steps down the corridor, which grew ever more shadowed. The sounds of moans and twisted cries of pleasure disappeared behind us until all I heard was the shuffle of our feet across the stone. The place was like a crypt to begin with, but as the path wound along, the torches lighting the way grew farther and farther between. The air was cooler, damp, as if we were descending into the bowels of the earth. The titillation of watching the obscene began to wear off, and I began to grow nervous about Andreisa's intent. She seemed very accommodating… almost too much so. Was she really taking me where I needed to go, or…

The next words she said didn't make me feel any better.

"Here it is," she said, gesturing at two large wooden doors. The path dead-ended into them. You either went forward, or turned around. The tops were both curved in an arch that met in the middle, and the wood appeared to be carved with a number of strange symbols. It reminded me of the entryway to a very old church, only there were no symbols of doves or crosses here. There were eyes, and chains and strangely intersecting circles and jagged lines.

"This is the entryway to the Field of Flesh," Andreisa said. "And this is as far as I'll take you. I really would suggest that you just sneak a peek through the doors, satisfy your curiosity and then come back with me without going inside. I can show you so many other exciting things."

As she said it, she slipped a hand across my belt buckle and down, trying to raise my lusts again. I took her hand in mine and squeezed it.

"Thanks for your help," I said. "But I feel like I really need to do this. Maybe I'll see you again in the club, later

tonight."

She gave me a humorless grin and nodded. "Maybe," she said, as I released her hand.

I could almost hear what she was thinking. "Maybe, but I don't think so."

She turned away and disappeared around the bends in the corridor. I took a deep breath and turned back to the doors. They were easily ten feet tall, but when I reached out to pull the handle, the door swung toward me without a sound.

I stepped into the room beyond.

"Holy Mother of God!" I whispered. I stood in an alcove, but just a few steps ahead of me, the floor was much brighter. The room ahead seemed to stretch out forever, but it wasn't the enormity of the place that shocked me.

It was the bodies.

The Field.

There were thousands of men and women ahead of me, all of them tied to row after row of heavy wooden stakes. They all appeared to be nude, but that wasn't the shocking part. It was what their nudity revealed that was frightening. Just a few yards ahead of me, a woman shivered and moaned faintly on her pillar. She was missing her left arm. But it looked as if the arm had just recently been severed. Blood flowed in a thick, rhythmic pulse down her side from the ragged hole in her shoulder. It was collected in a trough near her feet, and sluiced away in the gutter.

Her other arm remained whole, and she was using it to masturbate. Her moans appeared to be related to that activity, rather than the fact that she appeared to be bleeding to death. When her head raised momentarily from staring at the ground, I thought for a second that her eyes were closed. But then I realized that her eyelids were open. There were just no eyeballs beneath them.

I looked away, only to have my gaze fall upon a man without legs. He was strapped to the wooden pole with a harness.

His body wept blood from a dozen gashes that seemed to all run parallel his ribs. But like the woman next to him, his hand was busy, masturbating himself with the lubrication of his own blood. As he arched his chest in apparent orgasm, the slits in his chest also opened, spilling more blood down his sides to splash in the gutter alongside his stake. This man had eyes, but he was looking somewhere that I couldn't follow. His eyes were wide, but when I stepped a few steps closer, he seemed stare right through me.

"Jesus Christ," I murmured. As my eyes slipped over the bodies behind and around these two horrid figures, I quickly realized that they were not nearly the worst abominations in the room. Everybody appeared to be missing some "pound of flesh," and many were clearly getting off to some invisible porno show that must have been playing in their heads. Others hung limp, and apparently lifeless.

The most horrible part was that there were so many of them. I couldn't see where the rows began or ended. There was no way in hell I was going to find Lucas in all this.

I looked from right to left, taking in the sea of humanity ahead, and then looked back the way I'd come.

The door had closed as quietly as it had opened. I stepped back to push it open, to escape back into the corridor to consider. I didn't think that I could do this job for Mrs. D anymore. And I had a really creepy feeling about being in this place. A sense of dread that I couldn't contain. Maybe it was time to give back the retainer, and cut bait.

The door wouldn't budge.

Great.

My heart froze. If I couldn't go back… then how was I going to get Lucas out of here if I actually managed to find him?

I thought about what Mrs. D had said. She'd talked about me finding a back door to the place and sneaking her in.

One bridge at a time, I thought, and turned back to the bodies. The first thing to do was actually *find* Lucas. Then we'd figure out how to get back out of the room. I suspected the former was going to take a lot longer than the latter.

I looked out at the Field before me and considered my strategy. I wondered if the people were arranged here in some order. If they were staked in order of entry, presumably Lucas shouldn't be buried too far into the middle.

Only one way to find out.

Ask.

It's what a good detective does.

I walked up to a guy who seemed to have all of his limbs, though his body was a mess of scars and oddly formed bumps where the flesh hadn't knitted back together evenly. He looked like he'd survived a walk through the threshing machine.

"Hey," I said. "Can I ask you a question?"

One of his eyelids slowly raised, revealing a cotton white orb behind it.

I swallowed hard, but asked my question. "How long have you been here?"

"Not long," he said. "And not long enough."

Great. That was really helpful.

"I mean… have you been here a week? A month? I need to find someone, so I need to see where they've put the most recent arrivals."

His head tilted slowly to the left, and he opened the blind eye again. "We reap. We rotate."

"How can I find the man I'm looking for?" I asked once more.

"Close your eyes," the man advised. "In the Field, you see what you wish."

I gave up and began walking down the row, looking right and left for a chest tattooed with a man in chains. This was going to be a long night.

I walked past men holding their entrails in slick fingers, and women massaging the raw meat holes where they had once had breasts. I saw an old, gray-haired guy with no lower jaw, and a beautiful blonde girl who looked right out of the sorority. Her body was flawless, but when her blue eyes turned to follow me as I stepped closer, she opened her mouth to smile… and a stream of blood slipped over her lips. She had no teeth.

Damn.

I passed what seemed like 100 people bound to stakes when I finally came within sight of the shadowed wall on the other side of the room. The sight gave me comfort; I had started to believe there really was no end to this chamber of horrors.

As I reached the end of the row, finally, I then began to walk back. This time I counted the rows. When I got to the other side, I was pretty sure I had just walked past 216 people bleeding from any number of gashes and amputations. My guess was that there were at least that many going longitudinally as well.

My feet were going to hurt.

I started down the next row and caught my breath as I slowed to stare at a tall redhead. Her hair was striking, hung in long curls down her shoulders and trailing strands almost all the way to her elbows. Her breasts were small, but her entire body looked to have been poured from cream—she was flawless and shockingly white. Without a freckle or mole.

And she was masturbating herself with a frenzy I had rarely seen.

I felt myself growing hard, something I would not have thought possible in this room of abominations.

She moaned and cried out, louder and louder, eyes closed the whole time. I didn't think she knew I was there, until she suddenly opened two amazing large green eyes. Cat's eyes.

"Is this what you're looking for?" she asked. I was taken aback, since nobody else seemed to acknowledge me. But she was looking straight at me. No mistake.

"Well," I began, and stopped.

She stopped rubbing herself and instead offered me her palm.

It was thick with blood, and pink, fleshy petals that I could only believe were the shredded lips of her labia.

"Take it and eat," she said. "A feast for the beast. My body is yours to enjoy…"

Her thighs were running with scarlet, and now I could see the ragged shreds that she had made of her sex.

I backed away from her bloody fingers and hurried down the row, eyes looking right and left.

Sexual cannibalism had never been a part of my fantasy landscape.

I was midway through the fourth aisle, and my feet were already killing me. I stopped to take a breath. This could take forever. I wasn't sure how many more glimpses of the grotesque I could handle. And there was no place to avert the gaze; the abominations were everywhere. Blood and scars for what seemed like miles.

I closed my eyes and breathed deep. And then remembered what the first man I'd talked to had said. "Close your eyes. In the Field, you see what you wish."

If for no other reason than to try to wipe clear the images I would now see in my dreams forever, I held my eyes closed and pictured the photo that Mrs. D had given me. Of Lucas's broad chest, overprinted with another man's chest in chains.

It was weird, but instead of just seeing that tattoo, I suddenly saw a hazy maze of bodies all around it. In my head, I was looking to the left, and about 50 yards down, the chained man tattoo almost seemed to glow in the distance.

I stepped toward it, and realized that while the bodies looked faint as ghosts around me, I was seeing them in their actual positions, relative to where I stood. Without opening my eyes, I reached out to a woman with long dark hair, and touched her shoulder. My hand felt her flesh; I wasn't dreaming that she was really there, just in front of me.

Nor was I dreaming that my hand now felt sticky.

I had an idle thought that no amount of soap was going to wash this place from my body.

I held my eyes closed and slowly threaded my way through the bodies, occasionally reaching out to touch one, to validate that the ghosts that I saw in my head were really there.

They were.

In moments, I stood at the place where that glowing tattoo had lured me. I was afraid to open my eyes.

But I did. I was standing before a man.

It was Lucas.

And now I saw why the tattoo was glowing. Someone had carefully used a knife or a razor to trace the lines of his body art. They had painstakingly carved the tattoo into his skin. The flesh behind each link of the tattoo chains had been removed, turning the chains around his heart into a three-dimensional weeping wound. A chain of broken flesh and blood.

Lucas's eyes were already wide when I opened mine, and the ghostly vision of all the abominations around us turned undeniably real. How I had been seeing him with my eyes closed... I didn't want to know. I'd never really believed in dark magic until the past hour. But in a room filled with bleeding people who clearly should be dead yet seemed very much alive—and even happy with—their fate... I knew something was at work here that I didn't really want to understand.

"Were you looking for me?" Lucas asked. His eyes were piercingly blue, and his voice low. Soft with a hint of gravel. He would have made a good country music singer, I thought.

"Word on the street is you want to break those chains," I said.

He smiled. Slightly. "I think my chains have already been broken," he said. "But I would like to see my wife again. Is Patricia here?"

I shook my head. "She's outside. I'm supposed to call her now that I've found you—she sent me in to rescue you. She said they'd never let her past the door."

"Hmmm," the other man said. "They might have let her in, but probably not out again."

"I didn't know if I was really going to find you," I said. "The rows seem to go on forever."

Lucas shook his head. "Not forever. There are 216."

My eyes popped wide. "How did you know that?"

He smiled. "It's a special number. 6 times 6 times 6. There are never more and never fewer voyeurs watching here. The Field must always have exactly that number of people in it."

"What happens if too many die?"

"Nobody dies here."

"But I've seen them—there are people bleeding to death all around us."

"We bleed so that NightWhere lives," Lucas said. "So long as we are connected, we will not die."

"That's insane."

Lucas smiled, grimly. His face grew distant. "It is beautiful. The things I see every time I close my eyes..."

I heard murmuring coming from behind me. As if the Field was growing agitated suddenly. "Let's just get you out of here," I said, bending to look behind him, to see what chain or rope tethered him to the wooden pole.

There was nothing there. His naked back pressed against the wood, but there appeared to be nothing keeping him in place.

"You can walk away from this at any time!" I yelled. "Why are you just standing there?"

"No," he said. "There are things you do not see. Run your hand down the outside of the pole."

"And doing that will release you?" I now imagined that he was held by a line of hooks on the inside back of the pole, fastened deep inside his skin. Maybe by tripping a switch that he couldn't reach, those invisible bindings would be released?

I didn't see any such button or switch, but I grasped the pole and slid my hand down it. As I did, I heard laughter from one of the bodies beside me. I ignored it, as Lucas fell away from the pole, his body collapsing with a grunt on the stone next to me.

"Damn," he breathed. "My legs don't want to work. It's been a long time."

I pulled my hand from the pole to help him up but found that it wouldn't budge. I yanked it again, and then pulled my arm so hard I could feel my wrist bones threatening to crack.

"Help," I called to Lucas. "Now I can't get my hand free."

"No," Lucas agreed. "You can't."

He was slowly bending his legs at the knees, stretching and unstretching them as he kneaded the muscles with his hands. "There are many ways into the Field, but only one way out. There must always be 216 times 216 bodies to bleed. Forty-six thousand, six hundred and fifty-six pairs of eyes to watch."

"Please help me," I said. "You can't get out of here anyway. The door I came through is locked."

Lucas shook his head. "It's a one-way door," he said. "If you come in through it, you cannot go back out through it. You have to find a different way."

I suddenly realized why Mrs. D had hired me. It wasn't to find Lucas, it was to trade places with him. Now that I'd walked in... Lucas could presumably walk out.

"I can't stay here like this," I complained. "My hand is glued to the bottom of the pole!"

Lucas laughed. "Don't worry," he said. "The Harvester will be along soon. He'll get you up. With his blade he'll strip those clothes away, and set your blood free. You are lucky—you will be able to see things here you've never even dreamed of. You will watch the most beautiful, horrible things..."

The air slowly seemed to fill with whispers. At the same time, Lucas's face grew fuzzy, and my vision instead filled with images of men and women bound to iron racks with chains. They writhed and bled and groaned in obscene orgasm as a handful of young nude women with some of the most perfect breasts and bellies I had ever seen proceeded to flog them steadily. Bloodily. Mercilessly.

I blinked to try to clear my vision, and vaguely I could see Lucas leaning over me, rifling my pockets for my phone. I saw his grin when he found it and held it up in front of his face.

"Thanks man," he said. "I enjoyed it here for a while, but I really still wanted to do more than watch. This is something of an unorthodox way of leaving the Field, but it plays by the rules. An eye for an eye, your blood for mine. One voyeur in, one voyeur out."

The whispers in my head grew louder, a growing wind of moaning voices, all saying what sounded like the same thing. Lucas limped down the path, and just as he faded from view, I saw a dark shadow turn the corner, moving toward me. A tall man in a black cape and hood. Carrying a scythe.

I put my feet against the pole and pushed, trying to rip my hand from its grasp, but it was as if my flesh had grown into the wood. I felt my shoulder pop, but the hand would not rip free.

The visions Lucas had promised filled my head then, marvelous visions of blood and breasts and sex and pain that turned orgasmic.

I almost didn't feel it when the grim Harvester's blade descended.

At the same time, I finally realized what I had been hearing at the edges of my perception. It had been a fuzzy but persistent chant. And now its words were clear.

That drone in the back of my head had been the sound of forty-six thousand people whispering and moaning one word:

"Welcome."

I knew without a doubt that I wasn't going to be leaving, and so I closed my eyes, and thought about what I wanted to see.

What I *really* wanted to see.

January 2015

RED EQUINOX

DOUGLAS WYNNE

The Red Equinox has dawned, and the old gods who have slept for aeons are stirring.

Urban explorer and photographer Becca Philips was raised in the shadow of Miskatonic University, steeped in the mysteries of her late grandmother's work in occult studies. But what she thought was myth becomes all too real when cultists unleash terror on the city of Boston. Now she's caught between a shadowy government agency called SPECTRA and the followers of an apocalyptic faith bent on awakening an ancient evil.

As urban warfare breaks out between eldritch monsters and an emerging police state, she must uncover the secrets of a family heirloom known as the Fire of Cairo to banish the rising tide of darkness before the balance tips irrevocably at the Red Equinox.

"Dougas Wynne has accomplished a rare feat in *Red Equinox*. He has written a thrilling action-adventure story while at the same time melding it with hints–and more than hints–of chilling Lovecraftian cosmicism. Vivid characters, a keen sense of place, and a cleverly executed plot contribute to making *Red Equinox* one of the more notable novels in the Lovecraftian tradition."
–S. T. Joshi

February 2015

An ancient relic lost to the world ages ago surfaces in Missouri. Miles Knight, a skeptic suddenly threatened by forces he cannot comprehend, scrambles to stay alive.

Chased by a murderous hit man, assailed by unspeakable evils, Miles finds unexpected aid in Bartholomew Owens, the Forever Man, and his protégé, Katie Bethel.

From the sleepy heartland of America to the corrupt dangers of Africa, from the forgotten ruins beneath the Vatican to the simmering heat of Istanbul — they race to secure the safety of mankind, and to ultimately stop a deranged reverend from unleashing a holocaust that could bring civilization to its knees.

Revelation is the follow-up to Matthews' popular debut novel, Forever Man.

REVELATION
A Forever Man Novel

Brian
W. Matthews

Stalking the Sexy 32-Bit Nightmare

By Richard Dansky

CORLEN KRÜGER

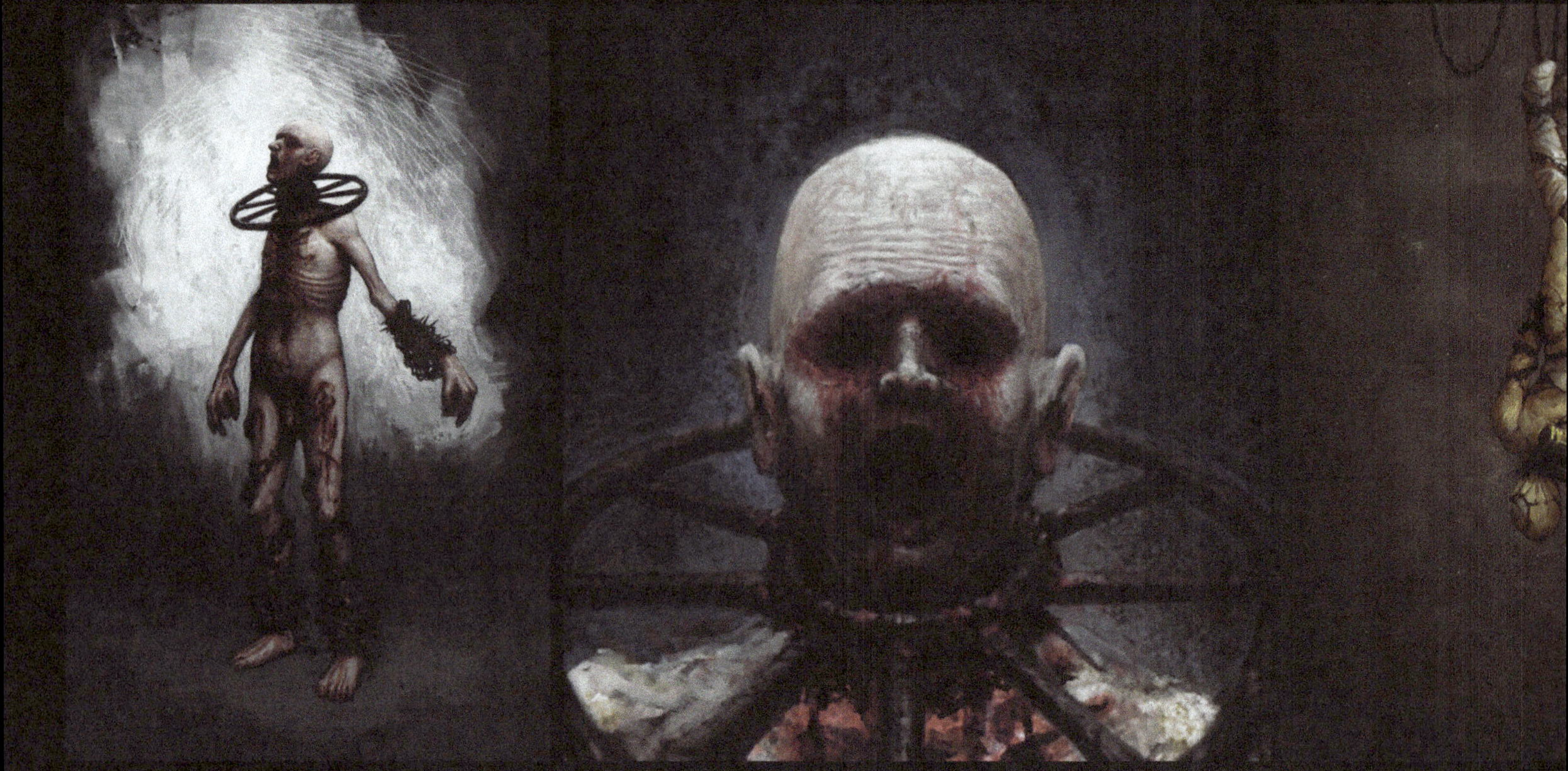

Justine Concept Images

While horror has been part of video games' DNA since the very beginning, it's largely been confined to certain very specific subgenres. *Resident Evil* and its ilk are very much about body horror, *Silent Hill* and *Fatal Frame* focus on psychological horror, Lovecraftian horror is everywhere from Eldritch to the original *Alone in the Dark*, and of course, there's always plenty of zombies.

Erotic horror, on the other hand, is an entirely different kettle of tentacles, one that's rarely attempted and almost never succeeded at. Game writer Iain Lowson (*Dark Harvest: The Legacy of Frankenstein*) notes "I genuinely don't know of any good erotic horror videogames," while Mikael Hedberg (*Amnesia*) says, "Good examples? I'm having a hard time thinking of any at all."

Hedberg ought to know; he remains one of the few game writers to have made a serious stab at writing erotic horror content. The well-received *Justine* DLC for *Amnesia: The Dark Descent* required "reading up a bunch on the Marquis de Sade," with "some sexual/erotic stuff tied into the horror." And of course mature sexual themes have entered the mainstream AAA space with the help of BioWare. But beyond that, Hedberg notes, "You almost specifically need to hunt down esoteric otaku games to get anything even resembling quality."

Zombiiu and comics writer Antony Johnston singles out *Silent Hill 2* as perhaps the most successful attempt at the subject material. "There's the mixture of unease and excitement when you're around Maria or the deliberately over-seal appearance of the Nurses and Mannequins, both designed to subvert the

Dark Harvest: The Legacy of Frankenstein
Image courtesy of Richard Dansky

Images courtesy of Richard Dansky

male gaze; and of course good old Pyramid Head himself, who penetrates everyone with his enormous sword…" That being said, Johnston also notes that *Silent Hill 2* avoids going juvenile or exploitative with even its most shocking transgressions. "For all its pushing at boundaries," he suggests, "*Silent Hill 2* is actually quite restrained and subtle."

Matt Forbeck (*Deadlands*) seconds the suggestion, and adds the succubus tale *Catherine* as another example. Hedberg agrees, calling out the mechanics of nightmare that the game employs as a particular high point. But at the same time, he thinks it could have gone further, noting that "eroticism comes largely from the fact that we know that seedy sex is involved and that brings a lot of guilt into the picture. In the end it's probably more nerve wrecking than truly exciting."

Even with missteps like *Jericho* or the erotic elements of *F.E.A.R. 2*, then, games like this prove it can be done. Why, then, aren't more developers tackling the subject matter?

"It's really hard to do well without simply being exploitative," says Johnston, noting the industry's tendency to go over-the-top—not the best approach with potentially delicate or trigger-laden material. Hedberg agrees, noting that "it's not so much that erotic horror is missing as sexuality in general is missing…. You almost specifically need to hunt down esoteric otaku games to get anything even resembling quality."

Lowson is more explicit in calling out the problem, noting that the male-dominated and sometimes misogynistic culture around game development doesn't go well with the delicate touch required to create something genuinely erotic. "Eroticism is a seduction, taking time and effort, and it's often subtle," he notes, suggesting that developers are unlikely to invest in a product that relies on subtlety to hit its target with both fans and critics.

That is, of course, if there's an understanding of erotic horror at all. Hedberg is wary in particular of making "porn stories without the porn," while Lowson agrees, suggesting that many developers confuse "gore porn" with erotic horror.

How, then, to bridge the gap and start making games that do justice to erotic horror? Lowson has a simple answer: "Lots of careful research." Knowledge of the market, he feels, is key, while Forbeck calls out the necessity of having the right mix of horror and the erotic. Hedberg takes a more straightforward approach, suggesting, "We might need to actually do the work of creating a good and interesting story while infusing it with horrific and sexy moments. That is, let the story be primarily about something else and then as an on-going theme add sex and horror, instead of treating it like a genre that needs its own set of rules."

But it's Johnston who offers the most basic prescription: "The first thing you'd have to do…is figure out *why* the game needs eroticism." Unless the eroticism is utterly intrinsic to the game concept, he argues, the entire thing is bound to fail. The additional challenges: PR, finding an audience, technical hurdles, avoiding what writer Maurice Broaddus (*Firefly* RPG) calls "crashing into skeevy"—all of those are meaningless if the erotic elements are merely tacked on to an experience that could be delivered just as well without them.

But with independent game development exploding, the potential for more games like *Catherine* exploding onto the scene exists.

HELLNOTES

THE HORROR REVIEW

HORROR, SCIENCE FICTION & FANTASY REVIEWS

FICTION, MOVIES, AND ART
DEDICATED TO THE HORROR GENRE

JOURNALSTONE
YOUR LINK TO ARTISTIC TALENT

Exponential
Adam Cesare
Samhain, December 2014
Trade paperback, 204pp., $14.00
Reviewed by Michael R. Collings

Devotees of classic 1950s and 1960s creature features—and their extended progeny—will enjoy re-living the action, the tension, the sheer gonzo brilliance of a small group of isolated people confronting an unstoppable monster in Adam Cesare's newest horror tale, *Exponential.* The cover boasts a blurb from John Skipp hailing Cesare as the "most cinematically savvy new writer kicking horror ass today" (*Fangoria*), and the praise is both well-deserved and well-demonstrated in this story of threat and survival.

In the beginning, there is only a mouse, named Felix by its would-be rescuer, a janitor in a highly classified laboratory. In keeping with the 1950s conventions, Sam Taylor is relatively unintelligent, vastly unimaginative, and focused only on the possibility of saving one experimental animal from certain death, even though there are sufficient indicators for readers to understand the folly of the act. Taylor learns all too soon for himself that, just as man should not meddle in some things, some things should not be rescued, especially when it means liberating a creature that absorbs, consumes, and grows…exponentially.

The opening chapters follow one of two patterns. Either they introduce the creature's next victims, reveling in the blood and gore that accompanies Felix wherever it goes; or they bring one of the small cast of key participants a step or two closer to their final destination—a run-down bar in the middle of the Nevada desert, miles from anywhere (but, as it turns out, far too close to Las Vegas for comfort). Finally, however, the main characters are assembled, and they too turn out to follow the conventions of horror films perfectly—two men, two women, each crippled in some central way, each bringing baggage from past experiences that will play major roles in meeting and—each hopes—defeating the monster.

Part of the interest in *Exponential* lies in the interactions of these four…five, if one counts the requisite barkeep. In the face of the unknown, surrounded by death and darkness, each reacts both as expected and in unexpected ways, penetrating the veneers of convention to bring new twists and turns to the plot. Strengths emerge from weakness, freedoms from inhibitions, successes from failures.

Exponential makes no secret of its reliance on film. In fact, it embraces its cinematic heritage. Chapters are visual scenes, fully developed around a single significant action that moves the story forward. Setting is archetypally filmic, although the fact that Rose's Tavern is a bar ultimately becomes more important than merely providing an excuse for a gathering place with little or no communication with the outside world. Similarly, the fact that two of the central characters are fleeing from a botched drug heist also becomes less a cliché than an integral element in the plot. Throughout, characters—and the narrator—remind readers to watch for connections with films: a reference to Steve McQueen's first leading role in *The Blob* (1958) and several subsequent sideways glances at the film and the actor's subsequent career. *Teen Wolf* (1985) has a cameo spot, as does Billy Jack from *Born Losers* (1967). M. Night Shyamalan's *Signs* (2002) becomes a source for one theory about the monster and how to combat it. While not specifically mentioned, Dean R. Koontz's breakaway novel *Phantoms* (1983) and the later film version (1998) seem to underscore some of the more specific traits the monster displays, particularly its vulnerability to chemicals that alter its internal structures and eventually—or possibly—destroy it.

Taken in all, *Exponential* is a quick, fast-paced read that builds on expectations…that invites them and helps define them…and arrives at a satisfactory conclusion—rather like the final frames of *The Blob,* as the stark white letters forming "The End" transform into a single, elemental "?"

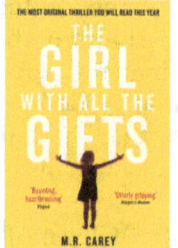

The Girl with All the Gifts
By M. R. Carey
Orbit Books
ISBN: 978-0316278157
2014; $25.00 hardcover; $12.99 ebook
Reviewed by Andrew Byers

If you're going to write a zombie novel in 2014, you have to give readers something truly new because by this point, if someone is interested in reading a story about zombies, they've undoubtedly read all the usual approaches by now. I am happy to say that M. R. Carey has indeed given us a fresh look at zombies in THE GIRL WITH ALL THE GIFTS. I'm not going to beat around the bush as some other reviews have and pretend that this is something other than a zombie novel. That's not a spoiler, simply read the back cover blurbs and you'll know just what you're in for. I'd also like to clarify that while this book is credited to "M. R. Carey," it is written by Mike Carey, prolific author of the Felix Castor supernatural detective series as well as the Lucifer comic/graphic novel series (a spin-off of Neil Gaiman's *Sandman*). Carey's got a great reputation as a wordsmith and world-builder, so I'm not sure why the publisher has resorted to initials here.

Some mild plot spoilers follow, though I promise not to ruin the book for you.

Melanie is a very smart, precocious girl forcibly enrolled in a special school that is as much a maximum-security prison as it is a place of learning. The world outside the school is a post-apocalyptic Britain, with the survivors trying desperately to find a cure for the disease that has brought down civilization. I don't want to say too much about the nature of the disease that brought down civilization, except to say that it is interesting and nuanced, and provides good scope for the story. Again, I don't want to offer too many spoilers, but Melanie, her favorite teacher, and a couple soldiers are forced to leave the fragile outpost of a heavily militarized civilization in which they have been living and travel through a ruined Britain, giving the reader the opportunity to learn what's going on along with the protagonists.

The zombies of THE GIRL WITH ALL THE GIFTS offer a nice, logical mix of shamblers, sprinters, and more enigmatic sorts, making their nature unpredictable and part of the novel's mystery for unraveling. I was also pleasantly reminded of David Gerrold's excellent (though still uncompleted after all these years) War Against the Chtorr series in which an alien – and highly lethal – ecosystem is gradually replacing our own.

Carey's writing is very clear and eminently readable; this was the longest piece of fiction I've read by Carey (I've loved several of his stories collected in various anthologies) and his prose remains as fine as ever. Characterization, dialogue, plot, and action sequences are all very well done. I am happy to say that action and combat are strengths for Carey.

I can't quite decide if THE GIRL WITH ALL THE GIFTS is a young adult novel or not, or if that's even a meaningful genre distinction (aren't YA novels mainly read by adults anyway?), and frankly, it doesn't matter either way. This was a very fast, enjoyable read. Hard to put down. Highly recommended.

Sex and the Cthulhu Mythos
Bobby Derie
Hippocampus Press
September 2014
Reviewed by David Goudsward

In spite of the rather salacious title, Bobby Derie presents an objective and scholarly (and in several spots, dry) analysis of love, sex, and gender in the life and work of H. P. Lovecraft and how the concepts evolved through his protégés and later devotees. The book consists of four sections, looking at Lovecraft the man, his works, the works of others built upon his foundation, and a survey of the range of "Cthulhurotica" from sex magick to shokushu goukan.

As one might suspect, Derie has his work cut out for him. Although Lovecraft professed to being uninterested in matters amatory, he was pursued by a number of women in his amateur journalism days – Winnifred Jackson, Hazel Heald, and of course, the future Mrs. Lovecraft, Sonia Greene. Derie uses his discussion of Lovecraft's relationship with his wife to segue into an analysis of Lovecraft's work, looking at the material from a sex-centric perspective. He finds both normal and unconventional sexuality in a surprisingly large number of tales. Some are discussed elsewhere, such as the Deep Ones miscegenation in "The Shadow over Innsmouth" and the homosexual implications of Edward Derby's marriage to Asenath Waite who is actually a vessel hosting the consciousness of her father in "The Thing on the Doorstep", but Derie also finds his topic well-represented by tales such as "The Dunwich Horror" where Yog-Sothoth impregnates Lavinia Whateley, the supernatural conception that gives birth to Wilbur Whateley and his twin.

Derie addresses the themes that will pervade the rest of the book, with a particularly well well-summarized look at the tentacle as a phallus. He then examines the writers who carried forth the Lovecraft tradition starting with peers such as Robert E. Howard, Clark Ashton Smith, Robert Bloch and August Derleth. He follows this thread to the modern titans such as Ramsey Campbell, W. H. Pugmire, Alan Moore, Edward Lee and Caitlín R. Kiernan. These modern authors are far more explicit than anything Lovecraft wrote or even inferred. Indeed, most of the modern mythos would have been banned as pornography under the ethos of Lovecraft's time, which Derie touches on lightly with the kerfuffle over the necrophilia-themed "The Loved Dead" collaboration with C.M. Eddy.

Derie wraps up the book by wading into the seething mass of erotica in other media, bravely delving into the occult forms of Lovecraftian, films, comic books, even exploring two of the scariest places on the Internet for Cthulhuroticsm – the old newsgroup alt.sex.cthulhu and Cthulhu fan fiction archives.

Derie's impartial façade is maintained throughout; this is a titter-free examination of what could easily slip into a voyeuristic romp. It is an aspect of Lovecraft scholarship not often examined, and certainly with some discomfort when it is brought up. *Sex and the Cthulhu Mythos* should be on the shelved of anyone with an interest in the analysis of the mythos and its evolution. However, it is important not to read too much into the sexual connotations of the mythos. As psychoanalyst Allen Wheelis once cautioned, although conscious aims are often a cover for the unconscious aims, it should not always be assumed that is true. In other words, to paraphrase Freud, sometimes a tentacle is just a tentacle.

SNAFU: Heroes—An Anthology of Military Horrors
Edited by Geoff Brown and Amanda J. Spedding
Cohesion Press, 2014.
Reviewed by Michael R. Collings

With the publication of *SNAFU: An Anthology of Military Horrors,* the editorial team of Geoff Brown and Amanda J. Spedding scored an undeniable win. Now, with the four novella-length tales in *SNAFU: Heroes—An Anthology of Military Horrors,* they demonstrate that the excellences of the earlier volume were not merely fortuitous. With contributions by Jonathan Maberry, Weston Ochse, James A. Moore, and Joseph Nassise, there is military action aplenty, enough monsters—and frightening enough monsters—to satisfy even the most discriminating of readers, and sufficient opportunities for snafus on every level, from individuals making faulty decisions to layers of bureaucratic red tape that threaten humanity's safety.

The first story, Joseph Nassise's "The Hungry Dark: A Templar Chronicles Mission," takes Knight Commander William Cade and his Echo Team through a nightmarish encounter with zombies and demons in a village in Germany's Black Forest. Darkness is a theme throughout: the darkness of night falling over the infected village, the darkness of death and betrayal as the team and a handful of survivors struggle to endure until the dawn, the darkness of a powerful storm that isolates Cade and the others from any hope of help, the darkness of demonic powers intent upon emerging into this world and controlling it. To make matters immeasurably worse, in the early stages of infection, there is no way to identify the infected from the healthy, enemies from friends. Eventually, everything relies on Cade's intuitiveness, his courage and drive, and his willingness to sacrifice himself for all.

Weston Ochse's tantalizingly titled "Tarzan Doesn't Live Here Anymore" is essentially a parable about a broken world and a broken mind. It begins cataclysmically: "The earth was rent as if a leviathan had burst free to sail the galaxy for better worlds to chew." And from there, we are introduced to an earth fissured and cracked, to innumerable monsters of varying sorts emerging from the scars to wreak havoc on their surroundings. The Sonoran Rift, in the middle of the desert near Bisbee, Arizona, is the setting; among the battalion sent in to destroy any monsters that might rise from it is an incognito reporter, gambling his life in the hopes of garnering a once-in-a-lifetime exposé. And there *are* monsters—gigantic tarantulas and, more frightening perhaps, equally gigantic tarantula hawks, huge wasps that lay their eggs in the still-living bodies of tarantulas paralyzed by a venomous sting. But that is not the end of the monsters. Andy Fryerson becomes convinced that one of his fellows intends to rape an innocent woman and—just as Fryerson had tried to come to the aid of a girl he had known years before, imagining himself a wrong-righting Tarzan dropping from the trees—he now vows to stop the attack…no matter what. No one and no *thing* will stop him.

James A. Moore's "War Stories" represents in some ways a retreat from the expansiveness of the first two. It begins quietly, intimately, with two characters: a young man fresh from appalling experiences in Viet Nam (and equally appalling ones upon returning to the States); and his grandfather, a veteran of both World War II and Korea. Realizing that his grandson is on the brink of a breakdown, the old man sits with him on the family porch and, for the first time, opens up about his wartime experiences and inviting his grandson to reciprocate. Moore skims through this part, as the two establish a powerful bond… powerful enough for the grandfather to relate one final encounter, with Nazis, death-camp victims used for experimentation, unbelievable monsters created from humans, and one anomalous individual who might or might not have been human, or a monster. The story accentuates the inhumanity of war by expanding its characters—literally and physically—as the grandfather and a few others fight against seven-foot-tall monstrosities and the human-monsters that created them.

The final story is Jonathan Maberry's "Changeling: A Joe Ledger Adventure." It begins shortly after Ledger has witnessed the death of the second woman he had ever loved, Grace Courtland, and his subsequent descent into a distanced coldness, a ruthlessness that he himself describes as monstrous. Now he is summoned from the prospect of enjoying a baseball double-header on a perfect May afternoon to investigate a supposedly empty scientific laboratory. The place had recently been raided by multiple alphabet-agencies, none of which fully trust the others. Ledger's enigmatic boss, Mr. Church, is convinced that there is more inside than simply empty rooms, particularly since a dozen or so of the scientists who should have been inside have never been found. Angry at the interruption in his life and at the multiple administrative snafus that prevent *anyone* from going in, Ledger enters the building. There he discovers—no great surprise, of course—monsters beyond his imagining. But more importantly, he discovers another person already inside, already searching for answers, already more knowledgeable about the lab that anyone should be…or *could* be. And worse, she triggers excruciating memories of Courtland.

Each of the stories is well handled, deftly written, approaching questions of what constitutes a monster and what constitutes a hero from vastly different directions. Each answers some of those questions; each leaves others frustratingly unanswered. But in the ambiguities inherent in each story, in the unresolved possibilities of the natural and the supernatural, lie the strengths that makes each powerful.

SNAFU: Heroes is the first in several advertised follow-up anthologies to the original *SNAFU,* that will include *SNAFU: Wolves at the Door* and *SNAFU II: Survival of the Fittest.* From the evidence in the first two volumes, these are books to watch out for, the purchase, and to enjoy thoroughly.

Shrieks and Shivers from The Horror Zine
Edited by Jeani Rector
January 2015
Reviewed by David Goudsward

Shrieks and Shivers from The Horror Zine is the third anthology selected from pages of the e-zine by Jeani Rector. Rector is no slouch when it comes to writing horror, with highly respected novels and short stories to her credit, but as an editor and anthologist, she is even better—I might even suggest phenomenal. In five years, she has catapulted *The Horror Zine* into an innocuous little website into an award-winning e-pub juggernaut, where best-selling scribes (the current issue includes a Piers Anthony story) and lesser-known authors intermingle freely in the table of contents.

The only change from the previous two books is the new publisher, Post Mortem Press. Everything else remains unchanged–Rector has again selected an exceptional collection of the best of the best: 33 stories in a well-balanced collection of emerging writers blended with tales from such luminaries as Joe McKinney, William F. Nolan, Ray Garton, Elizabeth Massie, Tim Waggoner, P.D. Cacek, and Tom Piccirilli. Just to add to the name-dropping, the book also features a foreword by Bentley Little and an introduction from John Russo.

More importantly, there is little repetition in the stories; Rector gleefully bounces from haunted castles to sideshow freaks, from parasitophobics to somniphobics, and from organ harvesting to suicidal sky divers. Even when the standard beasties such as zombies, ghosts, lycanthropes, and witches appear, they are new twists, not the same tired tropes. As one example, "Reflector Eyes" by Garrett Rowlan is a modern retelling of *Frankenstein* (or Pygmalion and Galatea for the purists). Only instead of spare body parts and a mad scientist, you have spare auto parts and a sculptor, with a little *Wizard of Oz* on the side.

Bentley Little's foreword mentions his dismay that this could be the last Horror Zine anthology. I agree. The variety and quality offered by Rector and *The Horror Zine* is a standard to which other anthologies should strive, and the loss to the horror genre would be immeasurable.

The Starry Wisdom Library: The Catalogue of the Greatest Occult Book Auction of All Time
Edited by Nate Pedersen
PS Publishing
December 2014
Reviewed by David Goudsward

In 1935, Robert Bloch was completing "The Shambler from the Stars" and wrote to H.P. Lovecraft for permission to kill him off in the story. Lovecraft not only agreed, but returned the favor by offing horror writer "Robert Blake" in his sequel, "The Haunter of the Dark."

The Blake character becomes obsessed with a deserted church across the street from his apartment in Providence, RI. He learns the blighted building once was the home to the esoteric Church of Starry Wisdom. Exploring the church, Blake discovers that when the cultists vanished, they left behind their library of rare and ancient books on the occult and black magic. Blake reads from the tomes, translates a journal best left untranslated, and dies unpleasantly.

Nate Pedersen has returned to the moldering library of the lost cult in the new book *The Starry Wisdom Library*. He has developed the premise that in 1877, the Church of Starry Wisdom was preparing to leave Providence under their own terms (didn't happen), and approached the infamous Arkham auction house of Pent & Serenade, specialists in discreetly selling off occult collections.

In preparation for the auction, Pent & Serenade, well aware of the value of the library, commissioned 19th-century scholars and specialists to write essays on the histories of the books for the catalog of items being auctioned. This catalog has only been recently rediscovered in the Miskatonic University Library and this book is the "facsimile reproduction" of the original publication.

The "19th-century scholars" who have contributed essays on the malignant books are some of the top writers and researchers in the weird fiction field today. Here, firmly formatted as a Victorian pamphlet, are Lovecraft's history of the *Necronomicon*, as well as contributions from F. Paul Wilson, Ramsay Campbell, Joseph Pulver, Pete Rawlik, Robert Price, W.H. Pugmire, E.P. Berglund, and 37 other scholars.

If you play Call of Cthulhu RPG, it's a priceless tome unto itself, providing ample background material to obliterate the players. For readers of weird fiction, it is a delightful compilation of notorious texts of varying degrees of familiarity, all carefully formatted by antiquarian bookseller Jonathan Kearns. It is gorgeously styled, quirky, and a unique addition to any weird fiction bibliophile's shelf.

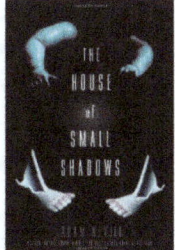

The House of Small Shadows
Adam Nevill
St. Martin's Press
2014
Reviewed by David T. Wilbanks

I'd be shocked to discover a horror fiction fan who had not heard the name "Adam Nevill" by now; with the Guardian dubbing him "Britain's answer to Stephen King" you can assume he's something special. I'm not so sure the comparison to King is completely accurate; to me Nevill is a bit closer to Clive Barker, and as far as I'm concerned that's just as great a compliment. On the other hand, Nevill's like neither one; he has his own thing going.

The author has a new novel out in the UK as I write this (October 2014) but the focus here is on the previous one and if you have not yet read *The House of Small Shadows* you are in for a harrowing time. When it comes to blood-chilling, claustrophobic terror, this book has few rivals. The lead character Catherine is sent to an eccentric old woman's home, called Red House, to evaluate the treasure trove contained therein. But she finds more than she expects in the way of antiques and in the way of the old woman's eccentricities. The longer she stays at the Red House, the more unsettling things become as she uncovers its dark history. At times she would like nothing better than to drop the whole affair and leave the place, but Catherine has much to prove to herself and to the world, and it is this battle between self-preservation and self-worth that builds tension throughout the novel.

To reveal more would spoil the fun, perhaps. Let's just say fans of the weird will find plenty of old dolls, grotesque puppets, twisted taxidermy and even worse things. Yet it is the expanding cloak of inescapable dread that Nevill conjures, like a coffin lid slowly closing over the reader, that is most impressive, leaving one breathless and more than a little disturbed.

Horror novels don't get much better than this.

The Deep
Nick Cutter
Gallery Books
January 2015
Reviewed by Josh Black

The Deep is the sophomore novel from Nick Cutter, pseudonym of literary fiction writer Craig Davidson. While his first horror outing, *The Troop*, was a thick slab of gross-out horror with an interesting spin on Lord-of-the-Flies style savagery, this is a different beast entirely. It's a much more psychologically driven, internal book, with some well-placed moments of the pure body horror that Cutter excels at.

It begins with the 'Gets, a disease of catastrophic proportions. Passingly similar to Alzheimer's in its initial stages, the 'Gets affects memory, causing people to forget at first minor things, then major ones, and finally subconscious things as their internal organs forget how to function and simply shut down. It's a scary thing to think about, and Cutter's gift for description drives that fear home. As far as fear goes, though, that's only the tip of the iceberg. The 'Gets is merely the catalyst that drives the story into the heart of *The Deep* and what it's really about.

Amidst the quiet, degenerative chaos wrought by the 'Gets, veterinarian Luke Nelson is called by his scientist brother to the Trieste, a deep sea research lab where a small group of people are studying a possible cure. They've discovered a mysterious amorphous substance they call Ambrosia, which they hope will act as a panacea for physical illnesses, including the 'Gets. The trouble is, it seems to have its own opinion on the way it should act.

The Deep is a slow-burn at first, unraveling its mysteries slowly as the tension escalates. It focuses on a small cast of characters in a confined and very isolated space, cut off from the world above by malfunctioning equipment and sporadic water conditions that could eviscerate them if they attempted a return.

The main focus here is on Luke. Having lost his wife and son, he'd had nothing to lose and everything to gain in joining his brother in the search for a cure. His loss comes back to haunt him, though, as his mind begins to deteriorate under the pressure of the deep, the darkness, and the unknown things that lurk within the shadows of the lab. The title has more than one meaning – the deep is both a physical thing and a mental one, as the uncanny occurrences in the lab and the darkest corners of Luke's mind and memory converge. Flashback segments flesh out Luke's character, and some dark aspects of his past gradually resurface in the worst conceivable ways.

Like all good haunted house novels (and yes, this can be considered a haunted house novel, albeit one with a unique skin), the setting is a character in itself. It's likened to a living thing, with its succession of tubes and tunnels that mirror the veins and organs of a gigantic creature that's swallowed everyone and doesn't intend to let them out. Given the stillness and silence, every noise and moving shadow has the characters – and readers, by extension – on edge.

Some of the imagery in later sections could have been off-putting and ludicrous in the hands of a less skilled writer, but Cutter has a way of molding the mundane into something outright horrifying. For the most part, though, this is the kind of horror that creeps its way inside you, that has you watching over your shoulder and looking inside yourself. *The Deep* has all the hallmarks of a horror classic, and comes highly recommended.

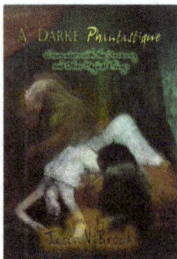

A Darke Phantastique: Encounters with the Uncanny and Other Magical Things
Jason V. Brock, ed.
Cycatrix Press, 2014
Trade paperback, 728 pages
Reviewed by Michael R. Collings

At 728 pages, it would seem that Jason Brock's anthology, *A Darke Phantastique*, has the thickness, the length, and the physical weight to qualify for instant *tome*-dom; at the least, it meets the size requirements to be categorized with long, heavy, densely academic-looking, dry-as-dust, antiquated volumes that no one ever willingly picks up.

Except that in this instance, size is the least of the characteristics that immediately strikes readers. No one seeing the richly evocative cover by Samuel Araya, then opening the book at random to be greeted by page after page of stunning interior artwork, will ever shrug *A Darke Phntastique* aside as a *tome*. Even before reading any of the stories (including a television script and a number of poems), readers will note that the illustrations on almost every page and the highly creative use of margins and print overlays throughout do more than illustrate—they *illuminate*, both in the sense of widening and deepening the stories themselves and in the sense of creating a seamless blend of verbal and visual that has its beginnings in Medieval illuminated manuscripts. That many of the pieces are manipulated photographs, blending modern technique with ancient effect, only serves to make the experience more remarkable. In spite of these excellences, however, *A Dark Phantastique* is *not* a coffee-table art book; the art serves to highlight *stories,* many already remarkable in their own right.

The title and the subtitle are crucial to understanding what the book contains. It is about the "darke phantastique"—both words suggesting, with the art inside, an awareness of past traditions. The additional *-e* on the first throws the phrase back several centuries to late Medievel, Renaissance, and early Modern English. *Phantastique* is an archaic form of *fantastic,* stemming from a time when the word referred more directly than now to things grotesque or bizarre, when *fancy* was a pejorative. As with the other elements already considered, the words suggest a collision between past and present, between staid literary traditions and stories that determinedly expand, undermine, and re-define those traditions.

The subtitle provides even more information: "Encounters with the Uncanny and Other Magical Things." Here is where the anthology differentiates from more narrowly conceived collations of horror, science fiction, or fantasy. In the 1970s, Tzvetan Todorov defined the fantastic using structural principals. During its telling, a story may hesitate between the "fantastic uncanny," in which events seem impossible within the confines of the world as we know it; and the "fantastic marvelous," in which events can ultimately be traced to possibilities within the real world. For the duration of that hesitation, readers are in the realm of fantasy; once readers decide that the events either *are possible,* or *are not possible,* the story shifts to the uncanny (*unknown*) and depends upon supernatural or inexplicable causations; or to the marvelous (*wondrous* or *surprising*) and depends upon a reexamination of physical laws.

Taken together, the title of this book warns readers that what follows will be grotesqueries of the darker sort, stories that will be unsettling, discomforting, frightening, even perhaps horrifying. And the subtitle shifts and clarifies that intention: the stories will be mysterious, enigmatic, baffling, and bizarre. They will be, in a word, *magical.*

The overall tone of the anthology is introduced in a 1951 essay by Ray Bradbury on "The Beginnings of Imagination," followed by Jason V. Brock's "An Abiding Darkness, A Phantastique Light," a fairly lengthy discussion of what readers might expect. The bulk of the book divides into thematic sections: "Magical Realities," "Lost Innocence," "Forbidden Knowledge," "Hidden Truths," and "Uncanny Encounters"—each focusing on an element of the book's title and subtitle while at the same time using wording that implies both tradition and innovation.

Of course, all of this is just prefatory to the most important constituent: more than fifty stories, poems, and (one) teleplay. That is where the true magic reveals itself, whether in a relatively direct ghost story like Joe R. Lansdale's "The Case of the Four-Acre Haunt"; a shorter, highly metaphorical tale about monsters, strangers,

perceptions, and revenge, such as Paul Kane's "Michael the Monster," in which Halloween takes on a new significance; a horrific transformation of a childhood tale in William F. Nolan's "The Last Witch"; or symbolic pieces that border on (and occasionally cross into) surrealism, such as Nathaniel Lee's "The Wisest Stone and the Zoo" and Derek Künsken's "The Buddha Circus." Some are short permutations on expectation, as in E.E. King's "Three Fables"; others are extended experiments in language and form that expand the definition of *narrative* and *story*, including Jason Maurer's "'In Your Dark': Differing Strategies in Subhuman Integration Through Monster Academies" and S.T. Joshi's "You'll Reach There in Time."

For anyone interested in the potentials for wedding traditional motifs to current social concerns, the sheer range of themes is inviting. Several stories deal with sexuality, from rigidly defined to subtly (and not so subtly) evolving—as well as sexual expression ranging from homosexuality to transsexuality to incest. A number of stories embody the empowerment of women; others deal with subtle difficulties inherent in religious belief, in the whole issue of diversity, in something as apparently direct as vegetarianism.

This is one of those few anthologies that captures the pulse of its time. The first time I came across such a book, it was definitely a *tome*—1080 pages long, a thick, grey-bound book with no dust jacket, with no illustrations at all, dusty from sitting on a shelf in a used-book store for who-knew-how-long. The volume was copyrighted 1944; I bought it in about 1968 for—as I recall—one dollar…fairly big money for a poor student back then. I opened it…and was both transformed and transported.

Reading *Great Tales of Terror and the Supernatural,* edited by Herbert A. Wise and Phyllis Fraser, introduced me to what horror could accomplish as well as to seminal stories from the finest practitioners of the late nineteenth and early twentieth centuries. I don't know how many times I've dipped into that book over the decades; I'm rather surprised that it has held up as well as it has. But I wouldn't trade it for anything—at least in terms of being able to trace the genesis of my engagement with things dark and frightening.

I can easily imagine new generations of readers opening *A Darke Phantastique: Encounters with the Uncanny and Other Magical Things*, becoming entranced initially by the artistry of the book, then progressing into the stories themselves and discovering new ways of looking at a new century of darkness…and new tales to explore it.

HELLNOTES

FICTION, MOVIES, AND ART
DEDICATED TO THE HORROR GENRE

UNSETTLE... EDIFY... INVOLVE...

DARK DISCOVERIES

SUBSCRIBE and never miss another issue of...

www.darkdiscoveries.com

FEATURES:

Weird Fiction & Film, Extreme Horror, Comics & Pulps, New Blood, Dark SciFi, Twilight Zone, H.P. Lovecraft, Horror in Rock, Forgotten Horror & SF TV...

INTERVIEWS:

Ray Bradbury, Bruce Campbell, Christopher Lee, Joe R. Lansdale, William F. Nolan, EC Comics Al Feldstein, Brian Keene, Jack Ketchum, David Cronenberg...

FICTION:

Richard Matheson, Ray Bradbury, Thomas Ligotti, Richard Laymon, John Shirley, William F. Nolan, Ramsey Campbell, Joe R. Lansdale, Lisa Morton, Edward Lee...

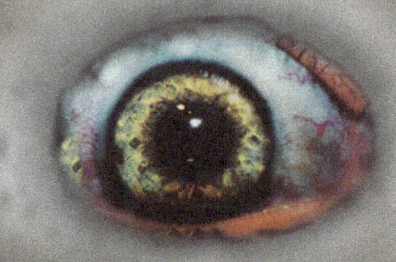

"Dark Discoveries is a very handsome publication..."

--Dean Koontz

"A bright new force in Dark Fantasy."

--William F. Nolan

"Dark Discoveries is a high quality mag... and it keeps getting better..."

--Horror Fiction Review

PRINT SUBSCRIPTIONS

4 issues (1 year): US ($37.95) Canada ($46.95) Overseas ($69.95)

8 issues (2 years): US ($74.95) Canada ($92.95) Overseas ($139.95)

(*Shipping is included on print subs)

ADVERTISERS!

Inquire via E-mail for rates!

Please Note: Future content subject to change without notice. All rights reserved.

DIGITAL SUBSCRIPTIONS

4 issues (1 year): $19.95
8 issues (2 years): $39.95
Payment accepted via PayPal:
christophercpayne@journalstone.com
Also by Check/M.O. (Payable to)

JournalStone Publications
439 Gateway Dr., #83, Pacifica
CA 94044, U.S.A.

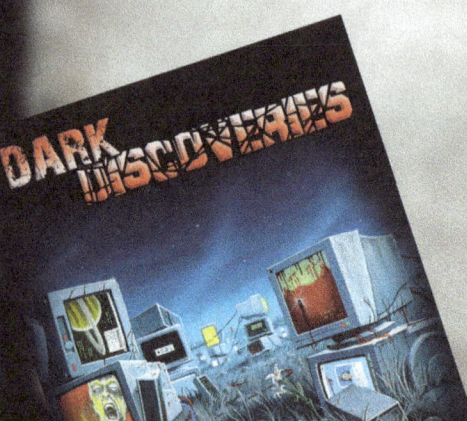

JOURNALSTONE
YOUR LINK TO ARTISTIC TALENT